THE JOHN HARVARD LIBRARY

BERNARD BAILYN

EDITOR-IN-CHIEF

THE MEMOIRS
OF AN
AMERICAN CITIZEN

BY

ROBERT HERRICK

Edited by Daniel Aaron

THE BELKNAP PRESS OF
HARVARD UNIVERSITY PRESS
CAMBRIDGE, MASSACHUSETTS

CONTENTS

INTRODUCTION

LOOKING back at the Harvard of the late 1880's after an interval
of a half century, George Santayana remembered it as intellec-
tually poor and uninspired. The earnest literati — he was thinking of poets like George Cabot Lodge, Trumbull Stickney,
and William Vaughn Moody — tried pathetically to cope with
the barren materials of American life,

but every day their own talent grew thinner and ghostlier, and
the subject-matter which American life offered them — when not
treated (as it is now-a-days) satirically — was woefully stifled and
starved. In the 1890's or thereabouts, I knew a half a dozen young
Harvard poets, Moody being the most successful of them with the
public: every one of them was simply killed, snuffed out by the
environment. They hadn't enough stamina to stand up to their
country and describe it as a poet could. It was not that they imi-
tated the English — they were ferocious anglophobes — but that,
being educated men, they couldn't pitch their voices or find their
inspiration in that strident society.[1]

Santayana's reflections here and elsewhere on Harvard's
bleached culture reveal his characteristic if indulgent bias; they
are partially belied, however, by his own invigorating presence
on the faculty and by the remarkable circle of young men who
attended college at the same time. And yet the number of
emigrés who abandoned New England for foreign parts rather
than suffocate in the "sad sterility" of Boston would seem to

[1] Santayana to V. F. Calverton, Nov. 18, 1934 (V. F. Calverton Papers,
New York Public Library).

bear him out. Some escaped to New York or to Europe; others carried their consciences and ancestral convictions to the uncultivated pastures of the Middle West. Among the latter was Robert Herrick, a young teacher and writer whom Santayana had known at Harvard.

In Herrick's case, the transplantation never "took." He camped in Chicago for thirty years, loathing the urban monstrosity which came to represent for him everything crude and careless in American life. But his move to Chicago in all likelihood saved him from the Boston sickness.[2] Furthermore, it challenged him as a writer, furnished him with texts for his Yankee sermons, exacerbated his Hawthornian conscience. The history of his prolonged conflict with the city of "greed" and "slouch" can be found in a series of Chicago novels, the best known of which is *The Memoirs of an American Citizen* (1905).

II

Herrick attributed his moral outlook to his "pure puritan ancestry" and to the "puritan" influences of his youth. The Herricks had been living along the New England coast since 1636, and his mother's family line included the Peabodys of Salem and the same Manning family into which Hawthorne's father married and by whom Hawthorne was brought up. In an unpublished autobiographical fragment, Herrick made a point of emphasizing his New England rootedness but not, he insisted, out of a spirit of "pride or self-congratulation." What he particularly treasured was the cultural and moral legacy of Massachusetts (entrusted since the Civil War, he believed, to "nerveless Brahmin hands"), that "intellectual and literary tradition of New England puritanism . . . the world of ideas,

[2] For a fuller statement about New England's "anemia," see Herrick, "New England and the Novel," *The Nation*, 111 (Sept. 18, 1920), 323–325.

the life of letters and scholarship, the pure tradition of New England." [3]

He felt the full force of his legacy during his undergraduate years at Harvard from 1884 to 1890. Entering as a freshman in his seventeenth year, and having neither the money nor the temperament for undergraduate high-jinks, he attached himself to that "distinctly unusual group of mature young men," as he put it later, all of them "readers and admirers of literature and philosophy": Santayana, Bernard Berenson, George P. Baker, Norman Hapgood, Robert Morss Lovett, and William Vaughn Moody. As a contributor to and later editor of the Harvard *Monthly*, Herrick profited from his association with these "brilliant interested minds" who stimulated each other's literary ambitions; he gained more from them, he afterwards confessed, than from his college courses or from the over-indulgent criticisms of his compositions by Professor Barrett Wendell.

Herrick and his friends were steeped in the popular Victorian writers, but his own self-professed models were Maupassant, Flaubert, Bourget, and Zola, "not bad models for a young man to aspire to in a country whose imaginative writing was and is so sloppily sentimental and romantic as is the case with ours." [4] His college writing, however, and the stories he published in the early nineties hardly sustained his ambition to become an American Maupassant. For the most part they were competent if sometimes trivial exercises in the Howells-James vein deal-

---

[3] Herrick, according to Blake Nevius, wrote this memoir, "Myself," around 1913. It is part of the Herrick collection in the Harper Memorial Library at the University of Chicago. Many of Herrick's statements and opinions below are quoted from this recollection, with permission of the custodian of the collection. See Blake Nevius, "The Idealistic Novels of Robert Herrick," *American Literature*, 21 (March 1949), 57. [Blake Nevius, *Robert Herrick: The Development of a Novelist* (Berkeley and Los Angeles, 1962), was published shortly after this book went to press.]   [4] "Myself."

ing with crises in love and courtship and involving the ubiqui-
tous Daisy Millerish heroines. And yet they already fore-
shadowed the qualities and attitudes that were to characterize
the mature novelist: a certain dourness and irony, a dry and
hard estimate of the American woman in all her stages and
roles, and a wary realism.

Some of these stories and two of his early novels bore a
Chicago dateline. After teaching English composition at the
Massachusetts Institute of Technology for three years following his graduation in 1890, Herrick accepted a teaching invitation from the persuasive William Rainey Harper, president of
the newly established university on the Midway. Herrick
stayed at the University of Chicago, with numerous leaves of
absence, until 1923, holding himself aloof from his students —
to whom he lectured with averted face on contemporary literature and composition — and confining his university friend-
ships to a favored few.

Although Harper's plant for higher education struck the condescending young author as "the strangest travesty of a university that I had ever dreamed of, — something between a boiler
house, the celibrated grain elevator, and an intelligence office,"
and although he blanched at "the god-forsaken landscape
and rivers of mud," [5] the writer in him responded to the challenge. Chicago was to be his big subject, and he examined it
outside and inside for the next two decades.

Herrick arrived in Chicago when the great World's Fair
still glittered on the shores of Lake Michigan, and he was at
first impressed by the "play city" rising out of a swamp. It
seemed to confirm what the Chicago novelist, Henry Blake
Fuller, hopefully called Chicago's urge "toward the amenities
and adornments of life," and to correct the national view of

[5] "Myself." Herrick described the first years of the University and
Harper's heroic labors in his novel, *Chimes* (New York, 1926).

Chicago "as the Cloaca Maxima of modern civilization." [6] Only in the fall of 1894 when the wind whipped through the lath-and-plaster skeletons of the Fair buildings and hordes of unemployed men slouched along the miles of squalid streets did the vision fade and a different Chicago begin to take shape in his consciousness.

Herrick's misgivings had already been anticipated by Fuller, whose realistic portrayal of Chicago society, *The Cliff-Dwellers* (1893), minced no words about the big dirty city and the rapacity of its business leaders. "Really I write about this town," Fuller confessed to William Dean Howells in 1895, "neither because I like it or hate it, but because I can't escape it and because I am so ashamed of it. If you are condemned to residence on a muckheap wouldn't you too edit it? Wouldn't you want to give it some credit, some standing (*as* a muckheap) by ordering, formulating, characterizing its various delectabilities? No — I am only devoting Chicago to literary manipulation . . . to raise this dirt pile to some dignity . . . by annexing it to the principality of literature." [7] As a native son, however, Fuller could not discount the civic pride of Chicago's leaders. If, as one of his characters remarked, Chicago was "the only great city in the world to which all of its citizens have come for the common, avowed object of making money," [8] these same dealers in hogs, oil, and a variety of other unpoetic commodities had provided the city with libraries, an art gallery, a symphony orchestra, and a university. "Renaissance" may not be the most exact word to describe Chicago's artistic and intellectual stirrings between the Columbian Exposition and World War I, but for a while it looked as if this great mid-

[6] Henry Blake Fuller, "The Upward Movement in Chicago," *The Atlantic Monthly*, 80 (Oct. 1897), 534.

[7] Fuller to William Dean Howells, June 3, 1895. Howells Papers, Houghton Library, Harvard University.

[8] Fuller, *With the Procession* (New York, 1895), p. 248.

western mart might at least challenge New York's claim as the cultural capital of the nation.

Herrick took part in Chicago's literary and artistic life without believing in its cultural future. Despite its distinguished journalists and publishers, its Art Institute, and its literary clubs, he was apparently too outraged by the city's pervasive materialism ever to become one of its celebrators. For Herrick, as well as for some of the other Chicago realists, no compromise, no accommodation, was possible between aesthetic and pecuniary values.

The Gospel of Freedom (1898), drafted during a vacation in Venice and the Austrian Tyrol and completed in New Hampshire, records Herrick's first bleak fictional look at Chicago — even though the larger part of the narrative takes place in Europe. He pictures the city in all its glaring contrasts, a city flung together by man "for his artificial necessities in defiance of every indifference displayed by nature," and he likens it to "a huge garment made of heterogeneous materials — here a square of faded cotton, next door a patch let in of fine silk." Railroads criss-cross "lines of streets built up on embankments with oily ditches, and intersected by cross streets that disappear into the marsh." And over the newly-landscaped parks, the factories, the cool houses of the rich, hangs "the pall of black smoke" periodically cleansed by the lake winds.[9]

In the next two novels, whose settings are wholly or largely confined to Chicago, new details and colors are added to the portrait of this pulsating and unlovely metropolis. Less is made, perhaps, of its brutal power and more of its "tawdriness, slackness, dirt, vulgarity," as Herrick describes it in *The Web of Life* (1900). Here is Cottage Grove Avenue, a South side thoroughfare, as seen from a cable car:

[9] *The Gospel of Freedom* (New York, 1898), pp. 101–102.

India, the Spanish-American countries, might show something fouler as far as mere filth, but nothing so incomparably mean and long. The brick blocks, of many shades of grimy red and fawn color, thin as paper, cheap as dishonest contractor and bad labor could make them, were bulging and lapping at every angle. Built by the half mile for a day's smartness, they were going to pieces rapidly. Here was no uniformity of cheapness, however, for every now and then little squat cottages with mouldy earth plots broke the line of more pretentious ugliness. The saloons, the shops, the sidewalks, were coated with soot and ancient grime. From the cross streets savage gusts of fierce wind dashed down the avenue and swirled the accumulated refuse into the car, choking the passengers and covering every object with a cloud of filth.[10]

But neither in this novel nor in its successor, *The Common Lot* (1904), did Herrick abandon his ulterior purpose for the mere cataloging of urban horrors. Chicago was a mighty fact, but it was also, and more significantly, an emblem of the industrial age, of "all the sharp discords of this nineteenth century." [11] The Chicago newspapers and the Windy City Boosters ("persons," said Herrick, "who proclaimed an unreasoned enthusiasm and loyalty to anything at all hours") [12] assailed him angrily for daring to suggest that Chicago "was not the Paris and Berlin of the United States combined with purely American advantages over anything that had been seen before." But they missed the more malign criticism that lurked beneath his realistic reporting of Chicago's noise and dirt and slovenliness. These were to Herrick the outward signs of an inner disease that affected not only the poor but also the leading citizens — businessmen in particular but also doctors, lawyers, architects, and their pampered and frustrated wives and imperious daughters.

Herrick, in these and other novels, may have been drama-

[10] *The Web of Life* (New York, 1900), p. 199.
[11] *Ibid.*, p. 167.
[12] "Myself."

tizing the social categories of his university colleague, Thor-
stein Veblen, but he was doing it as a latter-day Hawthorne,
not as a new-world Zola or Flaubert. "There was something
in me," he acknowledged, "as in every pure-blooded New
Englander, of the mystic, the transcendentalist, the idealist." [13]
He was far more appalled by the moral defilement produced
by Chicago's inveterate materialism than by its external ugliness. Thus at the conclusion of *The Common Lot*, he describes
the reflection of the architect Powers Jackson, who has yielded
to the goddess of Success and who has dishonored "himself
and his profession" in the process:

Greed, greed! The spirit of greed had eaten him through and
through, the lust for money, the desire for the fat things of the
world, the ambition to ride high among his fellows. In the world
where he had lived, this passion had a dignified name; it was called
enterprise and ambition. But now he saw it for it was, — greed and
lust, nothing more. It was the air of the city which he had breathed
for eight years . . . In his pride, he had justified knavery by
Success.[14]

Each of the three novels mentioned above, although redolent
of smoky Chicago, were parables on the theme of success, the
"unpardonable sin" of selling one's spiritual birthright for a
mess of dollars. Herrick confessed as much in his autobiography. Nurtured on what he called "the puritan faith," he had
migrated to the center of the world of fact and "had reacted
naturally against its rather coarse and obvious pursuit of personal satisfaction." At the same time, he had no wish to apply
the "narrowly puritanic 'be good or you will be punished'
sort of creed" in a different setting. He knew, as he afterwards
expressed it, that the "stinging consciousness of sin" which
had dignified early New England literature, had degenerated

[13] "Myself."
[14] *The Common Lot* (New York, 1904), p. 338.

into "a morbid anxiety about appearances," a "taste for spiritual window dressing"; [15] and he had escaped into the denser, richer atmosphere of the Middle West to free himself from the ghostly obsession.

Chicago quickened Herrick's imagination as the dark forests of sin, Cotton Mather's "Synagogues of Satan," had stimulated the fancies of his Puritan ancestors, but he considered it no more corrupt than any other big city in America. It served rather as a kind of bare stage where his characters, infected with its virus, could act out their sordid triumphs and defeats. "Is it strange," he asked in retrospect, "that with this ferment of impulses within me I should as a novelist present mankind as engaged in the world-old struggle between the spirit and the flesh? Or that I should harp, perhaps too insistently, upon that ancient motto, 'Sacra fames suri,' — the Cursed Thirst for Gold?" [16]

III

The most objective and 'historical' of Herrick's Chicago novels was *The Memoirs of an American Citizen* (1905), sketched in the summers of 1903 and 1904 and serialized in *The Saturday Evening Post* from April through July 1905. Herrick, who usually incorporated (despite his unconvincing disclaimers) real people and real situations into his fiction,[17] relied this time on his imagination and on his general acquaint-

---

[15] "New England and the Novel," p. 324.
[16] "Myself." See also Bernard Duffey, *The Chicago Renaissance in American Letters* (Lansing, Mich., 1954), pp. 116–120, for pertinent comments on Chicago and Herrick.
[17] See Herrick, "The Necessity of Anonymity," *The Saturday Review of Literature*, 7 (June 6, 1931), 886. Robert Morss Lovett scolded Herrick when "he had trenched upon private interests and violated personalities." Lovett, *All Our Years* (New York, 1948), p. 97. Probably the most egregious example of this 'violation' of personality was Herrick's almost venomous portrait of Bernard Berenson who appears as the character Simon Erard in *The Gospel of Freedom*.

ance with the life of the city he had been observing for about a decade.

He was pleased with the result, partly because his book exemplified one of his favorite contentions: that the novelist, even if he were a college professor supposedly isolated from the currents of life, could achieve a deeper reality than the journalist-writer who swallowed the raw facts but who lacked "the necessary repose and unconscious digestion" to assimilate them.[18] Although Herrick borrowed the idea of his morally obtuse but energetic hero from the "rogue" novels of Smollett, his method was essentially Jamesian. That is to say, he chose to penetrate what James called in the preface to *The Princess Casamassima* "the vast smug surface," through the eyes and consciousness of his picaresque narrator. He demonstrated James's assumption that if you "haven't, for fiction, the root of the matter in you, haven't the sense of life and the penetrating imagination, you are a fool in the very presence of the revealed and the assured; but if you *are* so armed you are not really helpless, not without your resource, even before mysteries abysmal." [19]

Now Herrick knew his Chicago as well as or better than James knew London, yet he proposed, he tells us,[20] to write the *Memoirs* completely out of himself, to pluck his hero from an Indiana farm, plump him down penniless in the Chicago maelstrom, and watch him scrabble out at the end "with his bagful of plunder, his work accomplished at the apex of his ambition" and preparing to mount "the long flight of granite steps before the Senate wing of the Capitol." To give Van Harrington's Chicago career the necessary actuality, moreover,

[18] "Myself."
[19] R. P. Blackmur, ed., *The Art of the Novel. Critical Prefaces by Henry James* (New York, 1934), p. 78.
[20] "Myself." The quotations in this paragraph and the next two are from the same source.

Herrick decided to conduct him through the mazes of Chicago "Business," that "one great American passion," and to dramatize his "morally interesting situation," as James would say, by projecting him against a grimy background of stockyards, packing houses, trusts, labor violence, and venal politics. Herrick, to be sure, knew little or nothing about business, but his ignorance and the very "impertinence" of his invention exhilarated him. The trick was to give the illusion of reality "without the realist's embarrassing worry about whether he is really doing it."

To his surprise and pleasure, the story wrote itself easily, and he never felt at a loss for material. He was stimulated by the excitement that the restless, roaring city had always produced in him. Even a professor on the Midway could not escape it. It was not the first time that "the outer machinery of business life — the elevators, plants, shops, warehouses, the streams of operatives and the small gatherings of operators" had stirred him, but in this novel he wanted to capture as well "the inner human feelings and motives that actuated the whole." The details of marketing meat products and the mysteries of finance (all checked by a knowledgeable friend) bulked far less in his mind than the problem of spiritual verisimilitude. "It is the seeing eye and the conceiving brain," Herrick said, "that always counts for more than the loaded notebook." He considered the documentary portions of the novel pure fakery, a subterfuge to induce belief, trimmings by which he might deceive the reader into believing that the author was an expert on the packing industry.

Happily in the *Memoirs*, the realistic details blended with the theme, and he took pains to verify them; but these concessions to outward realism, he felt, did not explain why his readers and reviewers assumed that he had mastered the complexities of his hero's business. The sections of his book that depended least on a fidelity to fact were singled out by some of his readers as the closest to experience. Herrick, they suspected, must have had a real person in mind. But the "self" masquerading in the image of Van Harrington was not an actual Chicagoan, but a type of American Citizen, able, ambitious, hardworking, impelled by the dream of success to skirt or subvert the law and to palliate his misconduct by playing the role of benefactor to his state and country. Musing over his achievements as he surveys the railroad yards and warehouses from his office window, Harrington can say:

I, too, was a part of this. The thought of my brain, the labor of my body, the will within me, had gone to the making of this world. There were my plants, my car line, my railroads, my elevators, my lands — all good tools in the finite work of this world. Conceived for good or for ill, brought into being by fraud or daring — what man could judge *their* worth? There they were, a part of God's great world. They were done; and mine was the hand. Let another, more perfect, turn them to a larger use; nevertheless, on my labor, on me, he must build.[21]

IV

Herrick's apparent satisfaction with *The Memoirs of an American Citizen* was confirmed by most of the reviewers, who gave it at least qualified approval. Some of them seemed a little distressed by its bleakness. One regretted Herrick's want of confidence "in the virtue of the American people, which will outlast transient vices";[22] another declared that he would not like to see the novel in "the hands of youthful readers," because it seemed too much "a cynical apologia for commercial dishonesty."[23] But these were the undiscerning critics who misconstrued Herrick's pervasive irony. The more perceptive

[21] See page 266, below.
[22] *The Independent*, 59 (Nov. 16, 1905), 1154.
[23] *The Nation*, 81 (Sept. 7, 1905), 205.

praised him for his shrewd selection of details and for his brilliant idea of making "the chief actor in this drama of modern commercialism" unconsciously reveal himself. No more convincing way could be devised to picture "the moral callousness, the color blindness in all matters of rectitude, which make many capable, indomitable and successful Americans as effective and as immoral as the representative men of action during the Renaissance." [24]

The most authoritative commendation came from Howells, the dean of the realists, who wrote to Herrick that he had restored his faith in "the *crucial* novel" and that he deserved particular credit for doing the unpopular thing well. Realistic novels, truthful portrayals of American life, found less favor with the reading public than did the paint-and-pasteboard fiction Howells detested, and it pleased him that Herrick could write "a novel of manners of the older sort, that now appeals to me." [25] Howells followed up his letter three years later with a long and appreciative essay on Herrick's work which contains the first searching appraisal of the *Memoirs*. He complimented Herrick for rendering the outer and inner significance of "the material and spiritual incidents" of the novel, and he savored its moral insight. Perhaps, he offered, the autobiographic form complicated Herrick's problem, for "the meaning has often to be suggested rather than expressed by the autobiographer's carefully unguarded consciousness of it"; but he praised his skill in triumphing over this hazard, and praised the veracity of his American portraits in the center of the New World, "now aging so rapidly into the image of the Old." [26]

Considered simply as documentary history, the *Memoirs* is

[24] *The Outlook*, 81 (Nov. 25, 1905), 708.
[25] Quoted in *The Bookman*, 68 (1928), 199.
[26] Howells, "The Novels of Robert Herrick," *The North American Review*, 189 (June 1909), 816.

probably better and certainly no worse than the spate of fiction of 'exposure' written between 1900 and 1910. Herrick's novel appeared during the presidency of Theodore Roosevelt when a legion of journalists, novelists, and reformers were invading the noisome corners of American political and economic life and sensationally reporting their discoveries in the popular magazines. Yet if Herrick added his voice to those who inveighed against what T.R. called "the dull, purblind folly of the very rich men" and the shrewd lawyers who helped them prosper, he was no "muckraker" in the popular sense of that word. He wrote his books neither to fire the indignation of his readers nor to supply the "low-down" on big city corruption as did Lincoln Steffens. Journalism or slick commercial fiction, in Herrick's opinion, never succeeded in interpreting life deeply or in helping Americans to understand themselves or their country. Although he often described the chicaneries of Roosevelt's "malefactors of great wealth," his real concern was with the society that could produce such mechanical "unfertile types, — men and women who spring, like the dragon-born, ready-made, and like the seed of Cadmus are somewhat hard and metallic in their nature." [27] He was historically minded, but the events he treated or alluded to were important to him less for themselves than for what they revealed about the people who were caught up in them.

Herrick kept looking back in his stories to America of the eighties and nineties (the Pullman strike and the Chicago World's Fair had figured prominently in *The Web of Life*), and in the *Memoirs* we catch glimpses of the Haymarket Riot of 1886, the World's Fair, and the Spanish-American War as well as slightly disguised allusions to state and local scandals. How reliable his novel is as a description of the meat-packing

[27] Robert Herrick, "The Background of the American Novel," *Yale Review*, 3 (Jan. 1914), 222.

industry and Chicago business practices circa 1900 it is hard to say. The details are true enough, but we may well ask with one of Herrick's reviewers whether future historians studying "our present epoch of frenzied materialism" ought to depend upon the highly colored portrayals of the novelists? Novelists, the reviewer said, were often overzealous in reflecting the sordid elements in business life while at the same time they were "sometimes over-awed by the gigantic forces they found at play in our commercial civilization." [28]

Herrick was far from being overawed by the rapacious Midwestern capitalists (Van Harrington, it should be noted, is much less of a Titan than Dreiser's or Norris' Nietzschean tycoons), but he probably was "overzealous" in the *Memoirs* in representing practically all of them as types like Strauss, Gooch, Dround, Carmichael, and Harrington. Here, and most noticeably in his next novel, *Together* (1908), he was contrasting these oafs and pirates with the already defunct honorable merchants who spurned the faro game of Wall Street and who earned their wealth without stealing from the government or gambling on the price of foodstuffs. The latter and their wives, unlike the splashy Chicago nabobs, lived simply and unostentatiously. For Herrick, these were the true aristocrats: "Their coat of arms bore the legend: Integrity and Enterprise." [29]

Harrington belongs to an entirely different breed. This "pal of Providence," as Howells calls him, still retains vestiges of his Indiana village origins and is never completely immune to the pangs of conscience, but he is spiritually coarse and he is deaf to the finer ethical vibrations. At moments Herrick seems to show a sneaking sympathy for Harrington, but he can never feel the delight in him that both Dreiser and Norris show in

[28] *The Dial*, 39 (Sept. 1, 1905), 114.
[29] *Together* (New York, 1908), p. 111.

recounting the exploits of their buccaneering financiers; the moralist author cannot brook the egoism of his agreeable, cynical, and thick-skinned hero. He finds nothing poetic in exalted appetite and greed, and he is more disgusted than fascinated by the self-deceived business predators. Thus Herrick's portrait of the businessman is less brilliant and dynamic than the fabulous inventions of his romantic-realistic contemporaries, at the same time that it is closer to the human dimension.

Yet if Herrick's presentation of Harrington and his kind is down-to-earth and unromantic, if he saw "steadily what other writers only saw in fits and starts," [30] his stern moral code may have led to the distortion of his business image. "There is Ambition," Floyd Dell remarked, "which even if it be directed to purely commercial ends yet retains a certain human dignity, if not a romantic beauty. But Mr. Herrick declines emphatically to respect, as he declines to romanticize Ambition — the ambition, that is to say, of the business man. It is to him a dirty affair." [31] With Herrick, business motives are usually as simple as they are base. The only honorable businessman in the *Memoirs* is Farson, a principled Maine banker of the old and honorable vintage, who is revolted by Harrington's shoddy practices. All the rest are conscienceless, dishonest, or weak. Herrick the puritan mercilessly condemns their gospel of success, and Herrick the environmentalist blames Chicago for warping and debauching them.

Did Herrick, for all this unblinking honesty, ever really see Chicago, or did it appear to him as a kind of twentieth-century Vanity Fair? Some years after he had written Van Harrington's "autobiography," Herrick published an article on the

[30] Newton Arvin, "Homage to Robert Herrick," *The New Republic*, 82 (March 6, 1935), 94.
[31] Floyd Dell, "Chicago in Fiction," *The Bookman*, 38 (Nov. 1913), 274.

American novel in which he declared that the novelist simply *had* to deal with the city, although he implied that it was a dirty job:

Our intensely modern cities are, at least externally and in mass, undeniably ugly — sprawling, uncomposed, dirty, and noisy. With their slovenly approaches, their needless crowding, they express the industrial greed and uncoordinated social necessities of a rapidly multiplying and heterogeneous people. They are huge industrial camps, with all their massive buildings, rather than agreeable homes of human beings. A system of local government, curiously lax and susceptible of abuse by interested power, to which for generations our busy people have tamely submitted, has made it hitherto impossible to organize and develop the American city for the benefit of its citizens. One and all, our great cities are — at least superficially — convincing proofs of the terrible power of uncontrolled selfishness.[32]

Dreiser did not see Chicago through these moral spectacles although he would not have quarreled with the burden of Herrick's reflections. He had a far more intimate knowledge of its sores and blights than Herrick did, but he responded, like his open-eyed Carrie Meeber, to its power and poetry in a way that the ironical and inhibited Herrick never could. No one, not even Howells, had a clearer understanding of the limitations and the possibilities of the American novel than Herrick did, or was readier in theory to deal honestly and fearlessly with American realities. His novels do have verisimilitude; they abound with concrete details. But Herrick takes no relish in the city's sensuous integument. What really absorbs him are the disclosures of his moral X-ray, the shadows of disease which will ultimately destroy the body politic.

Herrick's realism was moral or emblematic, then, and consistent with his temperament, for he was incapable of immersing

[32] "The Background of the American Novel," *Yale Review*, 3 (Jan. 1914), 224.

himself without constraint in the seething society. Chicago diverted him from his somewhat tepid initial experiments in the fiction of manners, but it did not relax his New England preoccupation with sin and salvation. On the contrary, as his best informed critic has said, its "blustering, impenitent materialism" enhanced the "ancestral blight," and Herrick "spent the rest of his life resolving Chicago's claim upon his excessively sensitive moral imagination." [33]

v

Herrick published eleven more novels after *The Memoirs of an American Citizen*, as well as quantities of critical and miscellaneous writing — some of it of more than historical interest. Both in his 'realistic' fiction, where he was primarily concerned with the factual and the verifiable, and in his self-styled 'idealistic' novels in which he intended, as he said, "to get at the essence of character and experience rather than to deal with appearance or with fancies," [34] he continued his lifelong commentary on America's spiritual illness and described its internal and external manifestations. In general, his novels dramatized the hazards and moral dilemmas of well-to-do middle class men and women trying to live a moral life in an immoral society. What Herrick called "the complex of triviality" of their world became the material for his fiction.

A good many of the male characters in these books bore Harrington's brand of greed and egoism, and so did most of their handsome yet morally repulsive women. Some of the latter were half-men, like Harrington's feminine alter ego, Jane Dround, whose response to business enterprise was more intense even than Harrington's — and more romantic; more of them resembled his spoiled and pampered wife, Sarah, and her

[33] Nevius, "Idealistic Novels of Herrick," pp. 60–61.
[34] *Ibid.*, p. 62.

parasitical equivalents who were the beneficiaries of "the most material age and the most material men and the least lovely civilization on God's earth." [35] Women of integrity like Harrington's sister-in-law and former sweetheart, May, were the exceptions.

Never popular among the largely feminine consumers of fiction, Herrick's novels became increasingly neglected as his pictures of American society darkened and as his hope for its moral rehabilitation declined. He was probably right in attributing this neglect to the harsh truths of his message and his refusal to pander to the current romantic tastes, but there may have been another and less flattering explanation. More and more, he was indulging in the kind of sermonizing so conspicuously absent in the *Memoirs*. He was beginning to sound querulous as his bitterness deepened. All his integrity and talent, his eye for the salient detail and his power of satire failed to buoy up his fictional tracts, and his later novels — despite their flashes of life and moments of unfailing interest — seldom achieve the excellencies of *The Memoirs*. At their best, they are intelligent documents of considerable value to historians of the American business and professional classes and of American manners; at their worst, they are tedious jeremiads, verbose and sprawling.

For a very short time following the outbreak of the First World War, Herrick apparently thought that a cleansing idealism might restore the national spirit, but he quickly became disillusioned, and the next three Republican administrations seemed to confirm his direst apprehensions of America's moral collapse. As a younger man, his opinion of radicals had not differed markedly from that of his American Citizen; for the most part he portrayed them as a noisy greedy lot in greater need of moral regeneration than the society they proposed to

[35] *Together*, p. 517.

reform. Gradually, however, in his articles at least, he began to sound more and more like the anarchists in the *Memoirs*. The snobbish anti-Semitism implicit in some of his early fiction and his distaste for the new immigration that had changed the character of his beloved New England yielded to a genuine concern for the discriminated-against ethnic groups and an anger against their 'Nordic' oppressors.

The martyrdom of the Haymarket rioters must have touched his humanity as it had Howells', but that episode in the *Memoirs* is ironically conveyed through the mouth of Harrington. Herrick was even more deeply shocked by the execution of Sacco and Vanzetti, and he denounced "the intolerant egotism of a dominant class" in his own words:

Sacco and Vanzetti! The shoemaker and the fish peddler, who had the temerity in these United States to avow their belief in anarchy and to dream of another and better form of society, paid for their naïveté with their lives. For over seven years they proclaimed to the world from prison how completely America has renounced the traditional role of devotion to Justice, Humanity, — the Square Deal! To the intellectuals of the world as well as to the masses the fate of Sacco and Vanzetti served notice that the Messianic ideal was no longer working in America. Even the spirit of Agrippa had gone out of the ruling class; a narrow intolerance or indifference, a ferocious nationalistic egotism had taken its place. Sacco and Vanzetti have been dead now three years; in the feverish rapidity of our daily interests their names no longer "make the front page." And yet their memory, the vivid illustration offered by their fate of the new Americanism, will not die from the consciousness of millions the world over, not in generations. It was a big price to pay to maintain the infallibility of Massachusetts justice! [36]

This explosion was written in 1930 after the Great Depression had already set in. He welcomed it grimly. "The idealist gets contumely on earth here in the United States as elsewhere

[36] "America: The False Messiah" in *Behold America!* ed. S. D. Schmalhausen (New York, 1931), pp. 60–61.

for his visions, but his revenge comes in the revolution of time."
Perhaps, he said, economic adversity would cure "our besotted
arrogance," deflate our false ideals, and "chasten, enlighten, and
restrain the national spirit." [37]

The Depression, he wrote to Malcolm Cowley in 1934, might
also prove a boon to literature. Not only economics and politics had suffered from "the delirious last dance of rampant in-
dividualism" but art as well. Cowley's *Exile's Return* demonstrated to Herrick that the art for art's sake philosophy was
merely "another phase of the individualistic debauch and collapse we are passing through":

Luckily for myself, I was never tempted to follow that path. I
knew from the very start of my consciousness as a writer that whatever force I had in me was solely due to my tradition, my blood and
the soil I was born to (however much I might dislike, loathe it at
times!), that I was a medium for the expression of forces not myself. Concretely I avoided instinctively the patter and chatter about
letters and art, the literary "schools" already forming in the Nineties. I avoided as a rule contacts with men of my two professions,
teaching and writing, preferring the talk of a drummer in a Pullman
or a sailor on a boat to the conversations about Art and Life. My
own contacts with reality I felt were limited by the cloistered profession forced upon men, and whenever I was free to move I preferred to touch any bit of experience rather than swap ideas
with another practitioner of the arts. Theories, ideas seem to me
the easiest things to achieve for the artist; conceptions, impressions,
illuminations the rarest and the most essential . . . So, in a word,
all this discussion about the enervating influence of environment,
the futility of life, self-expression and self-fulfillment, merely convinced me that the individuals and periods in which they are felt
and expressed are self-condemned. They are fated to be swept
aside in the next surge of life as the foot marks on the beach today
by tonight's tide.

The proletarian literature (perhaps he was responding to the
new brand of Marxist puritanism) already underlined "these

[37] *Ibid.*, pp. 65–66.

elementary truths," and the coming years of hardship, he concluded, would teach many more. "We have not yet had enough
Depression for the good of American letters!" [38]

For several decades Herrick had been saying in his novels and
essays that "man cannot live unto himself alone and survive,"
and despite his hard and bitter appraisals of American failure in
domestic, business, professional, and political life, he had never
abandoned his belief in human plasticity. More and more, he
had shown his sympathies with minority groups, with the un-
derprivileged, with simple hardworking people everywhere.
Thus the Roosevelt administration was not being whimsical
when it offered Herrick the post of Government Secretary of
the Virgin Islands in January 1935. He had first visited the
Bahamas and Cuba while he was an undergraduate in 1887 and
had never lost his interest and affection for the Caribbean island-
ers. The new assignment gave him greater satisfaction, he
wrote to a friend, than either his teaching or his writing had
done. He died in St. Thomas in 1938 after a highly successful
tenure of office.

V I

Herrick's career, one is tempted to say, is of less interest to
the literary critic than to the social historian who might study
it as an exercise in human ecology. He is an example of the
misplaced New Englander, less distinguished than Henry
Adams but alienated from his contemporaries and contemptu-
ous of their values for some of the same reasons. Not even his
intelligence and taste, perhaps, were enough to compensate for
his unremitting didacticism and a certain bloodlessness in his
writing, but he deserves a more honorable place in the annals
of American literature than he has enjoyed.

[38] Herrick to Malcolm Cowley, November 30, 1934. Cowley Papers,
The Newberry Library, Chicago.

His attachment to the puritan verities helps to explain both his limitations and his peculiar merits as a novelist. Like the doleful hero of Santayana's *The Last Puritan*, Herrick was "convinced on puritan grounds that it was wrong to be a puritan." [39] Very likely it was this ingrained puritan bias which kept him from enjoying and savoring his American world. And yet if he relentlessly judged it by his own inflexible criteria, if he probed in a cold, unsympathetic, or angry spirit, it was the puritan's hatred for shams and compromises, the puritan's "bitter merciless pleasure in hard facts," [40] as Santayana put it, that enabled him to see Chicago and the Chicagoans with a clarity denied the morally confused.

The Memoirs of an American Citizen, the best constructed and most readable of his novels, shows both the defects and advantages of his crusty temperament. Like most of the fiction of the Howellsian realists, it wants passion and poetry; and if it is free from those lapses in taste we take for granted in the works of Norris, London, and Dreiser — free too of their philosophical pomposities — it demonstrates Herrick's incapacity ever to subordinate conscience to the fictive imagination. The reader might well wonder at moments whether Herrick understood the impulses of Harrington very much better than the upstart from Indiana understood them himself, or whether such an unyielding and fastidious moralist could ever be a completely trustworthy interpreter of the rank American scene in which the Harringtons flourished.

No one, however, can read Harrington's candid and damning self-revelations without having a deeper understanding of a familiar American type — the kind of 'fool' or 'Man of Understanding' in the Emersonian sense, who mistakes the gross ephemera for the Real. Herrick's book, tough and unsentimen-

[39] George Santayana, *The Last Puritan* (New York, 1936), p. 6.
[40] *Ibid.*, p. 7.

tal, dispells the cant that pervades so many fictional attempts to romanticize business, and echoing through its pages are the voices of ancestral New England gods warning a materialistic generation of the failure of success and declaring that life without principle is not life but death.

Daniel Aaron

August 1962

A NOTE ON THE TEXT

For this reprint of *The Memoirs of an American Citizen*, I
have followed the text of the Macmillan first edition of 1905.
Herrick revised his novel extensively after it had been serialized for *The Saturday Evening Post* publication in the late
spring and early summer of 1905, although none of the more
than one hundred changes altered the essential theme or struc-
ture of the book. The majority of them consisted of modifica-
tions of phrasing which made a particular comment or description more explicit or concrete, or which indicated more
precisely what action was occurring or had occurred. They
might almost be called extended stage directions.

In addition to these minor revisions, the book version contains new passages, sometimes of paragraph length, sometimes
running to a page or more. These help to illuminate the character of Herrick's narrator or to reinforce the logic of his
behavior. For example, the section running from the middle
of page 120 through the end of the sentence on the next page
is Harrington's somewhat oblique explanation of why he was
drawn to Jane Dround and why his wife proved inadequate as
a sympathetic listener to his deepest confidences. Apparently
Herrick's afterthoughts were intended to underscore the character and personality of his hero, to enhance the irony of his
protestations, and perhaps to make him more likeable. They
might also be described, in James's phrase, as "responsible

re-seeing." Although Herrick was not usually a painstaking craftsman (and, as Howells gently suggested, was even at times a careless one), he seems in this novel at least to have taken particular care in the preparation of his manuscript.

THE MEMOIRS
OF AN
AMERICAN CITIZEN

TO WILL PAYNE

[William Morton Payne (1858–1919), librarian, high school teacher, journalist, essayist, translator, editor, and critic, played an important part in Chicago's cultural life from the 1880's until the early twentieth century. For a number of years he was literary editor of the *Chicago Daily News* and the *Chicago Evening Journal* and contributed extensively to the Chicago *Dial* while serving as its associate editor. Payne's books and articles reflected the traditional literary standards of his times.]

"O Commander of the Faithful," said the other, "shall I tell thee what I have seen with my eyes or what I have only heard tell?"

"If thou hast seen aught worth telling," replied the Khalif, "let us hear it: for report is not like eye-witness."

"O Commander of the Faithful," said the other, "lend me thine ear and thine heart."

"O Ibn Mensour," answered the Khalif, "behold I am listening to thee with mine ears, and looking at thee with mine eyes, and attending to thee with mine heart."

CHAPTER I

THE LAKE FRONT IN CHICAGO

I sleep out — A companion — Hunting a job — Free lunch and a bad friend — Steele's store and what happened there — A positive young woman — Number twelve

---

It was a raw, blustering September night when I rounded up for the first time at the lake front in Chicago. There was just a strip of waste land, in those days, between the great avenue and the railroad tracks that skirted the lake. In 1876 there were no large hotels or skyscrapers fronting a tidy park; nothing but some wooden or brick houses, and, across the tracks, the waves lapped away at the railroad embankment. I was something more than twenty, old enough, at any rate, to have earned a better bed than a few feet of sand and sooty grass in a vacant lot. It was the first night I had ever slept out, — at least, because there was no place I had a right to go to. All that day I had been on the tramp from Indiana, and reached the city with only a few cents in my pockets.

I was not the only homeless wanderer by any means. Early in the evening a lot of bums began to drop in, slinking down the avenue or coming over from the city through the cross streets. It was early in the season; but to-night the east wind raked the park and shook gusts of rain from the low clouds, making it comfortable to keep moving. So we wandered up and down that sandy strip, footing it like dogs on the hunt for a hole, and eying each other gloomily when we passed.

Early in the evening a big wooden building at the north end

was lighted up, and some of us gathered around the windows and hung there under the eaves watching the carriages drive up to the door to leave their freight. There was a concert in the hall, and after it began I crawled up into the arch of a window where I was out of the rain and could hear the music. Before the concert was over a watchman caught sight of me and snaked me to the ground. He was making a round of the building, stirring up the bums who had found any hole out of the reach of the wind. So we began once more that dreary, purposeless tramp to keep from freezing.

"Kind of chilly!" a young fellow called out to me.

"Chillier before morning, all right," I growled back, glad enough to hear a voice speaking to me as if it expected an answer.

"First night?" he inquired, coming up close to me in a friendly way. " 'Tain't so bad — when it's warm and the wind don't blow."

We walked on together slowly, as though we were looking for something. When we came under the light of the lamps in the avenue we eyed each other. My tramp companion was a stout, honest-looking young fellow about my age. His loose-fitting black clothes and collarless shirt made me think that he too had come from the country recently.

"Been farming?" I ventured.

"Pine Lake, across there in Michigan — that's where I come from. Hostetter, Ed Hostetter, that's my name."

We faced about and headed toward the lake without any purpose. He told me his story while we dragged ourselves back and forth along the high board fence that guarded the railroad property. He had got tired of working on his father's farm for nothing and had struck out for the big city. Hostetter had a married aunt, so he told me, living somewhere in Chicago, and he had thought to stay with her until he could get a start on fortune's road. But she had moved from her old address, and his money had given out before he knew it. For the last week he had been wandering about the streets, hunting a job, and looking sharp for that aunt.

"We can't keep this up all night!" I observed when his story had run out.

"Last night I found an empty over there in the yards, but some of the railroad fellers got hold of me toward morning and made me jump high."

A couple of tramps were crouching low beside the fence just ahead of us. "Watch 'em!" my companion whispered.

Suddenly they burrowed down into the sand and disappeared. We could hear their steps on the other side of the fence; then a gruff voice. In a few moments back they came, burrowing up from under the fence.

"That's what you get!" Ed grunted.

Well, in the end we had to make the best of it, and we camped right there, hugging the fence for protection against the east wind. We burrowed into the loose sand, piling it up on the open side until we were well covered. Now and then a train rushing past shook us awake with its heavy tread. Toward morning there were fewer trains, and though it began to mist pretty hard, and the water trickled into our hole, I managed to get some sleep.

At daylight we got up and shook ourselves, and then wandered miserably into the silent streets of the downtown district. Between us we had fifteen cents, and with that we got some coffee and a piece of bread at a little shanty stuck on the side of the river. A fat man with a greasy, pock-marked face served us, and I can see him now as he looked us over and winked to the policeman who was loafing in the joint.

After our coffee we began the hunt for an odd job, and Ed talked of his hopes of finding that aunt — Mrs. Pierson. We kept together because we were so lonesome, I suppose, and Ed was good company — jolly and happy-hearted. That night we slept on the back porch of an empty house 'way south, where the streets were broad, and there were little strips of green all about the houses. The owners of the large house we picked out must have been away for the summer. Toward morning we heard some one stirring around inside, opening and shutting doors, and we made up our minds there were thieves at work in the house.

Ed stayed to watch, while I ran out to the avenue to get some help. It was a long time before I could find a policeman, and when we got back to the house there was Hostetter sitting on the curbstone hugging his belly. One of the thieves had come out of the house the back way, and when Ed tried to hold him had given him such a kick that Ed was glad to let him go. The officer I had brought evidently thought we were playing some game on him or weren't quite straight ourselves, and he tried to take us to the station. We gave him a lively chase for a couple of blocks; the last we saw of him he was shaking his fist at us and cussing loud enough to wake the dead.

That day was much like the one before, only worse. The weather was mean and drizzly. I earned a quarter lugging a valise across the city, and we ate that up at breakfast. At noon we turned into one of the flashy saloons on State Street. We hoped to be overlooked in the crowd before the bar while we helped ourselves to the crackers and salt fish. We were making out pretty well when a man who was standing near the bar and drinking nothing spied us and came over to the lunch table.

"Wet day," he observed sociably.

"That's about it," I replied cautiously, looking the man over. He wore a long black coat, a dirty light-colored waistcoat, and a silk hat, underneath which little brown curls sprouted out. He fed himself delicately out of the common bowl, as if the free lunch didn't tempt his appetite.

"Seeing the town?" he asked next, looking pointedly at Ed's dirty shoes.

"Some part of it, I reckon," Ed laughed.

"Looking for a job?"

"You bet we're looking!" Ed growled back. "Know where we can find it?"

Before long we were on easy terms with the stranger. He insisted on paying for beer all around, and on the strength of that Ed and I made another raid on a platter of beans. Dinner that night didn't look very promising.

"It seems to me I know of the very thing for you young fellers," our friend finally remarked, and we pricked up our ears.

He said he had a friend in one of the large stores on State Street, who had found fine places for some young men he had recommended. They were making big money now. Ed's eyes began to glisten. But suddenly another idea struck our good friend. He lowered his voice and drew us to one side. Would one of us like a fat job, where there wasn't much work except special times — a gay kind of place, where we could see something of life? Ed was pretty eager, but I rather suspected what he was after.

"I guess the other place is more what we want," I said.

"Ain't up to snuff just yet?" he giggled. "Wait a week or two, and you will be as quick as the next one."

As we made no reply, and I was moving toward the door, he remarked: —

"Sure, it's stopped raining! Let's be moving up the street, and see what my friend can do for you."

So we started up State Street with the man in the silk hat. At the door of a big dry-goods store, where we had tried unsuccessfully that morning to obtain work, he remarked: —

"We'll just look in here. I know a man in the gents' underwear department, and p'r'aps he can help you."

I didn't think it very likely, for I hadn't much faith in our smooth acquaintance. But there was nothing better to do. So we all passed in through the heavy doors of Steele & Co.'s establishment. Even on that rainy afternoon the place was pretty well filled, mostly with women, who were bunched together at certain counters. We had some trouble in following our guide, who squirmed into the thick of every jam. I began to think that, having talked big to two green young fellows, he now wanted to give us the slip. But I determined, just to tease him, he shouldn't get out of our sight as easily as he thought to.

The "gents' underwear" department, as I happened to have observed in the morning, was on the State Street side, near the door which we had just entered. Nevertheless, our friend was leading us away from that part and seemed to prefer the most crowded aisles, where "ladies' goods" were displayed. At the glove counter there was a press of women who were trying to get near a heap of niney-eight-cent gloves. Our guide was just ahead of us at this point, and near his elbow I noticed an old gentleman and a young lady. The latter, who was trying on a pair of gloves, kept asking the old gentleman a string of questions. He was smiling at her without taking the trouble to reply. The girl was pretty and nicely dressed, and I suppose I must have looked at her hard, for she suddenly glanced up at me and then turned her back and faced the counter. As she turned I noticed something white drop from her hand, and I pressed closer to her to pick it up. It was a little handkerchief. As I reached down I saw a thin hand stretch out around the young lady's waist and then give a little jerk. I had just straightened myself with the handkerchief in my fingers when I heard the young lady exclaim: —

"Father! My purse has gone!"

"Why, why!" the old man stammered. "Your purse has gone? Where could it have gone to?"

Just then some one grabbed my arm, and a voice said in my ear: —

"Not so slick as that, young feller!"

A man who looked like an official of the store had hold of me.

"Don't make any fuss, and hand over that lady's purse," he added in a low voice.

"I haven't got her purse. I was just going to give her this handkerchief, which I saw her drop," I protested, holding up the silly thing I had picked from the floor.

"That's all right," the man said with a grin. "And now hand over the purse, too."

He began to feel my pockets, and, of course, I resented his familiarity, and, like a country jake, kicked up a muss then and there. A crowd began to collect. The floor-manager rushed up at this point, and between them I was hustled across the store and into one of the private offices. The first thing I heard when I got there was the old gentleman just behind me, stuttering, too much excited to talk plain.

"Yes, yes, my daughter's purse! She just lost it!"

"That's all right," I said. "And I saw the fellow who took it. . . ."

"I saw this man take it," I heard the girl say to the manager.

"Yes, yes, my daughter saw the thief take her purse," the old man put in excitedly.

"I was watching him all the time," said the man who had laid hold of me first. "He came in at the State Street entrance a few minutes ago with a green one and an old sneak. I didn't think he had the time to pass the stuff over."

I was cool now, and laughed as the manager and the detective went through my pockets carefully.

"The old one's got the stuff fast enough," the detective remarked disgustedly. "Shall we have this one locked up, Mr. Marble?"

"You'll do it at your risk!" I put in loudly.

"Where's the young woman?" the manager demanded.

"It happened just while my daughter was buying a pair of gloves," the old man began to chatter. "You were asking me, my love . . ."

The young woman looked a little confused, I thought, and not so sure of herself. But she answered the manager's questions by saying promptly: —

"He must have taken it!"

"You saw him?" the detective questioned.

"Yes — I must have seen him — I saw him, of course!"

"I don't believe you could have seen me, ma'am," I said with a grin, "for you had just turned your back on me."

"How did you know that?" she asked triumphantly.

"I know it because when I first began to look at you, you didn't like it, and so you turned your back on me to show it."

"You know too much, young man," the manager remarked. "You'll prosecute him?" he added, turning to the old man.

"Prosecute? Why, yes, of course," he stammered; "though, if he hasn't the purse —"

"Come on, m'boy," the detective said to me. "You and I'll take a stroll down the street and find a good night's lodging for you."

That was before the day of patrol wagons. So the detective

locked his right arm securely in my left, and in this intimate fashion we walked through the streets to the police station.

When we reached that foul-smelling pen we were kept waiting by a large "order" that had just been rounded up from a gambling-house in the neighborhood. There were about twenty men and women in this flock. They were filing, one by one, before the desk-sergeant. I had never heard such a family gathering of names. They were all Smiths, Browns, and Joneses, and they all lived a good way from town, out in the fifty-hundreds, where there are many vacant lots. At the end of the file there was a little unshaven Jew, who seemed very mad about it all. He was the only one who had any money; he gave up a fat roll of bills that took the officer some time to count.

"I know who did this!" the Jew sputtered at the man behind the desk. "And I can make it hot for some of youse, all right."

"That's good," the sergeant replied pleasantly. "Another time you'll have the sense to know when you are well off."

I thought this was fatherly advice addressed to the Jew for his moral health. I congratulated myself that I had fallen into clean hands. So when my turn came, I said to the desk-sergeant confidentially: —

"I am quite innocent!"

"Is that so, m'son?" he remarked pleasantly.

"They haven't any right to arrest me. I was —"

"Of course, of course! Keep all that for his Honor to-morrow morning. What's your name, m'son?"

"E. V. Harrington," I replied quite innocently.

"And where do you hail from?"

"Jasonville, Indiana."

It did not occur to me then that, guilty or innocent, it made no difference after I had given my real name and home. Thanks

to the enterprise of metropolitan journalism, the folks in Jasonville, Indiana, would be reading at their breakfast to-morrow
morning all about how Van Harrington had been taken up as
a thief.

"Here!" the fat sergeant called out to one of the officers, after
I had handed over to his care the few odds and ends that I still
had about me; "show the gent from Indiany to number twelve."

CHAPTER II

THE HARRISON STREET POLICE COURT

A night in jail — A rapid-fire judge — The young lady is not so positive — The psychology of justice — What's the matter with Jasonville? — I tell my story to his Honor

---

THERE was a greasy bench at one end of number twelve, where I sat myself down, feeling that I had come to the end of things in Chicago mighty quick. A measly gas-jet above the door showed what a stinking hole I had got myself into. I could hear the gambling party across the way, laughing and talking, taking their lot rather easily. Pretty soon a man was put into the cell next mine. He kept groaning about his head. "My head!" he would say, "oh, my head! My head! oh, my head!" until I thought my own head was going wrong.

I wondered what had become of Hostetter. Apparently he had cleared out when he saw his chance friend getting into trouble. Perhaps he thought I had been working with our smooth acquaintance all along. Then I thought what a fool I had been to give my real name and home to the desk-sergeant. To-morrow the wise ones down in Jasonville would be calling Van Harrington bad names all over again, and think how clever they had been.

Some bad-smelling mess was shoved at me for supper, but I had no stomach for food, good or bad. The jail quieted down after a time, but I couldn't sleep. My mind was full of the past, of everything that had happened to me from the beginning. Only forty-eight hours before I had been tramping my way into the city, as keen as a hungry steer for all the glory I saw there ahead of me under the bank of smoke that was Chicago. Boylike, I had looked up at the big packing-houses, the factories, the tall elevators that I passed, and thought how one day I should be building my fortune out of them as others had built theirs before me. And the end of that boyish dream was this bed in jail!

The next morning they hustled us all into court. I was crowded into the pen along with some of the numerous Smiths and Joneses who hadn't been able to secure bail the night before. These were disposed of first in the way of routine business, together with a few drunks and disorderlies. There were also in the pen some sickly-looking fellows who had been taken up for smoking opium in a Chinese cellar, a woman in whose house there had been a robbery, and a well-dressed man with a bandage over one eye. He must have been my neighbor of the bad head.

The court room was pretty well jammed with these prisoners, the police officers, and a few loafers. The air smelled like a sewer, and the windows were foul with dirt. The judge was a good-looking, youngish man, with a curling black mustache, and he wore a diamond-studded circlet around his necktie. Behind the judge on the platform sat the young woman whose purse I was accused of stealing, and her father. She saw me when I was brought into the pen, but tried not to let me know it, looking away all the time.

When I arrived on the scene the judge was administering an oath to a seedy-looking man, who kissed eagerly the filthy Bible and began to mumble something in a hurry to the judge.

"Yes, I know that pipe dream," his Honor interrupted pleasantly. "Now, tell me the straight story of what you have been doing since you were here last week."

"You insult me, Judge," the prisoner replied haughtily. "I'm an educated man, a graduate of a great institution of learning. You know your Horace, Judge?"

"Not so well as the revised statutes of the state of Illinois," his Honor snapped back with what I thought was a lack of respect for learning. "Two months. Next!"

"Why, Judge —"

There was a titter in the court room as the graduate of a great university was led from the pen. His Honor, wearing the same easy smile, was already listening to the next case. He flecked off a stray particle of soot that had lodged on the big pink in his buttonhole as he remarked casually: —

"Is that so? Twenty-five dollars. It will be fifty the next time."

The judge nodded blandly to the prisoner and turned to my neighbor of the night, the man who had had so much trouble with his head. I was getting very uneasy. That smiling gentleman up there on the bench seemed to have his mind made up about most folks beforehand, and it didn't seem to be favorably inclined this morning. I was beginning to wonder how many months he had me down for already. It didn't add to my peace of mind to see him chatting genially with the old gentleman and his daughter as he listened to the poor criminals at the bar.

His Honor went on disposing of the last cases at a rapid rate, with a smile, a nod, a joke — and my time was coming nearer. The sweat rolled down my cheeks. I couldn't keep my eyes off the young lady's face; somehow I felt that she was my only hope of safety. Finally the judge leaned back in his chair and smelled at his pink, as if he had 'most finished his morning's work.

The clerk called, "Edward V. Harrington." I jumped.

"Well, Edward?" the judge inquired pleasantly as I stood

before him. "The first time we have had the pleasure, I believe?"

I mumbled something, and the store detective began to tell his story.

"Is that it, Doctor?" the judge asked the old man.

"Why, I suppose so — I don't know. He was caught in the act, wasn't he?" Then, as the old man sat down, he added peevishly: "At least, that's what my daughter says, and she ought to know. It was her purse, and she got me down here this morning."

"How about it, miss?" the judge asked quickly, wheeling his chair the other way and smiling at the young lady. "Did you see the prisoner here take your purse?"

"Why, of course —" She was just going to say "yes" when her eyes caught mine for a moment, and she hesitated. "No, I didn't exactly see him, but —" her look swept haughtily over my head. "But he was very close to me and was stooping down just as I felt a jerk at my belt. And then the purse was gone. He must have taken it!"

"Stooping to beauty, possibly?" the judge suggested.

"Stooping to pick up the lady's handkerchief, which I saw her drop," I ventured to put in, feeling that in another moment I should find myself blown into prison with a joke.

"Oh! So you were picking up the lady's handkerchief? Very polite, I am sure!" His Honor glared at me for an instant for the first time. "And you thought you might as well take the purse, too? For a keepsake, eh?"

He had wheeled around to face me. A sentence was on his lips. I could feel it coming, and hadn't an idea how to keep it back. I looked helplessly at the young woman. Just as his Honor opened his mouth to speak, she exclaimed: —

"Wait a moment! I am not sure — he doesn't look bad. I

thought, Judge, you could tell whether he had really taken my purse," she ended reproachfully.

"Do you consider me a mind reader, miss?" the judge retorted, suspending that sentence in mid-air.

"Let him say something! Let him tell his story," the young lady urged. "Perhaps he isn't guilty, after all. I am sure he doesn't look it."

"Why, Sarah!" the old gentleman gasped in astonishment. "You said this morning at breakfast that you were sure he had stolen it."

Here the detective put in his oar.

"I know him and the one that was with him — they're old sneaks, your Honor."

"That's a lie!" I said, finding my tongue at last.

"Good!" the judge exclaimed appreciatively. "I am inclined to think so, too, Edward," he went on, adjusting his diamond circlet with one finger. "This young lady thinks you have a story of your own. Have you?"

"Yes, I have, and a straight one," I answered, plucking up my courage.

"Of course," he grunted sarcastically. "Well, let's have it, but make it short."

It did sound rather lame when I came to tell what I had done with myself since I had entered the city. When I got to that part about the house where Ed and I had been disturbed by thieves, the old gentleman broke in: —

"Bless my soul! That must be the Wordens' house. The officer said there were two suspicious characters who ran away up the boulevard. This fellow must be one of them. Of course he took the purse! You know the Wordens, don't you, Judge?"

His Honor merely nodded to the old gentleman, smiled at the young lady, and said to me: —

"Go on, young man! Tell us why you left home in the first place."

I got red all over again at this invitation, and was taken with a new panic.

"Who are your folks? What's the name of the place?" the judge asked encouragingly.

"Jasonville, Indiana."

"What's the matter with Jasonville, Edward?" he asked more sharply. "Why do you blush for it?"

"I had rather not tell with all these folks around," I answered, looking at the young lady.

His Honor must have found something in my case a little out of his ordinary experience, for he took me back into his own room. He got me started on my story, and one thing led to another. His manner changed all of a sudden: he no longer tried to be smart, and he seemed to have plenty of time. After that long night in the jail I wanted to talk. So I told his Honor just how it had been with me from the beginning.

CHAPTER III

JASONVILLE, INDIANA

---

*The Harringtons — The village magnate — A young hoodlum —
On the road to school — The first woman — Disgrace, and a girl's
will — An unfortunate coincidence — In trouble again — May loses
faith — The end of Jasonville — Discharged — A loan — Charity
— The positive young lady hopes I shall start right — The lake
front once more — I preach myself a good sermon*

THE Harringtons were pretty well known in Greene County,
Indiana. Father moved to Jasonville just after the war, when
the place was not much more than a crossroads with a prospect of a railroad sometime. Ours was the first brick house, built
after the kind he and mother used to know back in York State.
And he set up the largest general store in that district and made
money. Then he lost most of it when the oil boom first came.

Mother and he set great store by education, — if father hadn't
gone to the war he wouldn't have been keeping a country store,
— and they helped start the first township high school in our
part of the state. And he sent Will, my older brother, and me
to the Methodist school at Eureka, which was the best he could
do for us. There wasn't much learning to be had in Eureka
"College," however; the two or three old preachers and women
who composed the faculty were too busy trying to keep the
boys from playing cards and smoking or chewing to teach us
much.

Perhaps I was a bit of a hoodlum as a boy, anyway. The
trouble started with the judge — Judge Sorrell. He was a local
light, who held a mortgage on 'most everything in town (in-

cluding our store — after father went into oil). We boys had always heard at home how hard and mean the judge was, and dishonest, too; for in some of the oil deals he had tricked folks out of their property. It wasn't so strange, then, that we youngsters took liberties with the judge's belongings that the older folks did not dare to. The judge's fine stock used to come in from the field done up, raced to death, and the orchard by the creek just out of town (which had belonged to us once) rarely brought a good crop to maturity. We made ourselves believe that the judge didn't really own it, and treated him as a trespasser. So one night, when the judge made a hasty visit to our house after one of the "raids," my father found me in bed with a wet suit of clothes on, which I had been forced to sacrifice in the creek. The end of that lark was that father had to pay a good sum for my private interpretation of the laws of property, and I spent the rest of the summer on a farm doing a man's work.

Perhaps if it hadn't been for that ducking in the river and what followed, I might have come out just a plain thief. While I was sweating on that farm I saw the folly of running against common notions about property. I came to the conclusion that if I wanted what my neighbor considered to be his, I must get the law to do the business for me. For the first time it dawned on me how wonderful is that system which shuts up one man in jail for taking a few dollars' worth of truck that doesn't belong to him, and honors the man who steals his millions — if he robs in the legal way! Yes, the old judge knocked some good worldly sense into me.

(Nevertheless, old Sorrell needn't have hounded me after I came back to Jasonville, and carried his malice to the point of keeping me from getting a job when I was hoping to make a fair start so that I could ask May Rudge to marry me. But all that was some time later.)

May was one of that handful of young women who in those days stood being sneered at for wanting to go to college with their brothers. We were in the same classes at Eureka two years before I noticed her much. She was little and pale and delicate — with serious, cold gray eyes, and a mouth that was always laughing at you. I can see to-day the very spot where she stood when I first spoke to her. Good weather I used to drive over from father's to Eureka, and one spring morning I happened to drive by the Rudge farm on my way to school instead of taking the pike, which was shorter. There was a long level stretch of road straightaway between two pieces of green meadow, and there, ahead of me, I saw the girl, walking steadily, looking neither to the right nor to the left. I slowed up with the idea that she might give me a nod or a word; but she kept her pace as though she were thinking of things too far off to notice a horse and buggy on the road. Somehow I wanted to make her speak. Pretty soon I said: —

"Won't you ride to school with me, Miss May?"

Then she turned her head, not the least flustered like other girls, and looked me square in the eye for a minute. I knew she was wondering what made me speak to her then, for the boys at school never took notice of the college girls. But she got into the buggy and sat prim and solemn by my side. We jogged along between the meadows, which were bright with flowers and the soft, green grass of spring. The big timber along the roadside and between the pasture lands had just leaved out, and the long branches hung daintily in the misty morning air. All of a sudden I felt mighty happy to be there with her. I think her first words were, — "Do you come this way often?"

"Perhaps I shall be coming this way oftener now," I made bold to answer.

Her lips trembled in a little ironical smile, and the least bit of red sprang into her white face. I said, "It isn't as short as the pike, but it is a prettier road."

The smile deepened, and I had it on my tongue to add, "I shall be coming this way every morning if you will ride with me." But I was afraid of that smiling mouth.

(Of course I didn't tell his Honor all this, but I add it now, together with other matters that concern me and belong here. It will help to explain what happened later.)

So that fine spring morning, when I was seventeen, I first took note of what a woman is. The rest of that year I used to drive the prim little girl back and forth between her father's farm and school. I was no scholar like her, and she never went about with the other girls to parties. She wasn't in the least free and easy with the boys. In those days most girls didn't think much of a fellow who wouldn't take his chances to kiss them when he could. Evenings, when we called, we used to pull the parlor door to and sit holding hands with the young woman of our admiration. And no harm ever came of it that I know: most of those girls made good wives when the time came, for all they were easy and tender and ready to make love in the days of their youth.

But once, when I tried to put my arm about May Rudge, as we were driving along the lonely road, she turned and looked at me out of those cold gray eyes. Her mouth rippled in that little ironical way, as if she were laughing down in her mind. She never said a word or pulled away from me, but I didn't care to go on.

May gave me ambition, and she made me want to be steady and good, though she never said anything about it. But now and then I would break away and get myself into some fool scrape. Such was the time when I came back from a Terre Haute party pretty lightheaded, and went with some others to wake up the old Methodist president of the college. I don't remember what happened then, but the next morning at chapel the old boy let loose on "wine and wantoning," and called me by name. I knew that I had done for myself at Eureka, and I was pretty mad to be singled out for reprobation from all the offenders. I got up from my seat and walked out while the school stared. As I was getting my horse from the place where I kept it, May Rudge came into the yard.

"You aren't going this way?" she demanded quickly.

"I don't see as there's much use waiting for bouquets."

"You aren't going without apologizing!" she flashed out.

To tell the truth, that had never occurred to me. It seemed she cared less for the disgrace than for the way I took it. So in the end, before I left town, I drove up to the president's house, apologized, and got my dismissal in due form, and was told I should go to hell unless I was converted straightway. Then May drove down the street with me in face of the whole school, who contrived to be there to see my departure.

"I guess this ends my education, and being a lawyer, and all that," I said gloomily, as we drew near the Rudge farm. "Dad will never forgive this. He thinks rum is the best road to hell, the same as the old preacher. He won't sell a glass of cider in the store."

"There are other kinds of work," she answered. "You can show them just the same you know what's right."

"But you'll never marry a man who isn't educated," I said boldly.

"I'll never marry a man who hasn't principles — and religion," she replied without a blush.

"So I must be good and pious, as well as educated?"

"You must be a man" — and her lips curved ironically — "and now you are just a boy."

But I held her hand when I helped her from the buggy, and I believe she would have let me kiss her had I wanted to then.

Father and mother took my expulsion from school very hard, as I expected. Father especially — who had begun to brag somewhat at the store about my being a lawyer and beating the judge out — was so bitter that I told him if he would give me fifty dollars I would go off somewhere and never trouble him again.

"You ask me to give you fifty dollars to go to hell with!" he shouted out.

"Put me in the store, then, and let me earn it. Give me the same money you give Will."

But father didn't want me around the store for folks to see. So I had to go out to a farm once more, to a place that father was working on shares with a Swede. I spent the better part of two years on that farm, living with the old Swede, and earning mighty little but my keep. For father gave me a dollar now and then, but no regular wages. I could get sight of May only on a Sunday. She was teaching her first school in another county. Father and mother Rudge had never liked me: they looked higher for May than to marry a poor farm-hand, who had a bad name in the town. My brother Will, who was a quiet, church-going fellow, had learned his way to the Rudge place by this time, and the old people favored him.

After a while I heard of a chance in a surveyor's office at Terre Haute, but old Sorrell, who had more business than any ten men in that part of the country, met the surveyor on the train, and when I reached the office there wasn't any job for me. That night, when I got back from Terre Haute, I told my folks that I was going to Chicago. The next day I asked my father again for some money. Mother answered for him: —

"Will don't ask us for money. It won't be fair to him."

"So he's to have the store and my girl too," I said bitterly.

"May Rudge isn't the girl to marry a young man who's wild."

"I'll find that out for myself!"

Always having had a pretty fair opinion of myself, I found it hard to be patient and earn good-will by my own deserts. So I said rather foolishly to father: —

"Will you give me a few dollars to start me with? I have earned it all right, and I am asking you for the last time."

It was a kind of threat, and I am sorry enough for it now. I suspect he hadn't the money, for things were going badly with him. He answered pretty warmly that I should wait a long time before he gave me another dollar to throw away. I turned on my heel without a word to him or mother, and went out of the house with the resolve not to return.

But before I left Jasonville to make my plunge into the world I would see May Rudge. I wanted to say to her: "Which will you have? Choose now!" So I turned about and started for the Rudge farm, which was about a mile from the town, beyond the old place on the creek that used to belong to us. Judge Sorrell had put up a large new barn on the place, where he kept some fine blooded stock that he had been at considerable expense to import. I had never been inside the barn, and as I passed it that afternoon, it came into my mind, for no particular reason, to turn in at the judge's farm and go by the new building. Maybe I thought the old judge would be around somewhere, and I should have the chance before I left Jasonville to tell him what I thought of his dirty, sneaking ways.

But there was no one in the big barn, apparently, or anywhere on the place, and after looking about for a little I went on to May's. I came up to the Rudge farm from the back, having taken a cut across the fields.

As I drew near the house I saw Will and May sitting under an apple tree talking. I walked on slowly, my anger somehow rising against them both. There was nothing wrong in their being there — nothing at all; but I was ready to fire at the first sign. By the looks of it, mother was right: they were already sweethearts. Will seemed to have something very earnest to say to May. He took hold of one of her hands, and she didn't draw it away at once. . . . There wasn't anything more to keep me in Jasonville.

I kept right on up the country road, without much notion of where I was going to, too hot and angry to think about anything but those two under the apple tree. I had not gone far before I heard behind me a great rushing noise, like the sudden sweep of a tornado, and then a following roar. I looked up across the fields, and there was the judge's fine new barn one mass of red flame and black smoke. It was roaring so that I could hear it plainly a quarter of a mile away. Naturally, I started to run for the fire, and ran hard all the way across the fields. By the time I got there some men from town had arrived and were rushing around crazily. But they hadn't got out the live stock, and there was no chance now to save a hen. The judge drove up presently, and we all stood around and stared at the fire. After a time I began to think it was time for me to move on if I was to get to any place that night. I slipped off and started up the road once more. I hadn't gone far, however, before I was overtaken by a buggy in which was one of the men who had been at the fire.

"Where be yer goin', Van?" he asked peremptorily.

"I don't know as I am called on to tell you, Sam," I answered back.

"Yes, you be," he said more kindly. "I guess you'll have to jump right in here, anyways, and ride back with me. The judge wants to ask you a few questions about this here fire."

"I don't answer any of the judge's questions!" I replied sharply enough, not yet seeing what the man was after. But he told me bluntly enough that I was suspected of setting fire to the barn, and drove me back to the town, where I stayed in the sheriff's custody until my uncle came late that night and bailed me out. Will was with him. Father didn't want me to come home, so Will let me understand. Neither he nor my uncle thought I was innocent, but they hoped that there might not be enough evidence to convict me. Some one on the creek road had seen me going past the barn a little time before the fire was discovered, and that was the only ground for suspecting me.

The next morning I got my uncle (who wouldn't trust me out of his sight) to drive me over to the Rudge place. He sat in the team while I went up to the house and knocked. I was feeling pretty desperate in my mind, but if May would only believe my story, I shouldn't care about the others. She would understand quick enough why I never appeared at the farm the day before. Old man Rudge came to the door, and when he saw me, he drew back and asked me what my business was.

"I want to see May," I said.

"I guess she don't want much to see you."

"I must see her."

The sound of our voices brought Mrs. Rudge from the kitchen.

"Mother," old Rudge said, "Van wants to see May."

"Well, Cyrus, it won't do any harm, I guess."

When May came to the door she waited for me to speak.

"I want to tell you, May," I said slowly, "that I didn't have any hand in burning the judge's barn."

"I don't want to believe you did," she said.

"But you do all the same!" I cried sharply.

"Every one says you did, Van," she answered doubtfully.

"So you think I could do a mean, sneaky thing like that?" I replied hotly, and added bitterly: "And then not have sense enough to get out of the way! Well, I know what this means: you and Will have put your heads together. You're welcome to him!"

"You've no reason to say such things, Van!" she exclaimed.

"There ain't no use in you talking with my girl, Harrington," put in Rudge, who had come back to the door. "And I don't want you coming here any more."

"How about that, May?" I asked. "Do you tell me to go?"

Her lips trembled, and she looked at me more kindly. Perhaps in another moment she would have answered and not failed me. But hot and heady as I was by nature, and smarting from all that had happened, I wanted a ready answer: I would not plead for myself.

"So you won't take my word for it?" I said, turning away.

"The word of a drunkard and a good-for-nothing!" the old man fired after me.

"Oh, father! don't," I heard May say. Then perhaps she called my name. But I was at the gate, and too proud to turn back.

I was discharged the next week. Although there was nothing against me except the fact that I had been seen about the barn previous to the fire, and the well-known enmity between me and the judge, it would have gone hard with me had it not been for the fact that in the ruins of the burned barn they found the remains of an old farm-hand, who had probably wandered in there while drunk and set the place on fire with his pipe.

When I was released my uncle said the folks were ready to have me back home; but without a word I started north on the county road in the direction of the great city.

"So," said his Honor, when I had finished my story in the dingy chamber of the police court, "you want me to believe that you really had no hand in firing that barn any more than you took this lady's purse?"

But he smiled to himself, at his own penetration, I suppose, and when we were back in the court room that dreaded sentence fell from his lips like a shot, — "Officer, the prisoner is discharged."

"I knew he was innocent!" the young lady exclaimed the next instant.

"But, Judge, where is the purse and my friend Worden's fur coat?" the old gentleman protested.

"You don't see them about him, do you, Doctor?" the judge inquired blandly. Then he turned to me: "Edward, I think that you have told me an honest story. I hope so."

He took a coin from his pocket.

"Here's a dollar, my boy. Buy a ticket for as far as this will take you, and walk the rest of the way home."

"I guess I have come to Chicago to stay," I answered. "They aren't breaking their hearts over losing me down home."

"Well, my son, as you think best. In this glorious Republic it is every man's first privilege to take his own road to hell. But, at any rate, get a good dinner to start on. We don't serve first-class meals here."

"I'll return this as soon as I can," I said, picking up the coin.

"The sooner the better; and the less we see of each other in the future, the better, eh?"

I grinned, and started for the door through which I had been brought into court, but an officer pointed to another door that led to the street. As I made for it I passed near the young lady. She called to me: —

"Mister, mister, what will you do now?"

"Get something to eat first, and then look for another purse, perhaps," I replied.

She blushed very prettily.

"I am sorry I accused you, but you were looking at me so hard just then — I thought . . . I want you to take this!"

She tried to give me a bill rolled up in a little wad.

"No thanks," I said, moving off.

"But you may need it. Every one says it's so hard to find work."

"Well, I don't take money from a woman."

"Oh!" She blushed again.

Then she ran to the old gentleman, who was talking to the judge, and got from him a little black memorandum-book.

"You see, my cards were all in the purse. But there!" she said, writing down her name and address on the first page. "You will know now where to come in case you need help or advice."

"Thank you," I replied, taking the book.

"I do so want to help you to start right and become a good man," she said timidly. "Won't you try to show your friends that they were mistaken in you?"

She turned her eyes up at me appealingly as if she were asking it as a favor to her. I felt foolish and began to laugh, but stopped, for she looked hurt.

"I guess, miss, it don't work quite that way. Of course, I mean to start fresh — but I shan't do it even for your sake. All the same, when you see me next it won't be in a police station."

"That's right!" she exclaimed, beaming at me with her round blue eyes. "I should like to feel that I hadn't hurt you — made you worse."

"Oh, you needn't worry about that, miss. I guess I'm not much worse off for a night in the police station."

She held out her hand and I took it.

"Sarah! Sarah!" the old gentleman called as we were shaking

hands. He seemed rather shocked, but the judge looked up at us and smiled quizzically.

Outside it was a warm, pleasant day; the wind was blowing merrily through the dirty street toward the blue lake. For the moment I did not worry over what was to come next. The first thing I did was to get a good meal.

After that refreshment I sauntered forth in the direction of the lake front — the most homelike place I could think of. The roar of the city ran through my head like the clatter of a mill. I seemed to be just a feeble atom of waste in the great stream of life flowing around me.

When I reached the desolate strip of weeds and sand between the avenue and the railroad, the first relay of bums was beginning to round up for the night. The sight of their tough faces filled me with a new disgust; I turned back to the busy avenue, where men and women were driving to and fro with plenty to do and think, and then and there I turned on myself and gave myself a good cussing. Here I was more than twenty, and just a plain fool, and had been ever since I could remember. When I had rid myself of several layers of conceit it began to dawn on me that this was a world where one had to step lively if he wasn't to join the ranks of the bums back there in the sand. That was the most valuable lot of thinking I ever did in my life. It took the sorehead feeling of wronged genius out of me for good and all. Pretty soon I straightened my back and started for the city to find somewhere a bite of food and a roof to cover my head.

And afterward there would be time to think of conquering the world!

THE PIERSONS

"Hello! Here you be! Ain't I glad I found yer this soon," and Ed's brown eyes were looking into mine. His seemed to me just then about the best face in the world. "Seems though I was bound to be chasin' some one in this city!" he shouted, grabbing me by the arm. "But I've found all of 'em now."

He had missed me at the police station by a few minutes, and I had left no address. After looking up and down a few streets near by, Ed had thought of lying in wait for me on the lake front, feeling that unless some extraordinary good luck had happened to me I should bring up at that popular resort. He had not seen the little incident when the detective grabbed me in the great store, for just at that moment his attention had been attracted to a girl at one of the counters, who had called him by name. The girl, who was selling perfumes and tooth-washes, turned out to be his cousin Lou, his Aunt Pierson's younger daughter. After the surprise of their meeting Ed had looked for me, and the floor-walker told them of my misfortune. Then the cousin had made Ed go home with her. Mrs. Pierson, it seems, took in boarders in her three-story-and-basement house on West Van Buren Street. She and the two girls had given Ed a warm welcome, and for the first time in many days he had

had the luxury of a bed, which had caused him to oversleep, and miss me at the station.

All this I learned as we walked westward toward Ed's new home. At first I was a little shy about putting another burden on the boy's relations. But my friend would not hear of letting me go. When Ed tucked his arm under mine and hauled me along with country heartiness, saying I could share his bed and he had a job in view for us both, I felt as though the sun had begun to shine all over again that day. Through all the accidents of many years I have never forgotten that kindness, and my heart warms afresh when I stop to think how Ed grabbed my arm and pulled me along with him off those city streets. . . .

So it happened at dinner-time that night I found myself in the basement dining room and made my first bow to some people who were to be near me for a number of years — one or two of them for life. I can remember just how they all looked sitting about the table, which was covered with a mussed red table-cloth, and lit by a big, smelly oil lamp. Pa Pierson sat at the head of the table, an untidy, gray-haired old man, who gave away his story in every line of his body. He had made some money in his country story back in Michigan; but the ambition to try his luck in the city had ruined him. He had gone broke on crockery. He was supposed to be looking for work, but he spent most of his time in this basement dining room, warming himself at the stove and reading the boarders' papers.

The girls and the boy, Dick, paid him even less respect than they did their mother. They were all the kind of children that don't tolerate much incompetence in their parents. Dick was a putty-faced, black-haired cub, who scrubbed blackboards and chewed gum in a Board of Trade man's office. Neither he nor his two sisters, who were also working downtown, contributed much to the house, and except that now and then Grace, the older one, would help clean up the dishes in a shamefaced way, or bring the food on the table when the meal was extra late or she wanted to get out for the evening, not one of the three ever raised a finger to help with the work. The whole place, from kitchen to garret, fell on poor old Ma Pierson, and the boarders were kinder to her than her own children. Lank and stooping, short-sighted, with a faded, tired smile, she came and went between the kitchen and the dining room, cooking the food and serving it, washing the dishes, scrubbing the floors, and making the beds — I never saw her sit down to the table with us except one Christmas Day, when she was too sick to cook. She took her fate like an Indian, and died on the steps of her treadmill.

There were two other regular boarders besides myself and Ed — a man and a woman. The latter, Miss Hillary Cox, was cashier in the New Enterprise Market, not far from the house. She was rather short and stout, with thick ropes of brown hair that she piled on her head in a solid mass to make her look tall. She had bright little eyes, and her rosy face showed that she had not been long in the city.

The man was a long, lean, thin-faced chap, somewhat older than I was. His name was Jaffrey Slocum; he was studying law and doing stenographic work in a law office in the city. When I first looked at him I thought that he would push his way over most of the rocks in the road — and he did. Slocum was a mighty silent man, but little passed before his eyes without his knowing what it meant. I learned later that he came from a good Maine family, and had been to college in the East. And he had it much on his mind to do several things with his life — the first of which was to buy back the old home in Portland, and put his folks there where they belonged. Old Sloco, we called him! For all his slow, draggy ways he had pounds of pressure on the gauge. He and I have fought through some big fights

since then, and there's no man I had as soon have beside me
in a scrap as that thin-faced, scrawny-necked old chip of Maine
granite.

When Ed introduced me at the table, Grace made a place
beside her, and her sister Lou hospitably shoved over a plate
of stew. Then Lou smiled at me and opened fire: —

"We read all about you in the papers this morning, Mr.
Harrington!"

"Heh, heh!" Pa Pierson cackled.

"Say, Lou, I don't call that polite," Grace protested in an
affected tone.

"Don't mind me," I called out. "I guess I'm a public character, anyway."

"What did the lady say when she found she was wrong?"
Lou went on. "I should think she'd want to die, doing a mean
thing like that."

"Did she give you any little souvenir of the occasion?" Dick
inquired.

"If they are real nice folks, I should think they'd try to make
it up some way," Grace added.

"But what we want to know first," Slocum drawled gravely,
"is, did you take the purse, and, if so, where did you put it?"

"Why, Mr. Slocum!" Miss Cox sputtered, not catching the
joke. "What a thing to insinuate! I am sure Mr. Harrington
doesn't look like that — any one could see he wouldn't *steal*."

In this way they passed me back and forth, up and down
the table, until the last scrap of meat was gnawed from the
bone. Then they sniffed at Jasonville. Where was it? What did
I do there? Why did I come to the city? Miss Cox was the
sharpest one at the questions. She wanted to know all about
my father's store. She had already got Ed a place as delivery
clerk in the Enterprise Market, and there might be an opening

in the same store for me. I could see that there would be a place
all right if I met the approval of the smart little cashier. It has
never been one of my faults to be backward with women, —
all except May, — and as Miss Hillary Cox was far from un-
prepossessing, I fixed my attention on her for the rest of the
evening.

The Pierson girls tired of me quickly enough, as they had
already tired of Ed. Lou soon ceased to smile at me and open
her eyes in her silly stare when I made a remark. After dinner
she went out on the steps to wait for a beau, who was to take
her to a dance. Grace sat awhile to chaff with the lawyer's
clerk. He seemed to make fun of her, but I could see that he
liked her pretty well. (It must be a stupid sort of woman, indeed,
who can't get hold of a man when he has nothing to do after
his work except walk the streets or read a book!) There was
nothing bad in either of the girls: they were just soft, purring
things, shut up all day long, one in a big shop and the other in
a dentist's office. Of course, when they got home, they were
frantic for amusement, dress, the theatre — anything bright and
happy; anything that would make a change. They had a knack
of stylish dressing, and on the street looked for all the world
like a rich man's daughters. Nothing bad in either one, then —
only that kind gets its eyes opened too late! . . .

The next morning I stepped around to the Enterprise Market, and Miss Cox introduced me to the proprietors. They were
two brothers, sharp-looking young men, up-to-date in their
ideas, the cashier had told me, and bound to make the Enterprise the largest market on the West Side. Miss Cox had evidently said a good word for me, and that afternoon I found
myself tying up parcels and taking orders at ten dollars a week.

Not a very brilliant start on fortune's road, but I was glad
enough to get it. The capable cashier kept a friendly eye on me,
and saved me from getting into trouble. Before long I had my

pay raised, and then raised again. Ed had taken hold well, too, and was given more pay. He was more content with his job than I was. The work suited him — the driving about the city streets, the rush at the market mornings, the big crates of country stuff that came smelling fresh from the fields. The city was all that he had hoped to find it. Not so to me — I looked beyond; but I worked hard and took my cues from the pretty cashier, who grew more friendly every day. We used to go to places in the evenings, — lectures and concerts mostly, — for Miss Cox thought the theatre was wicked. She was a regular church attendant, and made me go with her Sundays. She was thrifty, too, and taught me to be stingy with my quarters and halves.

The first day I could take off I went to the police station and paid my loan from the judge. I had to wait an hour before I could speak to him, while he ground out a string of drunks and assaults, shooting out his sentences like a rapid-fire battery. When I finally got his attention, he turned one eye on me: —

"Well, Edward, so you haven't gone home yet!" And that was all he said as he dropped the coin into his pocket. (I hope that my paying back that money made him merciful to the next young tramp that was cast up there before him!)

After I had paid the judge I strolled down to the South Side, into the new residence district, with some idea of seeing where the young lady lived who had first had me arrested and then wanted to reform me. When I came to the number she had written in the memorandum-book, there was a piece of crape on the door. It gave me a shock. I hung around for a while, not caring to disturb the people inside, and yet hoping to find out that it was not the young lady who had died. Finally I came away, having made up my mind, somehow, that it was the young lady, and feeling sorry that she was gone. That night I opened the memorandum-book she had given me, and began a sort of diary in a cramped, abbreviated hand. The first items read as follows: —

September 30. Giv. this book by young la. who tho't I stole her purse. She hopes I may take the right road.

October 1. — Got job in Ent — mark., 1417 W. VanB St. $10. Is this the right road?

October 23. — Went to address young lad. gav. me. Found crape on the door. Hope it's the old man.

From time to time since then I have taken out the little black memorandum-book, and made other entries of those happenings in my life that seemed to me especially important — sometimes a mere list of figures or names, writing them in very small. It lies here before me now, and out of these bare notes, keywords as it were, there rise before me many facts, — the deeds of twenty-five years.

When I got back to the Piersons' for dinner, Miss Cox was curious to know what I had done with my first day off.

"I bet he's been to see that girl who had him arrested," Lou suggested mischievously. "And from the way he looks I guess she told him she hadn't much use for a butcher-boy."

Pa Pierson laughed; he was a great admirer of his daughter's wit.

"I don't think he's that much of a fool, to waste his time trapesing about after *her*," Hillary Cox snapped back.

"Well, I did look up the house," I admitted, and added, "but the folks weren't at home."

After supper we sat out on the steps, and Hillary asked me what kind of a place the young woman lived in. I told her about the crape on the door, and she looked at me disgustedly.

"Why didn't you ask?" she demanded.

"I didn't care to know if it was so, perhaps."

"I don't see as you have any particular reason to care, one way or the other," she retorted. And she went off for that evening somewhere with Ed. For the want of anything better to do I borrowed a book from the law student, who was studying in his room, and thus, by way of an accident, began a habit of reading and talking over books with Slocum.

So I was soon fitted into my hole in the city. In that neighborhood there must have been many hundreds of places like Ma Pierson's boarding-house. The checkerboard of prairie streets cut up the houses like marble cake — all the same, three-story-and-mansard-roof, yellow brick, with long lines of dirty, soft stone steps stretching from the wooden sidewalks to the second stories. And the group of us there in the little basement dining room, noisy with the rattle of the street cars, and dirty with the smoke of factory chimneys in the rear, was a good deal like the others in the other houses — strugglers on the outside of prosperity, trying hard to climb up somewhere in the bread-and butter order of life, and to hold on tight to what we had got. No one, I suppose, ever came to Chicago, at least in those days, without a hope in his pocket of landing at the head of the game sometime. Even old Ma Pierson cherished a secret dream of a rich marriage for one or other of her girls!

Hillary Cox smiled on me again the next day, and we were as good friends as ever. As I have said, the energetic cashier of the Enterprise Market had taken me in hand and was forming me to be a business man. She was a smart little woman, and had lots of good principles besides. She believed in religion on Sundays, as she believed in business on week days. So on the Sabbath morning we would leave Ed and Lou and Dick Pierson yawning over the breakfast table, while Slocum and I escorted Grace and Hillary downtown to hear some celebrated preacher in one of the prominent churches. Hillary Cox had no relish for the insignificant and humble in religion, such as we might have found around the corner. She wanted the best there was to be had, she said, and she wanted to see the people who were so much talked about in the papers.

Perhaps the rich and prominent citizens made more of a point of going to church in those days than they do now. It was a pretty inferior church society that couldn't show up two or three of the city's solid merchants, who came every Sunday with their women, all dressed in their smartest and best. Hillary and Grace seemed to know most of these people by sight. Women are naturally curious about one another, and I suppose the girls saw their pictures and learned their names in the newspapers. And in this way I, too, learned to know by sight some of the men whom later it was my fortune to meet elsewhere.

There was Steele, the great dry-goods merchant, and Purington, whose works for manufacturing farming tools were just behind Ma Pierson's house; Lardner, a great hardware merchant; Maybricks, a wholesale grocer; York, a rich lumberman — most of them thin-faced, shrewd Yankees, who had seized that tide of fate which the poet tells us sweeps men to fortune. And there were others, perhaps less honorably known as citizens, but equally important financially: Vitzer, who became known later as the famous duke of gas, and Maxim, who already had begun to stretch out his fingers over the street-car lines. This man had made his money buying up tax titles, that one building cars, and another laying out railroads, and wrecking them, too. They were the people of the land!

One fine winter morning, as the four of us idled on the sidewalk opposite a prominent South Side church that was discharging its prosperous congregation into the street, Slocum nudged me and pointed to a group of well-dressed people — two or three women and a short, stout, smooth-shaven man — who were standing on the steps of the church, surveying the scene and bowing to their neighbors.

"That's Strauss!"

It was not necessary to say more. Even in those days the great Strauss had made his name as well known as that of the father of our country. He it was who knew each morning whether the rains had fallen on the plains beneath the Andes; how many cattle on the hoof had entered the gates of Omaha and Kansas City; how tight the pinch of starvation set upon Russian bellies; and whether the Sultan's subjects had bought their bread of Liverpool. Flesh and grain, meat and bread — Strauss held them in his hand, and he dealt them forth in the markets of the world!

Is it any wonder that I looked hard at the portly, red-faced man, standing there on the steps of his temple, where, with his women and children, he had been worshipping his God?

"My!" said Grace, "Mrs. Strauss is plain enough, and just common-looking."

(I have noticed that women find it hard to reconcile themselves to a rich man's early taste in their sex.)

"She don't dress very stylish, that's true," Hillary observed thoughtfully. "But it weren't so very long ago, I guess, that she was saving his money."

Strauss, surrounded by his women folk, marched up the avenue in solemn order. We followed along slowly on the other side of the street.

"He didn't make his pile at the Enterprise Market," Grace remarked. She spoke the idea that was in all our minds: how did he and the others make their money?

"I guess they began like other folks," Hillary contended, "saving their earnings and not putting all their money in their stomachs and on their backs."

This last was aimed at Grace, who was pretty smartly dressed.

"Well," said Slocum, dryly, "probably by this time Strauss has something more than his savings in the bank."

Thus we followed them down the street, speculating on the

great packer's success, on the success of all the fortunate ones in the great game of the market, wondering what magic power these men possessed to lift themselves out of the mass of people like ourselves. Pretty simple of us, perhaps you think, hanging around on the street a good winter morning and gossiping about our rich neighbors! But natural enough, too: we had no place to loaf in, except Ma Pierson's smelly dining room, and nothing to do with our Sunday holiday but to walk around the streets and stare up at the handsome new houses and our well-dressed and prosperous neighbors. Every keen boy who looks out on life from the city sidewalk has a pretty vigorous idea that if he isn't as good as the next man, at least he will make as much money if he can only learn the secret. We read about the rich and their doings in the newspapers; we see them in the streets; their horses and carriages flash by us — do you wonder that some poor clerks on a Sunday gape at the Steeles and the Strausses from the sidewalk?

What was the golden road? These men had found it — hundreds, thousands of them, — farming tools, railroads, groceries, gas, dry-goods. It made no matter what: fortunes were building on every side; the flowers of success were blooming before our eyes. To take my place with these mighty ones — I thought a good deal about that these days! And I remember Grace saying sentimentally to Slocum that Sunday: —

"You fellers keep thinkin' of nothin' but money and how you're goin' to make it. Perhaps rich folks ain't the only happy ones in the world."

"Yes," Hillary chimed in, "there's such a thing as being too greedy to eat."

"What else are we here for except to make money?" Slocum demanded more bitterly than usual.

He raised his long arm in explanation and swept it to and fro over the straggling prairie city, with its rough, patched look.

I didn't see what there was in the city to object to: it was just a place like any other — to work, eat, and sleep in. Later, however, when I saw the little towns back East, the pleasant hills, the old homes in the valleys, and the red-brick house on the elm-shaded street in Portland, then I knew what Slocum meant.

Whatever was there in Chicago in 1877 to live for but Success?

CHAPTER V

A MAN'S BUSINESS

Signs of trouble at the Enterprise — A possible partnership — He travels fastest who travels alone — John Carmichael — Feeding the peoples of the earth — I drive for Dround

---

"Do you see that big, fat fellow talking with Mr. Joyce?" the cashier whispered to me one morning as I passed her cage. "He's Dround's manager — his name is Carmichael. When he shows up, there is trouble coming to some one."

Dround & Co. was the name of the packing firm that the Enterprise dealt with. I tied up my bundles and made up my cash account, thinking a good deal about the appearance of the burly manager of the packing-house. Pretty soon Mr. Carmichael came out into the front store very red in the face, followed by the elder Joyce, who had been drinking, and they had some words. The cashier winked at me.

The Enterprise had been doing a good business. It was run on a new principle for those days — strictly cash and all cut prices, a cent off here and there, a great sale of some one thing each day, which the house handled speculatively. The brothers Joyce kept branching out, but there wasn't any money to speak of behind the firm. The Drounds and a wholesale grocer had backed it from the start. Nevertheless, we should have got on all right if the elder Joyce had given up drinking and the younger one had not taken to driving fast horses. Latterly no matter how big a business we did, the profits went the wrong way.

That evening, as Hillary Cox and I walked over to the Piersons', she said to me abruptly, "There's going to be a new sign at the Enterprise before long!"

The smart little cashier must have divined the situation as I had.

"Cox's Market?" I suggested jokingly.

"Why not Harrington & Cox?" she retorted with a nervous little laugh. We were on the steps then, and Ed joined us, so that I did not have to answer her invitation. But all through the meal I kept thinking of her suggestion. It was nearly two years since she had introduced me to the Enterprise, and I had saved up several hundred dollars in the meantime, which I wanted to put into some business of my own. But it did not quite suit my card to run a retail market. After supper the others left us in the dining room, and when we were alone Hillary said: —

"Well, what do you think of the firm name? It wouldn't be so impossible. I've got considerable money saved up, and I guess you have some in the bank, too. It wouldn't be the first time in this town that a clerk's name followed a busted owner's over the door."

She spoke in a light kind of way, but a tone in her voice made me look up. It struck me suddenly that this thing might mean a partnership for life, as well as a partnership for meat and groceries. Hillary Cox was an attractive woman, and she would make a splendid wife for a poor man, doing her part to save his money. Between us, no doubt, we could make a good business out of the old Enterprise, and more, too!

"That firm name sounds pretty well," I answered slowly, somewhat embarrassed.

"Yes — I thought it pretty good."

Suddenly she turned her face shyly away from my eyes. She was a woman, and a lovable, warm-hearted one. Perhaps she was dreaming of a home and a family — of just that plain, ordinary happiness which our unambitious fathers and mothers took out of life. I liked her all the better for it; but when I tried to say something tender, that would meet her wish, I couldn't find a word from my heart: there was nothing but a hollow feeling inside me. And the thought came over me, hard and selfish, that a man like me, who was bound on a long road, travels best alone.

"I don't know as I want to sell coffee and potatoes all my life," I said at last, and my voice sounded colder than I meant to make it.

"Oh!" she gave a little gasp, as if some one had struck her. "You're very ambitious, Mr. Harrington," she said coldly. "I hope you'll get all you think you deserve, I am sure."

"Well, that wouldn't be much — only I am going to try for more than I deserve — see?" I laughed as easily as I could.

We talked a little longer, and then she made some kind of excuse — we had planned to go out that evening — and left me, bidding me good night as if I were a stranger. I felt small and mean, yet glad, too, to speak the truth — that I hadn't made a false step just there and pretended to more than I could carry through.

Some time later Slocum looked in at the door, and, seeing me alone, came into the room. He had a grim kind of smile on his face, as if he suspected what had been happening.

"Where's Grace?" I asked him.

"Just about where your Hillary is," he answered dryly; "gone off with another fellow."

I laughed. We looked at each other for some time.

"Well?" I said.

"He travels fastest who travels alone," he drawled, using the very words that had been in my mind. "But it is a shame — Miss Cox is a nice woman."

"So is the other."

"Yes, but it can't be — or anything like it."

And the difference between us was that I believe he really cared.

So the Enterprise Market crumbled rapidly to its end, while I kept my eye open for a landing-place when I should have to jump. One day I was sent over to Dround's to see why our usual order of meats hadn't been delivered. I was referred to the manager. Carmichael, as I have said, was a burly, red-faced Irishman — and hot-tempered. His black hair stood up all over his head, and when he moved he seemed to wrench his whole big carcass with the effort. As I made my errand known to him, he growled something at me. I gathered that he didn't think favorably of the Enterprise and all that belonged thereto.

"They can't have any more," he said. "I told your boss so the last time I was over."

I hung on, not knowing exactly what to say or do.

"I guess they must have it this time," I ventured after a while.

" 'Guess they must have it'! Who are you?"

He thrust his big head over the top of his desk and looked at me, laying his cigar down deliberately, as if he meant to throw me out of the office for my impudence.

"Oh!" I said as easily as I could, "I'm one of their help."

"Well, my son, maybe you know better than I what they do with their money? They don't pay us."

I knew he was trying to pump me about the Enterprise. I smiled and told him nothing, but I got that order delivered. Once or twice more, having been successful with the manager, I was sent on the same errand. Carmichael swore at me, bullied me, and jollied me, as his mood happened to be. Finally he said in earnest: —

"Joyce's got to the end of his rope, kid. You needn't come in here again. The firm will collect in the usual way."

I had seen all along that this was bound to come, and had made up my mind what I should do in the event.

"Do you hear?" the Irishman roared. "What are you standing there for? Get along and tell your boss I'll put a sheriff over there."

"I guess I have come to stay," I replied easily.

"Come to stay?" he said with a grin. "How much, kid?"

"All you will give me."

"What are you getting?"

"Twenty."

"I'll give you fifteen to drive a wagon," he said offhand, "and I'll fire you in a week if you haven't anything better with you than your cheek."

"All right," I said coolly, not letting him see that I was ruffled by his rough tongue.

In that way I made the second round of the ladder, and went whistling out of Dround's packing-house into the murky daylight of the Stock Yards.

I liked it all. Something told me that here was my field — this square plot of prairie, where is carried on the largest commissariat business of the world. In spite of its filth and its ugly look, it fired my blood to be a part of it. There's something pretty close to the earth in all of us, if we have the stomach to do the world's work: men of bone and sinew and rich blood, the strong men who do the deeds at the head of the ranks, feed close to the earth. The lowing cattle in the pens, the squealing hogs in the cars, the smell of the fat carcasses in the heavy wagons drawn by the sleek Percherons — it all made me think of the soft, fertile fields from which we take the grain — the blood and flesh that enter into our being.

The bigness of it all! The one sure fact before every son and daughter of woman is the need of daily bread and meat. To feed the people of the earth — that is a man's business. My part was to drive a wagon for Dround at fifteen a week, but I walked out of the Yards with the swagger of a packer!

CHAPTER VI

FIRST BLOOD

Wholesale — The little envies of life — Learning how to read —
What there might be in sausage — Schemes — A rise in life — Big
John's favoring eye — Going short of pork — Uncertainty — Five
thousand dollars in the bank

I TOLD them all at the supper table that evening how I was going
into wholesale with Henry I. Dround & Co. Slocum nodded
approvingly, but before any one could say a word of con-
gratulation, Hillary Cox snapped this at me: —

"So you were looking out for yourself with that Carmichael
man! I thought the Enterprise wasn't big enough for your
talents. A desk in the inside office. I s'pose?"

"Not quite yet," I laughed; but I didn't say how little my
job was to be.

Miss Cox had given me up. I don't believe she meant to be
disagreeable, but somehow we had become strangers, all at
once. There were no more gossips on the front steps or Sunday
parties. Ed went to church with her in my place. They were
getting very close, those two, and it didn't take a shrewd eye
to see what was going to happen sometime soon.

The others were more generous than the little cashier and
inclined to make too much of my good fortune. For the first
time in my life I had the pleasure of knowing that folks were
looking up at me and envying me, and I liked the feeling of
consequence. I let them think I was to get big wages.

"I suppose you'll be leaving this ranch before long?" Lou
suggested.

"Oh, I shouldn't wonder if I might move over to the Palmer House."

A look of consternation spread over Ma Pierson's face at my joking words. She saw a quarter of her regular income wiped off the slate. After the others had gone I told her it was only a joke, and that I should stay with her "until I got married." She cried a little, and said things were bad with her and getting worse all the time. Lately Lou had taken to going with such kind of men that she had no peace at all. I tried to cheer her up, and it was a number of years after that before I could bring myself to leave her place, although the food got worse and worse, and the house more messy and slack.

Even when, later, I began to make a good deal of money, I did not care to change my way of life. At Ma Pierson's were the only people I knew well in the city, and though Grace, and Lou, and Ed, and Dick weren't the most brilliant folks in the city, they were honest, warm-hearted souls and good enough company. And the law clerk, Slocum, was much more. He meant a good deal to me. He taught me how to read — I mean how to take in ideas as they were thought out by those who put them in books. He lent me his own books, all marked and pencilled with notes and references, which showed me how a well-trained mind stows away its information, how it compares and weighs and judges — in short, how it thinks.

We had many a good talk, sitting on the dusty stone steps in our shirt sleeves late summer nights, when it was too hot to sleep. He had read a deal of history and politics and economics as well as his law, and when it came to argument, he could shut me up with a mouthful of facts that showed me how small my lookout on the world was. I remember how he put me through his old Mill, making me chew hard at every point until I had mastered the theory; then he fed me Darwin and Spencer, and Stubbs and Lecky, and a lot more hard nuts. And I think that I owe no one in the world quite so much as I do that keen, silent Yankee, who taught me how to read books and know what is in them.

Meantime I was not doing anything wonderful over at the Yards. For several months the big manager scarce looked my way when he came across me, while I drove and made deliveries to the city trade. Dround & Co.'s customers were mostly on the West Side, in the poorer wards along the river, where Jews and foreigners live. I used to wonder why the firm didn't try for a better trade; but later, when I learned something about the private agreements among the packers, I saw why each kept to his own field. I soon came to know our territory pretty well, and got acquainted with the little markets. My experience at the Enterprise gave me an idea that I thought to turn to some account with Dround's manager. One day, as I was driving into the Yards, I met the Irishman, and he threw me a greeting: —

"Hello, kid! What's the good word?" And he climbed affably into the seat beside me to drive up to the office.

Here was my chance, and I took it.

"Why don't Dround's handle sausage?" I said to the manager.

"What do you know about sausage?" he asked.

I told him what I had in mind. When I worked for the Enterprise we used to have trouble in selling our sausage. Women were afraid of it, thinking it was made from any foul scraps in the store. So, to make the customers take it, I hit on the plan when we had fresh sausage meat of putting some of the sausages by in clean little pasteboard boxes, and the next time a particular customer came in I would call her attention to one of the boxes, "which I had put aside for her specially." And she would take it every time. In this way the Enterprise built up a considerable trade in sausages. The same condition existed in other markets, as I knew; good customers were afraid to eat the ordinary sausage. So, I thought, why shouldn't the packing-house put up a superior kind of sausage in nice little boxes, with a fancy name? The marketmen could retail them handily. Carmichael seemed to be impressed with my idea: he asked questions and said he would think it over. That encouraged me to spring another scheme on him. Dround's trade was in the Jewish quarters, but of course we didn't sell to the real Jews.

"Why not get some old rabbi and make kosher meat — the real article? Strauss and the other packers don't handle it. We might have the market to ourselves, and it is a big one, too."

"Kid, you've got a head on you," big John said to me with warmth. And I saw myself a member of the firm next week!

It didn't work as easily as that, however. The next time I saw the manager I asked him about sausage and kosher meat, and he scowled. It seems he had presented my ideas to Mr. Henry I. Dround, and that gentleman had turned them down. He was a packer, so the head of the house said, and no cat's-meat man, to retail sausages in paper packages to the public. The same way with the kosher meat idea: his business was the packing business, and the firm wasn't trying any ventures. It seemed to me that Mr. Henry I. Dround lacked enterprise; I felt that his manager would have given my ideas a trial.

It was not long after that, however, before Carmichael took me into the office and made me a kind of helper to him, sending me up and down the city to collect accounts, look after the little markets that traded with Dround's, and try on the sly to steal some other fellow's business — that is, to break secretly one of those trade agreements which the packers were always making together, and always breaking here and there, and, when caught, promising each other to be good, and never do it again — until the next opportunity offered, of course! This was more or less confidential and delicate business, and I was not let into the inside all at once. But I said nothing, and kept my eyes open. I began to know some things about the business, and I could guess a few more. I learned pretty soon that Henry I. Dround & Co. was not one of the strongest concerns in the city; that it was being squeezed in the ribs by the great Strauss over the way — that, if it had not been for the smart Irishman, Strauss might take the bread out of our mouths.

Next to Slocum, I owe big John Carmichael more than I could ever pay in money. He was an ignorant, hot-tempered, foul-mouthed Irishman, who had almost been born in the Yards, and had seen little else than the inside of a packing-house all his life. He couldn't write a grammatical letter or speak an un-blasphemous sentence. But it didn't take me long to see that Dround & Co. was Carmichael, the manager, and that I was in the best kind of luck to be there under him, and, so to speak, part way in his confidence. . . .

Well, as I said, I got an inkling from time to time how there was a private agreement between the large firms to carve up the market, retail as well as wholesale, and that when one of the firms felt that they could do it safely they would sneak around the agreement (which, of course, was illegal) and try to steal their neighbors' trade. Carmichael managed this business himself, and now and then, when he saw I knew how to keep my mouth shut, he would trust some detail of it to me.

But I was getting only twenty dollars a week, and no rosy prospects. My little schemes of making sausages on a large scale and kosher meat had been turned down. I stowed them away in my mind for future use. Meantime, after working at the Yards for nearly two years, I had managed to lay by about a thousand dollars, what with my savings when I was at the Enterprise. That thousand dollars was in a savings-bank down-town, and it made me restless to think that it was drawing only three and a half per cent, when chances to make big money were going by me all the time just out of my grasp. I kept turning over and over in my mind how I might use that thousand and make it breed money. There were lively times then on the Board of Trade. Nothing much was done in the stock market in Chicago in those early days, but when a man wanted to take his flyer he went into pork or grain. I used to hear more or less about what was being done on the Board of Trade from Dick Pierson, who had been promoted from scrubbing blackboards to a little clerkship in the same office, which operated on the Board.

Dick had grown to be a sallow-faced, black-mustached youth who had his sisters' knack of smart dressing, and a good deal of mouth. He was always talking of the deals the big fellows were carrying, and how this man made fifty thousand dollars going short on lard and that man had his all taken away from him in the wheat pit. He was full of tips that he picked up in his office — always fingering the dice, so to speak, but without the cash to make a throw. Dick knew that I had some money in the bank, and he was ever at me to put it up on some deal on margin. Slocum used to chaff him about his tips, and I didn't take his talk very seriously. It was along in the early summer of my third year at Dround's when Dick began to talk about the big deal Strauss was running in pork. Pork was going to twenty dollars a barrel, sure. According to Dick, all any one had to do to make a fortune was to get on the train now. This time his talk made some impression on me; for the boys were saying the same thing over in the office at the Yards. I thought of asking Carmichael about it, but I suspected John might lie to me and laugh to see the "kid" robbed. So I said nothing, but every time I had occasion to go by the bank where I kept my money it seemed to call out to me to do something. And I was hot to do something! I had about made up my mind after turning it over for several weeks, to make my venture in Strauss's corner. Pork was then selling about seventeen dollars a barrel, and there was talk of its going as high as twenty-five dollars by the October delivery.

It happened that the very day I made up my mind to go down to the city and draw out my money I was in the manager's office talking to him about one of our small customers. Carmichael was opening his mail and listening to me. He would rip up an envelope and throw it down on his desk, then let the letter slide out of his fat hand, and pick up another. I saw him grab one letter in a hurry. On the envelope, which was plain, was printed JOHN CARMICHAEL in large letters. As he tore open the enclosure I could see that it was a broker's form, and printed in fat capitals beneath the firm name was the word SOLD, and after it a written item that looked like pork. As Carmichael shoved this slip of paper back in the envelope I took another look and was sure it was pork. I went out of the office thinking to myself: "Carmichael isn't buying any pork this trip: he's selling. What does that mean?"

As I have said, the manager had charge of those private agreements with which the trade was kept together. In this way he came in contact with all our rivals, and among them the great Strauss. After thinking for a time, it was clear to me that the Irishman had some safe inside information about this deal which Dick did not have, nor any one else on the street. That afternoon when I could get off I went down to the bank and drew my money. At first I thought I would take five hundred dollars and have something left in the bank in case I was wrong on my guess. But the nearer I got to the bank the keener I was to make all I could. I took the thousand and hurried over to the office on La Salle Street, where Dick worked. I beckoned him out of the crowd in front of the board and shoved my bunch of money into his hand.

"I want you to sell a thousand barrels of pork for me," I said.

"Gee!" Dick whistled, "you've got nerve. What makes you want to go short of pork?"

"Never you mind," I said; "go on and tell your boss to sell, and there's your margin."

"I'll have to speak to the old man himself about this," Dick replied soberly. "This ain't any market to fool with."

"Well, if he don't want the business there are others," I observed coolly.

Dick disappeared into the back office, and I had to wait some time. Presently a fat little smooth-shaven man shoved his head through the door and looked me over for a moment with a grin on his face. I suppose he thought me crazy, but he didn't object to taking my money all the same.

"All right," he called out with another grin, "we'll take his deal." And Dick came out from the door and told me in a big voice: —

"All right, old man! We sell a thousand for you."

When I got out into the street I wasn't as sure of what I had done as I had been when I went into the broker's office; but I had too much nerve to admit that I wished I had my money back in my fist. And I kept my courage the next week, while pork hung just about where it was or maybe went up a few cents. Then it began to slide back just a little — $16.87½, $16.85, $16.80, were the quotations — and so on until it reached $16.50, where it hung for a week. Then it took up its retreat again until it had slid to an even $16. Dick, who congratulated me on my luck, advised me to sell and be content with doubling my money. Strauss was just playing with the street, he said. This was only the end of August: by the middle of September there would be a procession. But my head was set. To be sure, when, after the first of September, pork began to climb, I rather wished I had been content with doubling my money. But I pinned my faith on Carmichael. I didn't believe he was selling yet. For a fortnight at the close of September, pork hung about $16.37½, with little variation either way. Then the last three days of the month, as the time for October deliveries drew near, it began to sag and dropped to $16.10. I hung on.

It was well for me that I did. October first Strauss began delivering, and he poured pork into the market by the thousand barrels. Pork dropped, shot down, and touched $13. One morning I called at the broker's office and gave the order to buy. I had cleared four thousand dollars in my deal.

It was first blood!

There was about five thousand dollars in the bank that day when I went back to the Yards, and I was as proud as a millionnaire. Somehow, I seemed to forget how I had learned the right tip, and thought of myself as a terribly smart young man. Perhaps I looked what I was thinking, for when the manager stepped out of his office a little later and eyed me there was a queer kind of smile on his lips.

"What's happened, kid?" he asked, quizzing me. "Been selling any more pork this morning?"

Then I suspected that somehow he had learned about my little venture in the market. I was doubtful just how he might take it.

"No," I said. "It's the time to buy now, isn't it?"

"Covering?" he chuckled. "Well, that's good. Say, some one telephoned out from Cooper's office for you this morning — about a little deal in pork. I answered the 'phone."

So that was the way he had learned! That fool Dick had got nervous, and been telephoning to me.

"I hope you made it all right," Carmichael added.

"You bet," I answered cheerily. And that was all that was ever said about the matter.

CHAPTER VII

THE BOMB

I become a packer on my own account — What there is in sausage — The Duchess — The Piersons' again — At the Haymarket — The path of the bomb — Another kind of evil

Not long after my little deal in pork Carmichael promoted me. Instead of running around the city to look after the markets, I was sent out on the road to the towns that were building up all along the railroad lines throughout the neighboring states. My business was to secure as many of these new markets as I could, and, wherever it was possible, to dispossess any rival that had got hold before. It gave me a splendid chance to know a great section of our country which was teeming with life.

That five thousand dollars in the bank burned worse than the first thousand. I took no more chances on pork, however, but I managed to turn a dollar here and there, and after a time something rather big came my way. There were a couple of German Jews, the brothers Schunemann, who were trying to run a packing business at Aurora. They had started as small butchers, and had done well; but they wanted to get into the packing business, and they were having a hard time to compete with the big fellows in Chicago. Their little plant was covered with a mortgage, and Dround and Strauss had taken away most of their trade. The Schunemann brothers were such small fish that they could make no agreements with the large companies, and they weren't important enough to be bought out.

That was what I told one of the brothers when he asked me

to say a good word for him with Carmichael. His concern was pretty near bankruptcy then, and it was plainly out of the question for them to go on as they had been without capital. If they had tried to build up a small business in *delicatessen* and such things, they might have succeeded better. I had never given up the idea of the money that might be made in putting up sausages and preparing kosher meat for the city market. Here, I thought, was just the opportunity. If I could buy out the Schunemann brothers or get a controlling interest, I might try my experiment. The scheme grew in my mind, and I went to Aurora several times to see the brothers. After a while I made the man an offer, and then we talked terms for several months. Slocum advised me and drew up the agreement. I was ready to put my stake into the venture, all that I had in the world. It hurt them to sell me the control of their business for seven thousand dollars, which was all that I could scrape together — and part of that was Slocum's savings, which he lent me.

At last we made the arrangement, and the Schunemann brothers put up the "Duchess" brand of sausage after my plan, and we began to handle kosher meat in a small way. I managed the sausage trade with Dround's business, working the two together very well; for the retailers who dealt with Dround's took to my idea and pushed our Duchess brand, which was packed in nice little boxes. It was a new idea in those days, and nothing takes like something that hasn't been tried before. We began to make money — not a fortune all at once; but the business promised to grow. Thus I became a packer, after a fashion!

In the years that immediately preceded the troublous times of 1886, I was a very busy man and often out of the city, too much engrossed with the growing business on my hands to consider very seriously the disturbances of that period. The fight with labor, which seems to be a necessary feature of our progress, had come to a kind of crisis in that year. But the events in Chicago during that crisis are still so near to many of us that even with the rapid forgetfulness of our days they have not quite escaped the memory of thoughtful men.

I remember that now and then, around Ma Pierson's table, the talk turned on the strike over at the harvesting works. We were all on the same side, I guess — the side of capital; there was enough for all of the good things of life, we thought, if men would only stop their kicking and keep at work. Slocum, for all that he was a lawyer, was the only easy one on the strikers: so long as they respected the laws he was with them in their struggle to get all they could from their employers.

"Mr. Renshaw says they're too well off now," Lou observed.

"Who is Mr. Renshaw?" I asked, surprised that Lou should take an interest in such matters.

Slocum looked across the table at me, and Grace quickly began on something else. . . .

Well, on the night of the fourth of May I was on my way to the Piersons' from the Union Station. It was very late, for I had just returned from Aurora, where I had been during the afternoon on my own business. As I got on the street car the men on the platform were talking excitedly about the shooting over at the harvester works. When I reached home, I was surprised to find no one on the steps, the door wide open, and a kind of emptiness in the whole place.

"What's up?" I asked old Pierson.

"That Cox girl's got her cheek blowed open with a bomb or suthin'. Times like this folks can't go gallivantin' about the streets," the old man snarled.

Slocum came in at the sound of my voice and told me what had happened. His face was white, and his long arms still twitched with the horror of what he had seen that night. It seems that Dick Pierson had come home to supper full of the news about the row between the police and the strikers. His talk had worked up the girls, — that is, Hillary Cox and Grace, — for Lou hadn't come home, — until all of them had started off after supper in the direction of the harvester works, where the trouble was reported to be.

Then they had strolled down to the Haymarket, where, instead of the great crowd they had expected to find, there were only some hundreds of men and women listening quietly to several workingmen who were speechifying from a cart. It didn't look very lively, and as a thunder storm was coming up in the north Sloco was for going home. But Ed, who, like a country galoot, was curious to hear what the orator in the cart had to say, pressed up close to the truck, in the front of the crowd, with Hillary Cox on his arm. Suddenly, so Slocum said, there was a shout from somewhere behind them: —

"The police! Look out for the police!"

In the rush that followed, Slocum and Grace were jammed back by the press and separated from the others. He remembered only a little of what happened those next moments. And what he did remember didn't tally with the stories that were told later at the trial. In the darkness of the lowering storm, above the heads of the close-packed, swaying mass in the square, there sounded a dull whir. Then came a terrific explosion. The next thing Slocum knew he was crawling on his hands and knees, groping in the darkness for Grace, while all around them crackled the pistol shots of the police. Then he heard Ed's voice shrieking: —

"The bloody brutes have shot her!". . .

"And Hillary?" I asked. "Is it bad?"

"A piece of iron ploughed across her cheek."

"Scar?"

Slocum nodded. (The truth is that if it hadn't been for the

ignorant doctor who got hold of the girl first her looks might have been saved. But he took eleven stitches, and there was left a long, ugly, furrowed scar across her pretty face!)

We went up to Slocum's room, and sat there far into the night, discussing what had happened.

"Oh, I suppose you law pills will mouse around in it considerable," I said. "The way to do is to string 'em up to the nearest lamp-post, as they do out West."

As I was saying that, a cab drove up hurriedly in the quiet street and stopped at our door. Slocum and I put our heads out of his window, curious to know what was happening now at two o'clock in the morning. We saw a man get out, then turn and lift a woman from the cab to the street. The woman staggered as she started to walk across the sidewalk.

"It's Lou Pierson!" Slocum exclaimed. He drew in his head suddenly and bolted from the room. I waited long enough to see the man who was with Lou pull the doorbell, and then leave the poor girl half-fallen on the steps, while he went back to the cab and spoke to the driver. Then I followed Slocum downstairs, two steps at a time. Slocum had wrenched open the house door and leaped down the long flight of steps, not pausing at the girl, who was making feeble attempts to rise and calling: "Fred! Fred!" But the man, having given his directions to the driver, paid no attention and got into the cab.

I helped Lou to her feet; she was still calling in a drowsy voice: "Fred! Fred!" I could see Slocum with his hand on the door of the cab. He spoke to the man inside, but I could not hear what he said. Suddenly his hand shot out; there was a tussle, half in and half out of the cab; the driver whipped up his horses, and Slocum was thrown to his knees. He picked himself up holding in his fist something that looked like a necktie.

As Slocum helped me carry the girl up the steps, he said: —

"That's who Renshaw is. A bit of a bomb would be about the right thing for him!"

Generalizations, I have learned, are silly things to play with. But there are some experiences in a man's life that tempt him to make them. It was only a mere accident that the man who was Lou Pierson's companion in the cab that night had taken a prominent part against the striking workmen. But when, later, I was called upon to sit in judgment on some hot-headed fools because they, in their struggle to get an eight-hour day, fomented strife, my thoughts would go back sourly to this example of the men I was expected to side with.

CHAPTER VIII

THE TRIAL OF THE ANARCHISTS

The terror of good citizens — Henry Iverson Dround — Righteous indignation — Leaders of industry get together "to protect society" — A disagreeable duty — Selecting the jury — The man from Steele's — What is evidence? — What is justice? — In behalf of society — Life is for the strong — All there is in it! — I take my side

THE morning after the fourth of May the city was sizzling with excitement. From what the papers said you might think there was an anarchist or two skulking in every alley in Chicago with a basket of bombs under his arm. The men on the street seemed to rub their eyes and stare up at the buildings in surprise to find them standing. There was every kind of rumor flying about: some had it that the police had unearthed a general conspiracy to dynamite the city; others that the bomb throwers had been found and were locked up. It was all a parcel of lies, of course, but the people were crazy to be lied to, and the police, having nothing better, fed them lies. At the Yards, men were standing about in little groups discussing the rumors; they seemed really afraid to go into the buildings.

In front of our office a brougham was drawn up — an unusual sight at any time, and especially at this hour. It was standing close to the door, and as I picked my way through the crowd I looked in at the open window. My eyes met the eyes of a woman, who was leaning against the cushioned back of the carriage. She was dressed in a white, ruffled gown that appeared strange there in the yards, and her eyes were half closed, as if she were napping or thinking thoughts far removed from the agitated city. But when I came closer she gave me the sharpest look I ever saw in a woman's eyes. It was a queer face, dark and pale and lifeless — except for that power of the eyes to look into you. I stopped, and my lips opened involuntarily to speak. As I went on upstairs, I wondered who she could be.

My desk was just outside the manager's private office, and, the door happening to be ajar, I could see Mr. Dround within, striding up and down in great excitement. Carmichael was trying to quiet him down. I could hear the chief's high, thin voice denouncing the anarchists: —

"It is a dastardly crime against God and man! It threatens the very foundations of our free country —"

"Yes, that's all right," big John was growling in his heavy tone. "But we don't want to make too much fuss; it won't do no good to poke around in a nest of rattlers."

"Let them do their worst! Let them blow up this building! Let them dynamite my house! I should call myself a craven, a poltroon, if I wavered for one moment in my duty as a citizen."

Carmichael sighed and bit off the end of a fat cigar that he had been rolling to and fro in his mouth. He seemed to give his boss up, as you might a talkative schoolboy.

Henry Iverson Dround was a tall, dignified gentleman, with thick gray hair, close-cut gray whiskers, and a grizzled mustache. He always dressed much better than most business men of my acquaintance, with a sober good taste. The chief thing about him was his manners, which, for a packer, were polished. I knew that he had been to college; there was a tradition in the office that he had gone into the business against his will to please his father, who had begun life as a butcher in the good old way and couldn't understand his son's prejudices. Perhaps that explains why all the men in the house thought him haughty, and the other big packers were inclined to make fun of him.

However that might be, Mr. Dround had a high reputation in the city at large for honorable dealing and public spirit. There was little set afoot for the public good that Henry I. Dround did not have a hand in.

I had met the chief once or twice, big John having called his attention to me, but he never seemed to remember my existence. To-day Mr. Dround blew out of the manager's office pretty soon and brushed against my desk. Suddenly he stopped and addressed me in his thin, high voice: —

"What do you think, Mr. Harrington, of this infernal business?"

My answer was ready, pat, and sufficiently hot to please the boss. He turned to Carmichael, who had followed him.

"That is what young America is thinking!"

Carmichael put his tongue into his cheek instead of spitting out an oath; but after Mr. Dround had gone, he growled at me: —

"That's all right for young America, but I am no damn fool, either! My father saw the riots back home in Dublin. It's no good sitting too close on the top of a chimney — maybe you'll set the house on fire. The police? The police are half thieves and all blackguards! They got this up for a benefit party, most likely. Why, didn't they kill more'n twice as many men over at McCormick's only the other day, just because the boys were making a bit of a disturbance? And nobody said anything about it! What are they kicking for, anyway?"

Mr. Dround's view, however, was the one generally held. That very evening there was a meeting of the prominent men of the city to take counsel together how anarchy might be suppressed with a strong hand. We little people heard only rumors of what took place in that gathering, but it leaked out that there had been two minds among those wealthy and powerful men — the timid and the bold. The timid were over-ridden by the bolder-hearted. Good citizens, like Strauss and Vitzer, so Carmichael told me with a sneer, talked strong about encouraging the district attorney to do his duty, and raised a fund to pay for having justice done.

"It means that some of those rats the police have been fer-reting out of the West Side saloons will hang to make them feel right. The swells are bringing pressure to bear, and some one must be punished. It's grand!"

He chuckled bitterly at his own wit. But the swells meant business, and when Henry I. Dround was drawn for the grand jury, to indict those anarchists that the police had already netted, big John swore: —

"He needn't have done that! There are plenty to do the fool things. It's his sense of duty, I s'pose, damn him! It's some of his duty to come over here and help us make enough money to keep his old business afloat!"

The Irishman thought only of the business, but Henry I. Dround was not the man to let any personal interest stand in the way of what he considered his duty to society. Perhaps he was a little too proud of his sacrifices and his civic virtues. Some years later he told me all about that grand jury. All I need say here is that this famous trial of the anarchists was engineered from the beginning by prominent men to go straight.

The hatred and the rage of all kinds of men during those months while the anarchists were on our hands, before they were finally hanged or sent to prison, is hard to understand now at this distance from the event. That bomb in its murder-ous course had stirred our people to the depths of terror and hate: even easy-going hustlers like myself seemed to look at that time in the face of an awful fate. The pity of it all was — I say it now openly and advisedly — that our one motive was hate. Stamp this thing out! that was the one cry. Few stopped to think of justice, and no one of mercy. We were afraid, and we hated.

Finally it came time for the trial; the *venire* for the jury was issued. One night, to my consternation, I found a summons at the house. When I showed it to a fellow-clerk at the office the next morning, he whistled: —

"I thought I saw the bailiff in here yesterday, looking around for likely men. They are after a safe jury this time, sure!"

I asked Carmichael to use his influence to get me excused, as I knew he usually did for the boys when they were summoned for jury duty. But all he said was: —

"You're a nervy youngster. You'd better do the thing, if you are accepted."

"It means weeks, maybe months, off," I objected.

"We'll make that all right: you won't lose nothing by it. But you mustn't mind finding a stick of dynamite under your bed when you go home after the trial," he grinned.

"I guess there's no trouble with my nerve," I said stiffly, thinking he was chaffing me. "But I don't want the job, all the same."

"Well, you'll have to see the old man this time. Maybe he can get you off."

So I went into Mr. Dround's private office and made my request. The chief asked me to take a chair and handed me a cigar. Then he began to talk about the privileges and duties of citizenship. From another man it might have been just slobber, but Henry I. Dround meant it, every word.

"Why don't you serve?" I asked him pretty bluntly.

He flushed.

"I haven't been drawn. Besides, it has been thought wiser not to give the jury too capitalistic a character. This is a young man's duty. And I understand from Mr. Carmichael that you are one of the most energetic and right-minded of our young men, Mr. Harrington."

He stood facing the window and talked along for some time in a general way. His talk was rather simple and condescending, but kind. He spoke of the future before me, of my having the right influence in the community. When I left him I knew perfectly well that the house expected me to serve on that jury if I was chosen, and that Mr. Dround would take personally the warmest interest in a young man who had the courage to do his duty "in behalf of society," as he kept saying.

Still I hoped to escape. I was tolerably far down the list. So day after day I listened to the wrangle among the lawyers over the selection of the jurors. It was clear enough from the start that the State wanted only one kind of man on that jury — an intelligent, well-to-do clerk or small manufacturer. No laboring man need apply: his class was suspect. As a clerk in Steele's store said to me while we waited our turn: —

"That bailiff came into our place and walked down past our department with the manager. I heard him say to Mr. Bent: 'I'm running this case. Let me tell you there won't be no hung jury.'"

"Do you want to serve?" I asked the man from Steele's.

"Well, I do and I don't." Then he leaned over and whispered into my ear: "It looks to me that there might be a better place for me at Steele's if everything goes off to suit and I am a part of it!" He nudged me and pulled a straight face. "I guess they ought to be hanged, all right," he added, as if to square himself with what he was ready to do.

After the defence had used up its challenges, which naturally was pretty soon, the real business of getting the jury began. Much the same thing happened in every case. First the man said he was prejudiced so that he couldn't render a fair verdict on the evidence. Then his Honor took him in hand and argued with him to convince him that his scruples were needless. His Honor drove him up and down hill until the man was forced to admit that he had some sense of fairness and could be square and honest if he tried hard. And then he was counted in. In every case it went pretty much as it did in the case of the man from Steele's.

"I feel," so the man from Steele's said, "like any other good citizen does. I feel that some of these men are guilty; we don't know which ones, of course. We have formed this opinion by general report from the newspapers. Now, with that feeling it would take some very positive evidence to make me think that these men were not guilty, if I should acquit them. . . . But I should act entirely upon the testimony."

"But," said the defence, "you say that it would take positive evidence of their innocence before you could consent to return them not guilty?"

"Yes, I should want some strong evidence."

"Well, if that strong evidence of their innocence was not introduced, then you want to convict them?"

"Certainly!"

Then the judge took him in hand, and after a time his Honor got him to say: —

"I believe I could try the case on the evidence alone, fairly."

And so they took him, and they took me in the same way, when it came my turn.

This is scarcely the place to tell the story of that famous trial. It has kept me too long as it is. The trial of the anarchists was an odd accident in my life, however, which, coming, as it did, when I had my foot placed on the ladder of fortune, had something to do with making me what I am to-day. Up to this time I had never reflected much upon the deeper things of life. The world seemed good to me — a stout, hearty place to fight in. I had made money in the scheme of things as they are, and I found it good. I wanted to make some more money, and I had little patience with the kickers who tried to upset the machine. But I had not reasoned it out. There in the court room, and later shut up in the jury quarters, day after day, cut off from my usual habits, I thought over some of the real questions of our life, and made for myself a kind of philosophy.

To-day, after the lapse of eighteen years, I can see it all as I saw it then: the small, dirty court room; the cold, precise face of the judge; the faces of the eight men whom the police had ferreted out of their holes for us to try. There wasn't much dignity in the performance: some pretty, fashionably dressed girls sat up behind the judge, almost touching elbows with his Honor. They came there as though to the play, whispering and eating candy. There was the wrangling among the lawyers, snarling back and forth to show their earnestness. But my eyes came back oftenest to the faces of those eight men, for whose lives the game was being played. Two were stupid; three were shifty; but the other three had an honest glow, a kind of wild enthusiasm, that came with their foreign blood, maybe. They were dreamers of wild dreams, but no thugs!

From the start it seemed plain that the State could not show who threw that fatal bomb, nor who made it, nor anything about it: the best the State could do would be to prove conspiracy. The only connection the lawyers could establish between those eight men and the mischief of that night was a lot of loose talk. His Honor made the law — afterward he boasted of it — as he went along. He showed us what sedition was, and that was all we needed to know. Then we could administer the lesson. Now that eighteen years have passed, that looks to me like mighty dangerous law. Then I was quick enough to accept it.

When we filed into the court room the last morning to listen to the judge's charge, the first face I saw was that of Hillary Cox. A big red scar, branching like a spider's web, disfigured her right cheek. It drew my eyes right to her at once. All her color and the plump, pretty look of health had gone for good. She looked old and sour and excited. And I wished she hadn't come there: it seemed as though she was waiting for her revenge for the loss of her youth and good looks. She was counting on me to give it to her! Ed sat beside her, holding her hand in a protecting way. He was an honest, right-feeling sort of fellow, and I guessed that her loss of good looks would make no difference in his marrying her.

Near the district attorney sat Mr. Dround. He listened to the judge's charge very closely, nodding his head as his Honor made his points and rammed conviction into us. . . .

"In behalf of society" — his phrase ran in my head all through the trial. That was the point of it all — a struggle between sensible folks who went about their business and tried to get all there was in it — like myself — and some scum from Europe, who didn't like the way things are handed out in this world. We must hang these rebels for an example to all men. To be sure, the police had killed a score or two of their kind — "rioters," they were called: now we would hang these eight in a proper, legal, and ordinary way. And then back to business! I suppose that the world seemed to me so good a place to hustle in that I couldn't rightly appreciate the complaint of these rebels against society. And at any rate I was convinced that we sensible folks who had the upper hand could not tolerate any bomb foolishness. "In behalf of society" — yes, before we had left our seats in the court room my mind was made up: guilty or not, these men must suffer for their foolish opinions, which were dead against the majority.

Thus I performed my duty to society.

When our verdict was ready, and we came in to be discharged, I saw Hillary Cox again. As the foreman rose to give our verdict, her scarred face flushed with excitement, and an ugly scowl crept over her brow. I turned away. Queer thoughts came into my mind — for the bad air and the weeks of close confinement had made me nervous, I suppose. . . . Society! I seemed to see old Strauss with his puffy, ashen face, and his broad hands that hooked in the dollars, dirty or clean, and Vitzer, who kept our honorable council on his pay-roll for convenience, and the man who had been with Lou Pierson that night, and many others. Were they better men before the eye of God than these eight misguided fools whom we were about to punish? Who did the most harm to society, they or that pale-faced Fielden, who might have been a saint instead of an anarchist? . . .

The judge was still making remarks; the jury were listening restlessly; the prisoners at the bar seemed little interested in the occasion. I kept saying to myself: "Society! In behalf of society! I have done my duty in behalf of society." But what was this almighty society, anyhow, save a lot of fools and scamps with a sprinkling of strong souls, who were fighting for life — all of them fighting for what only a few could get? My eyes rested on Hostetter's face in the crowd. His jaw was hanging open, and he was staring at the judge, trying to understand it all. Poor Ed! *He* wouldn't have much show in the scramble if society didn't protect him. Suddenly a meaning to it all came to me like a great light. The strong must rule: the world was for the strong. It was the act of an idiot to deny that truth. Yes, life was for the strong, all there was in it! I saw it so then, and I have lived it so all my life. . . .

The man from Steele's nudged my elbow: —

"My! I tell you I'll be glad to get home to-night. Won't the old woman's food taste slick to-night? You bet."

"The jury is discharged."

The play was over. The spectators were moving from the

crowded room. At the door my friends were waiting for me. Hillary Cox stretched up a thin hand.

"Thank you, Van," she said.

"You fellows did just right," Hostetter added.

Slocum said nothing, but there was a dubious smile on his lips.

"We're going to blow you off for a dinner at the Palmer House, the best you ever ate," Dick Pierson called out loudly. Then he added for the benefit of the onlookers, "To hell with the anarchists!"

"Quit that!" I said sharply, some of those queer doubts about the justice of the act I had been concerned in returning to me. "It's over now, and let's drop it."

It was good to be out on the streets once more, knocking elbows with folks, and my heart soon began to feel right. In the lobby of the hotel men I didn't know, who recognized me as one of the famous jury, came up to me and shook hands and said pleasant things. Before the dinner was far along I was quite myself again, and when Slocum set up the champagne for the party, I had begun to feel rather proud of the part I had taken in public affairs. After all, it was a fine thing to live and hustle with your neighbors for the dollars. I had done my part to make the game go on smoothly. At the Yards, the next morning, it was the same thing: my desk was covered with flowers, and the boys kept me busy shaking hands and taking in the cigars until I thought I was at a church presentation party. Big John was one of the first to welcome me back.

"Say! do you want a vacation? The old man thinks a month or two would be the right thing. Enjoy yourself, my boy, after your arduous duty!"

"Shoo!" I replied. "What would I do with a month's vacation, John? I've just pined to be back here at work. What do I want to light out for now?"

"Supposing some of 'em should try to fix *you?*" he grinned.

"I guess we've fixed *them* for good and all."

"Well, your nerve is all right."

So I sat down to my desk, quite the cock of the walk, and felt so pleased with myself that you would think I had saved the whole town from being blown up. I was for society as it is, first, last, and all the time, and I felt good to be in it.

Once, some months later, I saw those eight men again, when they were brought into court to be sentenced. They all had a chance to speechify, and I listened to them for a time. I didn't take much stock in Spies and Parsons — long-winded, talky, wild fellows. But the others, who weren't as glib as those two, had a kind of simple sincerity about them. They had the courage to stand up there in the face of death and say what they believed. No one plead for mercy. I was sorry for them.

But, nevertheless, it was comfortable to be of the strong. The world is for the strong, I said to myself as I left the court, and I am one of them!

CHAPTER IX

ANOTHER BOOST

*I become of importance in Dround's — Making money — The end
of Ma Pierson's — Rivals in sausage — I conclude to sell my business — Bluffing old Strauss — Carmichael regards me with respect*

AFTER the trial came another boost at Dround's. Thanks to the
big Irishman, I had done pretty well before; but now there
was some one at the top watching me. I was given a chance to
see what I could do to make markets in the new Southwest,
which was developing rapidly and in my opinion offered a
weak house like ours a better opportunity than the older fields.

And my little venture with the brothers Schunemann was
booming all the time. Ed and Sloco had looked out for my interests during the trial, and had kept my partners from robbing
me. Pretty soon I was able to buy out their interest in the
Aurora plant and get rid of them altogether, putting Ed in as
my manager. The Schunemanns took to peddling our kosher
meat in Chicago, and worked up a good trade. In my trips for
Dround & Co. I was able to make a large business for the Duchess brand of sausage, which soon began to attract attention.
One day Carmichael said to me: —

"So you're a sausage maker, after all, Van?"

"Yes, and coining money, too," I replied. "Perhaps Mr.
Dround would think differently now about the cat's-meat business."

Carmichael grunted. I suspected that he might like to have
me offer the firm a chance to come into my business, but I had

no such idea. I saw a great future in sausage, and, after that, other things — down a long vista of golden years.

About this time Lou Pierson disappeared from the house and never came back. Slocum went East and did his best to find the girl. He may have been too proud to marry her sister, but he felt badly enough over Lou's going that way. Later, when I saw the girl in New York, I concluded her return could do no good to any one, and said nothing. After Lou disappeared the old man began to drink pretty hard, and finally had to go to the hospital. The Van Buren Street house was a drearier place than ever, and Slocum and I decided to move and start housekeeping together. Ma Pierson needed us no longer. The Hostetters were keeping house for the old lady; for Ed married Hillary shortly after the trial, and together they tried running the Enterprise. But they could not make it go, somehow; so later I made Ed my manager, as I have said. Some time after this, when the old lady Pierson got sick, Slocum and I saw that she had a little rest and comfort to the end of her days. For her son Dick could never look after anybody but himself.

We had not been long in our comfortable flat on the South Side before an unexpected chance came to me to make a lot of money. As I have said, the Duchess brand of sausage, packed in dainty little boxes, was making a name for itself and attracting the attention of the trade. I began to have rivals, and my profits were cut somewhat; but they could never drive out the Duchess, which had a good start. One day Carmichael asked me if I would like to sell my sausage factory, as he called the Aurora plant. I told him jokingly he hadn't the money to buy it. But in reality I was ready to sell, for I saw that if the big packers went into the business in earnest, I could not compete. And it was only a matter of time before they would see, as I had seen, the immense profit in such small things. So when, a few days later, Carmichael said that one of Strauss's men had asked him to bring me over to their place, I went quick enough.

Carmichael took me into Strauss's office and introduced me to one of the men, a shrewd little fellow, who managed some of the old man's deals for him. After a little while, the man, Gooch, began to talk of my sausage business, praised the idea, and hinted that his boss might consider buying me out "for a proper figure." So we began to deal, and pretty soon Gooch named a figure, twenty-five thousand dollars or something of the sort, expecting me to bite. I laughed, and Carmichael, who was sitting by enjoying the fun, said: "He's no kid, Gooch, though he looks it. Better go your whole figure straight off." Gooch then said thirty-five thousand dollars — that was the limit. I began to talk about the kosher meat business the Schunemann brothers were handling for me, and I could see Gooch's eyes open. He got up and went back into an inner office, and when he returned he made the figure fifty thousand dollars. Carmichael expected me to take his offer, and if I had been asked that morning I should have said it was a big price. But suddenly it came into my mind that in that inner office was the great Strauss himself. He thought I was too small fry to deal with: he left me to his lieutenant. And I had a good mind to bring him out to buy my plant of me. So I talked on, and Gooch asked me to name my figure.

"Seventy thousand," I answered pretty quick.

Gooch turned to his desk, as if to tell me to go home, and Carmichael grunted, thinking how he would laugh at me about my cheek. I began to think I had gone too far, when the door of that inner office was pulled back and Strauss himself walked into the room. He nodded to Carmichael and gave me a look from head to foot, but said nothing. Gooch waited for the great man to speak.

"We'll take your figure, Mr. Harrington," Strauss said, after he had looked me up and down, and walked out again.

It took my breath away: the next moment I was sorry I hadn't said a hundred, it seemed so easy. But Strauss was back in his office and the door was pulled to.

The next I knew I was on the street, and big John was laughing so that men turned to look at him. "Pretty good for a kid," he kept saying between his bursts of laughter. "You had the old fox on the run. He wanted your cat's-meat place bad, though."

We went into a saloon, and I set up a bottle of champagne.

"You're all right," Carmichael said to me when we had drunk to my good luck. "You couldn't have run that place much longer. The big ones would have eaten you up, hide and all."

"I knew that!" I said calmly.

Carmichael looked at me with considerable respect, and that was one of the pleasantest moments of my life.

CHAPTER X

LOVE

A poor stenographer — The positive young lady under altered circumstances — Miss Gentles's story — A hard road for tender feet — Social and sentimental — A misunderstanding — Which is made right in the only way — My boss invites us to dinner — Another kind of woman — A woman's shrewdness — The social gift — At the opera — Business and pleasure — Sarah on Mrs. Dround

It was a hot day in August three years after the trial; I was sitting in Carmichael's office trying to get a breath of fresh air from his west windows. I called old Peters and asked him to send me up a stenographer.

"Haven't a good one in the place, Mr. Harrington," he said. "All the smart ones are off on their vacation. There's Miss Gentles, though — the old man generally keeps her for himself, but he's gone home by this time."

"Send up anything so long as it can write!"

"Well, she *ain't* much good," Peters replied.

I had my head down behind my desk when the stenographer came in, and I began to dictate without looking up. These stenographer ladies were all of a piece to me, — pert, knowing misses, — all but Miss Harben: she was fifty and sour, and took my letters like biting off thread. This one evidently wasn't in her class, for pretty soon she sang out: —

"Please wait! I can't go so fast."

So I waited, and looked up to see what I had to do with. This young woman was a good-looking, ladylike person, with a mass of lovely brown hair and long brown eyelashes. She was different from the other girls in the office, and yet it seemed to me I had seen her before. She was dressed in black, a sort of half mourning, I judged. Pretty soon she got stuck again and asked me to repeat. This time she looked at me imploringly.

"I am not very good," she said with a smile.

"No, you are not," I replied.

She laughed at my blunt answer — laughed pleasantly, like a lady who knows how to turn off a harsh truth, not flirtatiously, like most of her profession.

"Been long at it?" I asked the next time she broke down.

"Not so very. I graduated from the school about six months ago, and I have always worked for Mr. Dround since then. He doesn't talk as fast as you do, not nearly."

She smiled again at me, frankly and naturally. Suddenly I remembered where I had seen that face before, and when she looked up again I said: —

"Did you ever find that purse, Miss Gentles?"

She looked puzzled at first; then a light spread over her face, and she stammered: —

"Why, of course, you are *the* Mr. Harrington who — But you have changed!"

"Rather, I hope! And the light wasn't good in the police station that morning."

Miss Gentles leaned back in her chair and laughed, a blush spreading prettily over her face.

"It's all so funny!" she exclaimed.

"Funnier now than it was then," I admitted.

"I am very glad to meet you again. No, I never found that purse. The judge still twits me, when he sees me, about changing my mind. He thinks —" Then she stopped in embarrassment, and it was some time before I found out what the judge did think.

"Have you been back to that place in Indiana?" she asked.

And we had quite a chat. She talked to me like a young lady who was receiving a caller in her father's house. It took a long time to finish the few letters I had started to write. When she went, I got up and opened the door for her. I had to.

"Good afternoon, Mr. Harrington," she said, holding out her hand. "I am so glad to have met you again."

Old Peters, who was in the outer office, looked at us in considerable surprise. When Miss Gentles had gone he remarked in a gossiping way: —

"So you know the young woman?"

"I met her once years ago," I admitted. "How did she land here? She doesn't seem to have had much experience as a stenographer."

"No, she hasn't. Her father died several years ago, and didn't leave a cent. He was a very popular doctor, though — a Southerner. They lived kind of high, I guess, while there was anything. The Drounds knew them in their better days, and when the doctor died Mrs. Dround tried to help the girl in one way and another. Then they fixed up this job for her. I guess Mr. Dround don't work her very hard. Sorry you were troubled with her. We'll see that you get a rattler the next time, Mr. Harrington," he ended. (The men in the office were pretty nice to "Mr. Harrington" these days!)

"Oh, she isn't so bad!" I said to Peters. For I rather looked forward to seeing the pretty, pleasant-mannered girl again. "I'd just as soon have Miss Gentles next week when Mr. Dround goes East, if no one else wants her."

Old Peters had a twinkle in his eyes as he answered: —

"Just as you say, Mr. Harrington."

So I came to see a good deal of Miss Gentles that summer while Mr. Dround was away on his vacation. I can't say that the young lady developed much business ability. She forgot most things with a wonderful ease, and she was never very accurate. But she tried hard, and it seemed to worry her so when I pointed out her mistakes that I took to having in another stenographer in the afternoon to finish what she hadn't done.

Miss Gentles boarded with an old aunt of her mother's near where Slocum and I lived. I gathered that the aunt and her husband were not very kind to her. They thought she ought to marry, having good looks and no money. Miss Gentles let me call on her, and before the summer was over we were pretty well acquainted. For a long time the thought of May had kept me from looking at a woman; I always saw that little white face and those searching eyes, and heard that mocking laugh. But Miss Gentles was so different from May that she never made me think of the woman I had once loved.

I took Slocum to call on my new acquaintance, but they didn't get on well together. She thought his old Yankee ways were hard, and I suppose he thought I was bound on the voyage of life with a pleasure-loving mate. He used to growl to me about tying myself to a woman, but I always said he needn't worry about me — I wasn't the marrying kind.

"Oh, you'll be wanting to get married the same as the rest of the world," Sloco would answer, "and have a wife and children to spend your money on and make you earn more!"

But I thought differently. A man of my sort, I replied to him, works and fights just the same without wife or child, because of the fight in him, because he can't help himself, any more than the man who wants to drink can keep his lips from the glass. It's in his blood and bone. . . .

Miss Gentles had seen a good deal of society, — the best there was in the city in those early days. It was odd to hear her talking about people who were just big names to me, as if she had known them all her life. I must have struck her as pretty green. But she made me feel from the first like some one she had always known. She was proud enough, but simple, and not in the least reserved. She told me all about her people, the easy times and the hard times. And never a word of complaint or regret for all the parties and good things that were gone out of her life. She was one to take her beer with a joke when she couldn't have champagne. Of course, I told her, first and last, all my story. She made me take her to see the Hostetters at the old place on Van Buren Street. Then the four of us went up the lake on a picnic one Sunday. Hillary, I remember, was sullen because Ed paid so much attention to Miss Gentles on this trip.

So we became good friends. Yet I never felt really intimate with her, as I had with Hillary, and when I tried to step past a certain line she had her own way of keeping me off, not haughtily or pertly, but like a lady who knew how people of the great world, where I had never been, behaved to one another. One day, I remember, I was fool enough to send her a little fancy purse with a gold eagle in it, and a line saying that it was time for me to make restitution, or something of the sort. My gift came back quick enough, with a clever little note tucked inside, saying she couldn't let me admit that I had taken her purse. It was a good lesson for me.

When Mr. Dround returned in the fall she reported to him for work, and I was not altogether sorry. I had plenty of chances to see her outside of the office now, and I was desperately busy. In a few days, however, when I happened to be in Mr. Dround's office on some matter, he began to talk about Miss Gentles. Peters had told him that I had had her as my stenographer during his absence, and Mr. Dround would like to have me continue, as she wasn't adapted to his needs. Then he spoke of her people, and how he and Mrs. Dround had held them in the highest esteem, and had tried to do something for this girl. But there had seemed to be nothing that she was really fitted to do.

So we began again our work together, only it was worse; for her fashionable friends were back in the city now, and they kept inviting her out to parties and one thing and another, until she was too sleepy to do her work in the morning and was rather irregular. Then she was ill, off for a fortnight. I had Peters hire me another stenographer, a man, and Miss Gentles still drew her pay. Peters winked at me when I suggested that he needn't mention the fact of her absence in his report. I suppose, if I had stopped to think of it, I should have considered it more businesslike of her to quit her society and parties when she found they were interfering with her work. It was human, though, that she should want to get a little fun out of her life, and not lose sight altogether of the gay world where they have time to amuse themselves. And a pretty woman like her could hardly be expected to take stenography in a stock-yards office seriously.

Well, I missed her more and more, especially as I couldn't see her now that she was ill, and had to content myself with nice little notes of thanks for the flowers and fruit I sent. She came back at last, looking weak and droopy, for the first time rather hopeless, as if she saw that she wasn't fitted for the job and couldn't keep up with her friends, either. I felt very sorry for her. She wasn't made for work — any one could see that — and it was a cruel shame to let her boggle on with it. Just then I had to go to Texas on business; when I got back a week or so later, Peters told me that Miss Gentles had left five days before. A cold little note on my desk said good-by, and thanked me for my kindness to her — never a word of explanation.

I was so upset that I didn't wait to open my letters, but called a cab and started for the aunt's to find out what was the matter. It was just as well I had been in a hurry, for in another ten minutes Miss Gentles would have been on her way to Louisville, and it would have taken a week to hunt out the small place in Kentucky where she was going. Her trunk was packed, and she was sitting with her aunt in the large, ugly parlor, waiting for the expressman to come. When I walked in, following the servant, she didn't draw back her veil, but merely stood up and touched fingers with me. I saw that something was so wrong that it had to be made right at once, with no time to spare.

"You will kindly let me speak to Miss Gentles alone," I said to the aunt, who was inclined to stick. She went out of the room ungraciously.

"Now," I said, taking the girl's hand and looking through her veil into her eyes, "what is the matter? Tell me."

Her eyes were large and moist, and her lips quivered. But she shut her teeth down hard and said stiffly: "Nothing whatever, Mr. Harrington. You are very kind to come to see me before I leave."

"You aren't going to put me off with any such smooth answer as that," I said, "or you will have my company all the way you're going, wherever it may be. Tell me the straight truth, and all of it."

She began to laugh at my bluffing words, and ended with a nervous sob. After a while I learned the whole story. It seems that the man I employed talked out in the office about how he did all my work, and while I was South one of the "lady" stenographers had said something to Miss Gentles — a something she would not tell me. So she got up and took her leave, and knowing that her old aunt wouldn't want her around if she had no job, she had written some cousins in Kentucky and was going to them.

The expressman came about this time, but he didn't take her trunk. And when I left that chilly parlor we were engaged to be married. She said at the last, putting her hands on my coat: "You know I always liked you, even in the police station, Mr. Harrington — and — and I am so very, very happy, now, Van! It was terrible to think of going away. I had to, before you were due home. I was never so miserable before in my life!"

Something stirred from the bottom of my heart. I felt pitiful for all her trouble, her weakness, her struggle with a world she wasn't made for. Then she said trustingly, like a little child: —

"And you will always be good to me, as papa was with mamma, and patient, and love me a great deal, won't you? Yes, I know you will!"

I kissed her, feeling then that nothing in life could ever be like the privilege of loving and protecting this woman in her helplessness. I suppose that words like those she and I spoke then are common enough between men and women when they are in love. Yet those words have always been to me like some kind of sacred oath — the woman asking, out of her weakness, for love and protection from the one who holds all happiness and life for her, and the man, with his hasty passions, promising of the best there is in him.

Many a time in later years, when it hasn't always been easy to see things simply as it was then in our first joy, those words of hers have come back to me and given me that same soft tug at my heart. To hurt her would be to strike a child, to wring the neck of a bird that nestled in your hand. There are a good many kinds of love in this world, as there are of hate; perhaps about the best of all is this desire to protect and cherish a woman — the feeling that any man who is worth his salt has for the one he wants to marry. . . .

Sarah walked part way back to the office with me that morning, then turned north, saying she must try to find Mrs. Dround and tell her. She was so happy she couldn't go home and sit down quietly until I got back from the office. Mrs. Dround, she knew, would be specially glad to hear the news.

"For she thinks you are a very smart young man," Sarah added shyly.

"The lady must be a mind reader, then; for in the ten years I have been with the firm I can't remember seeing her once."

"Oh, yes, she has seen you. She said so. Anyway, Jane knows all about you, you may be sure. There isn't much that goes on around her that Jane doesn't know about."

With that she gave me a happy little nod and was off to the great stone house of my boss up north on the lake. It was a windy, dirty December day, but I was very content with the world as it was and thought Chicago was the finest city in the world. As I sat down to my desk my mind began to dance in a whirl of thoughts — of old plans and new combinations. I wondered what Sarah would say to some of my schemes to make our fortune. Perhaps they would merely frighten her; for a woman is a natural conservative. I hurried up my business to get back to her and tell her that some day, not so very distant, she would be a tolerably rich woman. For now it seemed only a step into the greater things I had seen all these years afar off.

The Drounds gave us a dinner not long afterward. I reached the house early, expecting to have a little time with Sarah before the others came. Pretty soon I heard the rustle of skirts, but, instead of Sarah, a tall, thin woman in a black lace evening-dress came into the room where the servant had left me. Instantly I knew that this was the face I had seen in the carriage the morning after the anarchist riot. She was a beautiful woman, with a dark, almost foreign look. She smiled cordially as she gave me her hand.

"Sarah is not quite ready. She wants to make herself very fine — the child! And Mr. Dround is late, too. I am glad, because it will give us a few minutes to ourselves. Come into the library."

She led the way into a long, stately room, with a beautiful ceiling in wood and gold. At one end, in a little arched recess, a wood fire was blazing. There were a number of large paintings on the walls, and queer Eastern idols and curios in cabinets. Mr. Dround had the reputation of being something of a traveller and collector. My first glance around that room explained a good deal to me about the head of our firm.

Mrs. Dround seated herself near the fire, where the light from a great candelabrum filled with candles flickered above her head. Her dark eyes gleamed under the black hair; it was a puzzle of a face!

She began pretty soon to talk of Sarah in a natural but terribly shrewd way.

"I wonder, Mr. Harrington, if you know your treasure," she said, half laughing. "It takes most men years to know the woman they marry, if they ever do."

"Well, I know enough now to begin with!"

"Sarah is such a woman — tender, loyal, loving. It needs a woman to know a woman, Mr. Harrington. But she hasn't a particle of practical sense: she can't keep an account straight. She has no idea what economy is — only want or plenty. She is Southern, so Southern! Those people never think what will happen day after to-morrow."

It seemed queer that she should be telling me this kind of thing, which I should be finding out fast enough for myself before long. Perhaps she wanted to see what I would say; at any rate I replied clumsily something about not expecting to make a housekeeper of my wife.

"Yet," she said slowly, studying me, "a woman can do so much to make or mar her husband's career."

"I guess I shan't lay it up against my wife, if I don't pull out a winner."

She laughed at that.

"So you think you are strong enough to win a fight without a woman's help?"

"I've done it so far," I said, thinking a little of May.

"You have made a beginning, a good beginning," she remarked judiciously.

She was reading me like a book of large print, leaning back in her great chair, her eyes half closed, her face in shade except when the firelight flashed.

"I suppose the only way is to keep on as you begin — keep your eyes open and take everything in sight," I continued lightly.

"It depends on how much you want, perhaps."

"I want pretty much all that I can get," I retorted quickly, my eyes roving over the rich room, with an idea that I might like to put Sarah in some such place as this.

Mrs. Dround laughed a long, low laugh, as though she were speculating why I was what I was.

"Well, you are strong enough, my friend, I see. As for Sarah, love her and don't look for what you can't find."

Just then we heard Sarah's laugh. She came into the room with Mr. Dround, a smile kindling graciously all over her face. The two women, as they kissed each other, made a picture — the dark head against the light one. Then Mrs. Dround gave Sarah a cool, motherly pat on the cheek, saying: —

"I have been offering your young man some advice, Sarah."

"He doesn't need it!" Sarah answered in a flash.

"Well, I don't know that he does," Mrs. Dround laughed back, kissing her again. Every one loved Sarah in the same protecting way! Soon after this Mr. Dround came up, smiling genially at the women's talk, and gave me his hand.

I had not seen the chief out of business hours before. I had never thought him much of a business man in the office, and here, in his own house, with his pictures and books and curios, he was about the last person any one would believe spent his days over in Packington.

It wasn't to be a simple dinner that evening. Sarah whispered that Jane had insisted on inviting a lot of people, some important people, she said, to meet her young man. And presently the guests arrived, — Lardner and Steele and Jefferson with their wives, and a number of others. About the only ones I knew were big John and his very fat wife. They seemed to be as much out of the crowd as I felt I was, with all my coolness. But Sarah was perfectly at her ease. I admired her all afresh when I saw how easily and gayly she took the pretty things those men said to her.

I was more at my ease in the smoking room after dinner, where I had to tell the story about the theft of the purse in Steele's store. The shrewd old merchant laughed heartily.

"I trust, Mr. Harrington," he drawled, "that now you are going to marry you will lose *your* purse there in place of taking one."

They paid me considerable attention all around, and it gave me a pleasant feeling — all of which, I knew, was due to Sarah. I was nothing but a newcomer among them, but she was the daughter of an old friend. And she had a wonderful way of her own of coming close to people.

I remember that we went later to the opera, which was being given in that big barn of an exposition building on the lake front where I had had my first experience of Chicago hospitality. We were in a box, and between the acts people came in to call. Sarah introduced me to some of them, and she held a reception then and there while Mrs. Dround looked on and smiled.

I forget the opera that was given, — some French thing, — but I remember how gay the place was, and all the important people of the city whom Sarah pointed out to me. Even as a matter of business, I saw it would be a good thing to know these people. Of course, the social side of life doesn't count directly in making money, but it may count a good deal in getting close to the crowd that knows how to make money. Perhaps I began to have even a little more pride in Sarah than I had before, seeing how she knew people and counted for something with them. In the game that we were going to play together this social business might come in handily, perhaps.

In one of the intervals of the opera Mrs. Dround remarked as if her mind had been on the same idea: —

"You see Sarah's sphere, Mr. Harrington?"

"Yes," I replied. "And the girl does it tip-top!"

She laughed.

"Of course! It's in the blood."

"Well, it isn't a bad thing, some of it," I went on with pride and content. "Strauss isn't here, is he?" I asked.

"The Strausses never go anywhere, you know."

"He's the biggest of them all, too," I said partly to myself.

"You think so? Why?" she asked, her brows coming together.

"He's the biggest dog, and it's dog eat dog in our business, as all over nowadays," I replied.

"Why now more than ever before?" she asked.

"It's in the air. There's a change coming over business, and you feel it the same as you feel a shift in the wind. It's harder work fighting to live now than ever before, and it can't go on like this forever. The big dog will eat up the rest."

"And you think Strauss is our big dog?" she asked with a smile.

I saw then where she had led me, but it was too late to be less frank.

"Yes," I answered, looking her in the eyes.

"Then how should one keep out of his jaws?" she went on, playing with her fan.

"Well, you can always get out of a scrap and stay out — or —" I hesitated.

"Or?" she persisted.

"Put up such a fight that the big fellow will give you good terms to get rid of you!"

"I see. You have given me something to think about, Mr. Harrington."

"The time is coming," I went on, careless whether she repeated to Mr. Dround my views, "and mighty quick, too, when that man Strauss will have the food-products business of this country in his fist, and the rest of us will be his hired men, and take what he gives us!"

"What are you two talking about in this intimate way?" Sarah broke in.

"The future," Mrs. Dround said.

"Business," I added.

"Business!" Sarah sniffed, and I knew I had done something I ought not to do. "And Nevada singing so divinely to-night! Come, Van, I want you to meet Mr. Morehead." And I was led away from our hostess to keep me out of mischief.

On our way home after the opera Sarah and I talked of Mrs. Dround. I had never met any woman like her, and I was loud in her praise.

"Yes," Sarah admitted slowly, "she seemed to like you. But did you see how she treated the Carmichaels? Just civil, and hardly that. Nobody can understand Jane. She just does as she wants always."

"I believe she must have a great head for business. If she were in Henry I.'s shoes —"

"I don't see why you say that! I am sure you never hear the least word about business in their house."

I smiled at Sarah's little show of temper, as she continued: —

"Anyway, it would be strange if she didn't know something about money-making. Her father was old Joe Sanson — they say he was a half-breed and made his money trading with the Indians and getting Government lands. Father used to tell stories about him. We heard that he left her a great deal of money, but nobody knows much about her or her affairs. She's so silent."

"I didn't find her so."

Sarah apparently did not altogether share my enthusiasm for Mrs. Dround.

"Tell me," she demanded, "just what she said to you, every word."

"I can't. She talks with her eyes, most."

"Oh, I hate to have men discuss business with women. It is such bad taste!"

"Why, Sarah, business is the whole thing for me. There isn't anything else I can talk about except you."

"Talk about me, then. I shall have to keep you out of Jane's way. I don't want you to talk to her about things I don't understand."

"Why not?"

She shivered and drew me closer to her.

"Because, Jane — I am afraid of Jane. She is so strong, and I am so weak. If she wanted you, or anybody, she would take you."

For all reply to this nonsense I kissed her good night.

MARRIAGE

JUST before we were married, Sarah and I went down to my
old home in Jasonville. She was determined that I should make
it up with my folks; it hurt her gentle heart to think that I had
lived all these years without any news of my kin. It was a
freezing January day when we drove up to the red brick house
next the store. As we rattled over the rutty streets in the depot
carriage, and passed the small frame houses all closed in for
the winter, I couldn't help feeling a most pharisaical pleasure
in knowing that I wasn't condemned to live in this bleak little
town.

When I knocked at the door, mother came to see who was
there. She knew me at once, but she looked at me slowly, in the
questioning way I remembered so well, before she said: —

"Well, Van! You've come back?"

"Yes, mother, and brought with me the best girl in the
world."

"I am glad to see you both," she said quietly.

"And how's father?" I asked nervously.

"Your father died nearly three years ago. We didn't know
where to send word to you."

There was no reproach in her voice; it was as if she expected nothing of me. We went into the house and sat down, and began to talk. It was solemn and painful all around, and if it hadn't been for Sarah I should have been taking an early train for Chicago. But she was sunny and light-hearted, and seemed to take pleasure in being there. While we were sitting in the front room talking to mother, a young woman came in with two small children hiding in her skirts.

"Your brother Will's wife," mother explained quickly.

"Why, May!" I exclaimed, a little embarrassed, "I didn't exactly look for this. Will didn't let me know — I —"

"We wanted to write you, but we didn't know where you were. I am very glad to see you, Van," May said quietly, a little smile curving up from her lips in a way that reminded me of the girl I once loved. She took both Sarah's hands and looked straight into her eyes.

"And this is your wife, Van?"

"Not quite, yet."

Of course I had told Sarah all about May, and I thought she might be cold to her, meeting her in this way of a sudden as Will's wife. She always said May had been hard that time before — had been too keen about her good principles to be a real woman. Yet, as they stood there looking into each other's eyes, I could see that they would come together very soon. Sarah smiled as if to say: "It's all right, my dear! You see, I am glad you turned him away that time. We have no reason to quarrel, have we?"

May began to blush under that smile, as though she knew what was in Sarah's mind. Then mother brought up May's two little boys, who went to Sarah at once. Will was away somewhere and didn't come home until supper. I though he looked pretty old for his age. Perhaps business was poor in Jasonville. The country ages a man fast when things go hard with him. At first he was stiffish to me, taken aback by our unexpected visit, but pretty soon he thawed to Sarah, who talked with him about his boys.

After dinner Will and I went to the barn and had a long smoke. He told me that the judge had pressed father pretty hard before he died, and after his death there wasn't much saved but the store, and that was mortgaged. And the business didn't amount to anything, according to Will. The mail-order business had cut into the country trade pretty badly by that time, and country people had begun more and more to go to the city to buy their goods. Moreover, time had shown that Jasonville lay to one side of the main lines of traffic. In short, Will had to scrape the barrel to get a living out of the old store.

He asked how it had been with me, and it gave me considerable pride to tell him what I had been doing. I told him about the packing business, my sausage factory, the deal with Strauss. He opened his eyes as he smoked my good cigar.

"So you struck it rich after all, Van!"

There was something on his mind, and after a time he managed to say: —

"I hope you won't have any more hard feeling for mother and me. We all treated you pretty harsh that time; we never gave you credit for what you had in you, Van."

"I guess it would have taken a prophet to see I had anything in me more than foolishness," I laughed. "Anyhow, it was the best thing that ever happened to me, Will, and I can't be too thankful that you folks in Jasonville threw me out."

"Yes, Jasonville ain't just the place for an ambitious man," he sighed. "And, Van, — about May, — it wasn't hardly fair. She cared most for you, then, at any rate; she wouldn't marry me, not for five years."

"Don't say another word, Will. May will make the best sort of sister. She's the right kind."

So that was the way we made it up as two brothers should. And the next morning, after doing some thinking over night about how I could best help my brother and May, I followed Will over to the store. On the way I met the old judge, looking hardly a day older than when I saw him last. He eyed me hard, as if he didn't know me from the last tramp, but I stopped him and greeted him.

"So you're loose once more," he grinned. "I see they shut you up as soon as you struck Chicago." He had a good time laughing at his little joke.

"Yes," I replied, "I am out once more, judge. And, from what I hear, the Harringtons have been paying you pretty well for all the green peaches I ever took off your place."

He mumbled something, but I turned on my heel, rather proud of myself if the truth be told, being well dressed, with an air of city prosperity.

Will was in the bit of an office behind the store. The old place was as mussy and dirty as ever, with fat files of dusty old letters and accounts. The old desk where father used to make up his bills was littered with last year's mail. It was Sunday, and the musty smell of the closed store came in through the door. It all gave me the forlornest feeling I had had in years.

"This will never pay, Will," I said to my brother, who was turning the leaves of a worm-eaten day-book. "The time when the small business would pay a man anything worth while is pretty nearly over for good."

"I suppose so," he replied despondently. "But somehow we must get a living out of it."

"Let the judge have it, if he'll take it. I can find you something better."

There was a place in Dround's that Will might work into; and before long he could be of use to me in a scheme that was coming around the corner of my mind into sight. As I talked,

Will's eyes brightened. Before we left the little office a new kind of look, the look of hope, had come over his face. I thought he seemed already some years younger. It takes the steps of a treadmill, downward faced, to crush the spirit in a man!

That was a happy morning. Surely, one of the joys of success is to give it away to the right ones. I remember a good many times in my life that I have had the pleasure of seeing that same look of hope, of a new spirit, come into a man's face, when I gave him his chance where he was least expecting it.

"But, Will, mind you, if you come to the city you'll no longer be your own man," I cautioned him. "Dround'll own you, or I shall. No doing what you want! To work with me is to work under me. Can you stand taking orders from your junior?"

"I guess, Van," he answered without any pride, "you have shown yourself to be the boss. I'll follow."

That night, when Will and May had left us at the junction where we were to take the Chicago train, Sarah brushed my arm with her cheek in a little intimate way she had and whispered: —

"May couldn't thank you. She feels it too much. You have made them so happy — there's a future now for them all. And I think, maybe, I can make you as good a wife as she could — perhaps better, some ways. May said so! Though May is a very nice woman, and I shall always love her."

"I guess you are both right," I replied, too happy to say much more.

A few weeks later and we were married. The Drounds gave us a pretty little wedding breakfast, to which came the few friends I had in the world and a few of the many Sarah had.

If Mrs. Dround was a careless hostess sometimes, that was not the day. She was specially gracious to Will and May, who were 'most strangers. It was all just as it should be, and I felt proud of myself to be there and to have this handsome, high-bred woman for my wife.

It was Sarah's idea that all the others should leave the house first, and that then we should slip away quietly to the train by ourselves. So at the last, while I was waiting for my bride to come downstairs, Mrs. Dround and I happened to be alone. She looked pale and worn, as if the people had tired her. She ordered the servants to take away the great bunches of roses that filled every nook in the room.

"They are too sweet," she explained. "I like them — but in the next room."

Her fastidiousness surprised me, and, as always, I began to wonder about her. Suddenly she leaned forward and spoke swiftly, intently: —

"I hope you and Sarah will be happy together — really happy!"

It was an ordinary kind of thing to say, but beneath the plain words there seemed to lie something personal.

"We shall be happy, of course!" I answered lightly. "There's nothing against it in sight."

"Ah, my friend, you can't count that way! Happiness is hard to get in this world, and you pass it by at odd corners and never know it." She smiled a little sadly, and then added in a more ordinary tone: "Sarah tells me that you are to be away only a few days. Does business tempt you so much that you can't resist it even now?"

"Well, I expect to love Sarah just as much when I get back to work. Business is a man's place, as the house is a woman's. Take either out of their places for long, and something is likely to go wrong with them."

She laughed at my satisfied wisdom.

"Are you so needed over there in the office?"

"You must ask your husband that."

"He says that you are the cleverest man they have had for years. Does that make you proud?"

"Thank you!"

"Will you let the big dog Strauss eat us?" she laughed on.

"I'll tell you a few years later, madam."

"Yes," she mused, "you are right. A man, a strong man — and that's the only kind that is a man — must be at work. The sweetest love can't keep him long."

Here Sarah's voice reached us: —

"You mustn't distract him to-day of all days, Jane!"

"He can't be distracted long, my child — by anybody!"

We had taken a pleasant house on one of the broad avenues to the south beyond the smoke bank, with a bit of a garden and a few trees. When we got back from New York we found supper waiting for us, roses on the table, a bottle of wine ready to open, and on the sideboard a box of cigars.

"The hand of Jane!" remarked my wife, as she rearranged the flowers and put the roses on the mantel-piece.

"The hand of Jane?" I repeated dully. "You mean Mrs. Dround did it all?"

"Yes, of course; it reaches everywhere."

And Sarah did not look as much pleased as I expected.

CHAPTER XII

AN HONORABLE MERCHANT

Mr. Dround's little weakness — An unpleasant occurrence — To the best of one's knowledge — "Kissing goes by favor," and other things — Switch-tracks and rebates — Carmichael talks — An item of charity — Our manager goes over to the enemy — I am offered his place — A little talk on the moral side — The dilemma of the righteous — What is, is good enough for me

---

"MR. DROUND seems to be doing a good deal of talking for the benefit of his neighbors," Slocum observed one day when I was in his office.

"Oh, he likes the job of making the country over! It suits him to talk more than to sell pork."

"Did you see what he said last night?" Slocum continued.

"No, what was it? Free trade or college education?" For Mr. Henry I. Dround was long on both subjects. He had always fooled more or less with politics, having come out as a mugwump and free-trader under Cleveland. That kind of doctrine wasn't much in favor among the business men of Chicago, but Dround liked being in the minority. He was an easy, scholarly speaker, and was always ready to talk at dinners and public meetings. "It seems to me I saw something in the papers of his speaking at the Jefferson Club banquet," I went on; "but I didn't pay any attention to it. The old man is rather long on wind."

"The papers missed most of the ginger. But I was there, and it was lively. Jimmy Birdsell, Hart's man, was there, too. It was this new Civil Service Bill that the silk stockings are trying

to push through the legislature. Of course, Hart and the machine are fighting it like fire. Well, your boss made the chief
speech, a good little talk about purity and business methods
in government and the rest of it. Birdsell sat just across the
table from me, and I could see from the way he knocked his
glasses about that he was getting hot. Maybe he came there for
a fight. At last he boiled over.

" 'Say, Mr. Dround,' he sang out in a pause between two
periods, 'how about your new switch-track over in Ada
Street?'

"Dround looked toward him over his glasses for a moment,
as though he hadn't heard what was said, and then he went
ahead with his talk. But Birdsell was some drunk and too mad
to care what he did. The men beside him couldn't keep him
quiet. 'I say, Dround,' he broke out again pretty soon, 'we
should like to hear what your firm does when it wants any little
favors from the city? That might be to the point just now!'

"This time Dround couldn't pass it over. He took a drink
of water and his hand shook. Then he said: 'I do not see that
this is the proper time to introduce a personal matter, but since
the gentleman seems concerned about my business honor, I am
glad to set his mind at rest. To the best of my knowledge,
Henry I. Dround & Co. have never asked and never accepted
any favors from the city. Is that satisfactory?'

" 'Come, now, Mr. Dround,' Birdsell sneered, 'that isn't
generally believed, you know.'

" 'I said,' your boss ripped back, '*to the best of my knowledge*, your insinuation is a lie!' He leaned forward and glared at
Birdsell. Well, there was a kind of awkward pause, everybody
waiting to see what would come next; and then Birdsell, who
must have been pretty drunk, called back: 'Ask your man John
Carmichael what he does when he wants anything from the
city. Ask him about your rebates, too. Then the next time you

come here telling us how to be good, you'll know more.' There was a cat-and-dog time after that, some yelling to put Birdsell out, and others laughing and clapping."

Slocum paused, and then added: —

"It put Mr. Dround in a tight place."

"What of it, anyhow?" said I. "Birdsell is nothing but a yellow dog. Hart keeps him to lick his platters. Every one knows that."

"Yes, that's so. But he said what most every one believes is true."

"That kissing goes by favor, and most other things in this world, too. Well, what of it?"

Slocum leaned back in his chair and laughed. Then he said to me seriously: —

"You aren't much troubled with scruples, Van!"

"Come, what's the use of talking good? You and I know well enough that there isn't any other way of doing business, not in any city in the country. You have got to pay for what you get, the same as elsewhere. Dround ought to know it, too, by this time, and not go 'round preaching loose — or else get out of business, which might be better!"

"I suppose so," Slocum replied solemnly. "But I always liked his sermons. Perhaps you and Carmichael could tone him down a bit just now."

"Oh, John don't mind his speeches, so long as he don't interfere with the business!"

We went out to lunch, and talked of other matters, and for several days I thought no more of the incident that Slocum had related. The switch-track business did not seem to me important. If the reformers wanted to get after us, or any other big firm, there were many more vulnerable points than that. Special privileges from the city we regarded as our rights. But there was the graft of railroad rates. Any fool could tell that, at the published tariff rates, there would be little business for the packers outside of Chicago. It was common knowledge that the trade was honeycombed with private agreements and rebate privileges, and that the fiercest part of the business was to get the right rate from the roads. Then there were the secret agreements between the packers, which were all illegal, but necessary to keep the trade from cutting prices all the time.

Carmichael attended to this end of the business for Dround, as he did of everything of real importance. He was a member of the firm now, and the wonder to me was that this smart Irishman could put up with Dround. It could hardly be a matter of sentiment with him. I had a warm feeling for the illiterate junior member, with a temper about an inch long, but a big, round heart open to any friend. He had bucked his way up in the world by main force, and I admired him. Besides, he had taught me how to eat, so to speak. In a word, I liked his way of doing things better than Mr. Dround's college talk.

Well, it happened that the cur Birdsell set some of the civil service reformers on the tracks of Brother Dround, and they got a smart newspaper reporter to work over the whole matter. There was a lively write-up in one of the papers, all about our switch-track over in Ada Street, with photographs and figures, and a lot more about the way the packers did business with the city. When I read the piece in the paper I took the trouble to pass by our new warehouse on my way to the office. The trackage was in, sure enough. Carmichael was just the man to have a thing done and settled by the time the public got around to talk about it!

Mr. Dround was in his office bright and early this morning, and sent for me.

"Harrington," he began, "what do you know about this talk in the papers?"

Mr. Dround seemed very nervous, not sure of himself.

"Why," I smiled, "I don't know much more than what the papers said. Mr. Carmichael, you know —"

"Yes," Mr. Dround interrupted impatiently, "Mr. Carmichael is in New York, gets back this morning; but I thought you might —" He hesitated, not wishing to admit his own ignorance. "I will send for you later when Mr. Carmichael comes in," he concluded.

So when John arrived he had us both in his office.

"You want to see me?" Carmichael asked gruffly, as if he hadn't much time that morning to waste on the senior member.

"Yes, I wish to talk over certain matters that concern us all, even though they may have no immediate bearing upon the business." Mr. Dround always talked like that when he got the least nervous.

"Well, what is it?" Carmichael asked. He had just arrived, and I suppose his letters interested him more than Mr. Dround's talk.

"You may not have seen the articles in the morning papers — about — about certain privileges which it is alleged —"

"What are the boys yapping about now?" Carmichael demanded, taking up a newspaper from the desk and thrusting his shoulders forward in an ugly fashion.

"It concerns our permit to lay that new switch-track," Mr. Dround explained.

Carmichael laid the paper down and looked at the senior member in a curious way, as if he were trying to make out just what kind of a fool he had to deal with. But as he said nothing, Mr. Dround continued: —

"Recently I had occasion to deny categorically that, so far as I knew, our firm ever made any such kind of arrangement as is here described. My word was challenged. It was a very painful situation, I need not say. Since then I have been thinking — I have been wondering whether this charge —"

He floundered pitifully, disliking to mouth the dreadful words. John helped him out brutally: —

"You wonder whether we had to grease anybody's paw about that switch-track over in Ada Street?"

Dround nodded. "The papers say so!"

"They have to print something, don't they? What harm does that do us? I wouldn't trust the whole d——n bunch of papers with a ten-dollar bill. They're a lot of blackmailers — that's what they are!"

John bit off the end of a cigar and spat it out in front of Mr. Dround.

"We are not concerned with the newspapers or their motives, Mr. Carmichael," the senior member observed with considerable dignity. "What I want is your assurance that this firm — that, so far as we are concerned, this accusation is false."

We waited for the Irishman's reply. It would be an easy matter to tell a fib and set Mr. Dround's mind at rest. But Carmichael seemed to be in a specially bad temper this morning. When he went to New York he was accustomed to enjoy himself, and it was not the right time to badger a man just off the cars. Pretty soon John said fiercely: —

"It's my business to look after such matters?"

Mr. Dround nodded.

"Don't I do it satisfactorily?"

Mr. Dround waived this point.

"Well, I guess you'll have to be content with that."

"Mr. Carmichael," the senior member leaped to his feet, "you forget yourself! You will be good enough to answer me yes or no, to my direct question. Did you or did you not pay money for this privilege?"

Carmichael's voice shook as he replied: —

"See here, Dround! If you don't know your own business

enough to know the answer, I don't see why I should tell you." His temper was going with every word he said. "But if you want to know, you shall! There hasn't been such a thing as a private switch-track put down in this city since you began doing business for less than seven thousand dollars. I paid the right people ninety-five hundred dollars for ours. There, you've got it! Now what are you going to do about it?"

The big Irishman plumped his two red fists on Mr. Dround's desk and glared at him. At that moment I pitied the old gentleman heartily; he was never born to do business, at least in our day. He seemed to shrivel up under Carmichael's words.

"How, may I ask," he said at last in a low tone, "was this done without my knowledge? How does it appear on the books?"

Carmichael laughed at the simple question.

"Charity! We are a very charitable concern!"

Mr. Dround's lips trembled, and he cried out rather than spoke: —

"No, never! Better to fail! Better to go bankrupt at once!"

He was talking to himself. Then he recollected us and said with dignity: —

"That is all, Mr. Carmichael. After this I shall attend to all such matters myself. Good morning, gentlemen."

He sat down at his desk, dismissing us. Carmichael was shaking with anger.

"No!" he cried, "it isn't all! Turn me out of your office like a boy, with my orders, when it's me that have stood between you and ruin any day these ten years! What would your business be worth if it weren't for John Carmichael? Ask Harrington here. Go out and ask your bank —"

"I don't believe we need to discuss this any further —" Mr. Dround began.

"Yes, we will! Get somebody else to do your dirty business

for you. For, let me tell you right here, Henry I. Dround, that I don't go broke with you, not for all your college talk and prin-ci-ples."

Mr. Dround pointed to the door. He was trembling again. I took the big Irishman by the arm and led him from the office. Outside the door he shook me off, and hurled himself into his own office.

That was the first wind of the storm, and the rest wasn't long in coming. Somebody told me that Carmichael had been seen with one of Strauss's lieutenants going into a law office that did some of the big packer's work. It looked as though he were making a deal with the Strauss crowd. It seemed natural enough to me that Carmichael should do this, but I was sorry for what must come. Meantime, Mr. Dround was more assiduous at business than I had ever known him to be. He came early, and instead of driving over to his club for luncheon took a bite in his office, and put in the afternoons going into all departments of the business.

In the end, the trouble came to a head in this way: in company with every large shipper at that period we made our bargain with the roads; no large firm and no railroad pretended to live up to the law in the matter of rates. The roads sold their transportation, as we sold ribs and lard — for the highest figure they could get. Before any considerable contract was entered into the thrifty shipper saw to his rate in advance. And some time later there came along from the railroad that got the business a check in the way of "adjustment." The senior member, in his new energy, discovered one of these rebates. He sent it back to the traffic manager of the road with a letter such as the roads were not in the habit of getting from their favored shippers. The second vice-president and general traffic manager of that line attended the same church the Drounds went to, and the president of the road, also, was one of Dround's friends. I wonder what they thought when their attention was called to this little matter!

Carmichael told me what had happened with a wicked grin on his face.

"Righteous man, Henry I. Dround, all right! D——n good business man, too," he commented. "What do you think is going to happen to this concern? He's chucked away the profits of that contract!"

"You aren't planning to stay, John?" I remarked casually.

He looked at me and laughed.

"Do you want to come with me when I get out?"

I smiled, but said nothing. There was no open row between Mr. Dround and the junior member of the firm this time. But a few weeks later Mr. Dround told me what I already knew — that he and Carmichael were about to part. I advised him bluntly to make it up with the Irishman if he could, — not to part with him at any cost.

"For, Mr. Dround, you will find him fighting on the other side; Strauss will have him."

He knew as well as I what that meant to his business, but he said with new determination: —

"Mr. Carmichael and I can never do business together again."

Then he offered to take me into partnership on the same basis that Carmichael had. I suppose he expected me to jump at my chance, but the prospect was not altogether inviting.

"I ought to say, Mr. Dround," I replied hesitatingly, "that I think Carmichael was right in this rebate business, and in the other matter, too. If I had been in his place I should have done the same thing — any man would. It's against human nature to sit still and be eaten alive!"

Mr. Dround's eyes lowered, and he turned his face away from me. His spirit was somewhat daunted: perhaps he began to realize what it meant to stand out alone against the commercial system of the age. Nevertheless, he said some things, perfectly true, about the honor and integrity of his firm. As it had been handed over to him by his father, so he would keep it, please God.

"That's all right," I said a little impatiently. "That might do in times gone by. But Carmichael and I have got to live in the present. That means a fight. I would like to stay on and fight it out with you. But I can't see the use on your basis. Look!"

I pointed out of his window to a new refrigerator building that Strauss was putting up under our noses.

"That is only one: you know the others. He is growing every day. You can't expect us to sit here twiddling our thumbs and thinking of our virtue while he gets the business! Better to sell out to Strauss right here and now, while there is something to sell."

"Never!" Mr. Dround cried with unaccustomed vehemence. "Never to him!"

"Well, then, we've got our work cut out for us, and let us waste no more time talking rebates and the rest of it."

"Yet that horrid scandal about the switch-track," he resumed in his old weak way. "Nothing has done so much to hurt my position in the city as that!"

"But what are you going to do about it?" I asked in Carmichael's very words. "Those thieves over there in the council hold you up. What good does it do the public for you to refuse their price? It's like paying for the right to put up a house on your own lot — it's tough, but you had better pay and not worry."

"Mr. Harrington, I refuse to believe that in our country an honorable business cannot be conducted successfully by honorable methods."

"That depends on what you choose to call honorable methods. At any rate," I concluded in disgust, "you are likely to have a good chance to try that proposition to the bitter end, unless you take my advice and sell to your chief competitor."

He waived this aside impatiently.

"Well, then, look for the fight of your life just to survive, not to make money. I tell you, Mr. Dround, Strauss is out there waiting to eat us all up. And you have thrown him your general for a beginning."

"But I trust that I have another as good or better," he said with his usual flourish of courtesy.

We had some more talk, he urging me to stay with him, although I let him see plainly where I stood on the matter of rebates, private agreements, and all the rest of the underground machinery of business.

"If I take your offer," I said at last, "I shall use the old weapons — you must know that. There are no morals in business that I recognize except those that are written on the statute book. It is dog eat dog, Mr. Dround, and I don't propose to be the dog that's eaten."

Even then he did not stop urging me, salving his conscience by saying: "It saddens me to hear as young a man as you take that cynical view. It is a strange time we are coming to. I pray it may not be a worse time for the country!"

To my mind there was something childish in the use of those words "better" and "worse." Every age is a new one, and to live in any age you have got to have the fingers and toes necessary for that age. The forces which lie in us and make those triumph who do triumph in the struggle have been in men from the beginning of time. There's little use in trying to stop their sweep, or to sit and cry like Dround by the road-side, because you don't like the game. For my part, I went with the forces that are, willingly, gladly, believing in them no matter how ugly they might look. So history reads: the men who lead accept the conditions of their day. And the others follow along just the same; while the world works and changes and makes itself over according to its destiny.

CHAPTER XIII

THE WILL OF A WOMAN

AFTER all, it was the will of a woman, perhaps of two women, that settled this business matter, for even in business — in the groping for position and money — the woman's share is large. Wherever a man's will is in play she brings her influence, soft and sure and hidden.

When I left Mr. Dround that afternoon, I was not ready to put the little fortune I had made, and, what was more, my life energy, into his forlorn enterprise. Not to hurt his feelings, I asked for time to consider his offer, and went home to tell my wife about the change in our affairs, considerably puzzled what to do. We had just moved into a larger house near the lake; the place had some pretty ground around it, and a large stable. It was all that our means warranted, and a little more. But Sarah had a passion for having people about, and there was a boy now to be considered. The air was supposed to be better for him farther away from the city smoke. Sarah had been delicate and nervous ever since the child was born, and I was glad to have her mind busy with the big new plaything.

A nurse in uniform was just coming into the gate when I

arrived. It seems that little Ned had a cold, and though he looked lively enough when I went into his room, Sarah was hovering over him as if he had lung trouble.

"The doctor thought I should have a trained nurse," Sarah explained. "Of course he doesn't expect any serious results, but one should take every precaution. And Mary is so careless, and we have those people coming to dinner to-night, and are going to the theatre."

I had forgotten that we were to have guests this evening. While we were dressing, I told Sarah about the trouble between Dround and his old manager, and how they had finally parted.

"That's just what I should have expected from Mr. Dround!" my wife exclaimed approvingly. "It must have been annoying for Mr. Dround to have such a dishonest person connected with him."

"Well, that is one way of looking at it I hadn't thought of!" I laughed.

"That Carmichael man is just an Irish brute! I suppose you have to put up with such people in the packing business, but I couldn't have them in my house."

"The Carmichaels don't trouble us much," I replied, smiling to myself at Sarah's ideas of things. "And John's all right — as honest as most men. This isn't just a case of stealing somebody's wash from the back yard, you know."

"But it's just as wrong! It's dishonest!" she cried with a proud tone in her voice. She came across the room and took hold of me by the shoulders. "Van, you don't believe in bribing people and such things? Why, you're too big and strong and handsome" — she gave me a kiss — "to do such common things!"

"Well, I don't know; it depends how you call it."

But she gave me another kiss, and before we could recover

from this argument there was a knock at the dressing-room door.

"My, Van! There's the first of them, and I haven't my dress hooked. You run and send Mary to me!" That rather closed the topic for the present.

There were ten of us at dinner, and we tried to keep up a chatter about the little things that Sarah had trained me to talk of when I was in company — the theatres and the opera, Mrs. Doodle's new place in the country, or old Steele's picture by the French painter. But to-night it was hard work: my thoughts would wander back to the Yards. At last the ladies left us to put on their wraps, and the men were lighting their cigars, when a servant told me that a man was waiting in the hall to see me. It was Carmichael.

"Why didn't you come right out, John?" I exclaimed. "Some of your friends are out there."

"No, thanks, Van," he growled. "I ain't got my fancy clothes on this trip, and maybe your wife wouldn't think me good enough for her friends" (which was pretty close to the truth). "But I come to see you about something important."

Sarah rustled into the hall just then.

"Van!" she said, bowing coldly to John, "we are all waiting for you."

"Better go, Harrington," Carmichael said sarcastically, reaching for his hat; "business don't count when there's a party goin' on."

"Oh, it's business!" Sarah's voice could carry a deal of scorn.

"Leave a ticket for me and I'll follow later," I replied impatiently, leading Carmichael into my library.

"Very well," Sarah answered, and swept out of the hall without a look for the Irishman.

Carmichael took a cigar, poured out a long drink of whiskey, and thrust his ungainly figure into a chair before the fire without saying a word. After a time he ripped out: —

"You aren't thinking of staying with old Dround?"

"That depends —" I began.

"Dround'll go broke inside of two years," he interrupted savagely. "His credit ain't much to boast of now, and when it gets around that I have drawn out, it won't improve."

"That's true enough," I admitted.

"The London and Chicago Company is going into the hands of receivers this week," he went on confidentially. "That was another of your tony houses managed from England! Strauss'll most likely get their plants at twenty cents on the dollar, and he'll get Dround when the time comes."

I made no remark, and after smoking for a time he leaned over toward me, saying impressively: —

"Young feller, do you reckon you can buck up against me and the Strauss crowd with that one-horse rig?"

It seemed to me highly improbable that any man could perform this feat, but I held my tongue. Carmichael should make his bid in his own way. Finally he whispered almost solemnly: —

"Want to make big money?"

And he began to bid, lowering his loud voice and beating the arm of his chair to clinch his argument. He spoke of the great revolution throughout the business world, coming consolidations, far-reaching plans that the Strauss people had had in mind for a long time, the control of railroads and steamship lines — all leading to one conclusion, one end — the complete mastery of food products by Strauss and his allies.

We had in more whiskey and cigars for the Irishman, who had a head like a rock. As he drank and talked, his brain was fired by a kind of rude imagination for the vast reach of what he saw. He opened himself to me without reserve, as if he already held me in his hand. The hours sped by; a carriage drove up to the house, and I knew that Sarah had returned from the theatre. But Carmichael talked on. Through his words I could see those vast industrial forces that had been shaping themselves for ages now fast rushing on toward their fulfilment. Ever since my head had been above the horizon, so to speak, I had seen straws borne on this wind. But now the mighty change was imminent; those who survived another decade would look out upon a very different world from that we had grown up with. That is what Carmichael and I saw that night, and when the door finally closed on my visitor I felt that it was settled: I should fight with the stronger army, side by side with Carmichael. . . .

I was standing before the dead fire, thinking, when the door opened and Sarah came in, her hair loosened over her white dressing-gown. She looked strangely pale and troubled.

"Van!" she cried sharply. "What have you to do with that dishonest Carmichael? What business has he with you? He makes me afraid; and you never came to the theatre at all!"

"You're dreaming, Sal." I took her on my knee. "John just came to tell me how to make your everlasting fortune."

"But you are not to leave Mr. Dround?"

"Just that."

"Leave Mr. Dround and go with that dishonest man! What are you thinking of, Van Harrington?"

That instinct of women, which people talk about, sometimes acts like a fog: it keeps them from seeing any one thing clearly. Sarah could only see the Drounds and the piece in the paper about bribing. So we talked it over, like husband and wife, arriving nowhere in particular, and finally I said at random: —

"You would like to be rich, to have a lot of money, more than you ever thought to have — millions, maybe?"

"Would it mean all that?" she asked slowly.

I laughed at the way she took my bait.

"Millions and millions, maybe."

"Would it be dishonest, Van?"

"We don't calculate on going to prison," I joked.

"Well," she reflected, "of course you know best. I don't believe a woman should interfere in her husband's business. But the Carmichaels and the Strausses are such common people, even if they are so awfully rich. They haven't the position the Drounds have."

When it came to that I kissed her and put out the lights.

In this life few intimacies fill the full orb of a man's being. Most men of affairs whom I have known, very wisely shut down their desks before coming home, and shut therein a good slice of themselves. Perhaps they do not care to trust any one, even a wife, with their secrets. Perhaps they do not need to share those restless hours of anxiety that come to all men who go into the market to make money. The wife should mean peace and affection: that is right and proper. Nevertheless, there come times when a man must talk out his whole soul to one who understands the language of it. For he hungers to say to another what he scarcely dares say to himself, what is shut up in the dark of his thoughts. It is not advice that he needs, but sympathy — to reveal to another that web of purpose which he has woven, which is himself. Many a man who has carried burdens silently long years knows what I mean. The touch of hand to hand is much: the touch of mind with mind is more.

Not that Sarah and I failed to be good married lovers. She was my dear wife. But there are some last honesties that even a wife penetrates not — moments when the building of years is shaking in the storm; moments of loneliness, when mad thoughts arise in a sober head, and a man gropes to find what there is not even in the heart of the woman he loves.

Dround was not at the office the next morning: they telephoned from his house that he was ill. Worry, perhaps, had brought on one of his nervous attacks. Meantime, it was easy to see the effect of Carmichael's loss all over the place. Down to the girls in the mailing room, the force knew that something was wrong with the concern. You can't keep real news from spreading: people are good conductors of electricity; their thoughts leak. In any business, the trouble at the head runs all along the line to the office boys.

Later in the day there came a message from Mr. Dround asking to see me at his house before I went home. It was plain enough what he wanted of me, and I disliked the coming interview. For I should have to tell him that I had decided to desert to his enemies. There was no other way, as I saw it. And yet it seemed like ingratitude. That was what his wife would think, and I saw her looking at me, a scornful smile on her lips. However, this was no matter for sentiment. If her husband had been another sort of man, — if he had any dare in him, — it might have been worth while to try a fall with Carmichael and Strauss. But as it was, I felt no desire to follow a funeral. Maybe she would understand. . . .

As I turned into the avenue near Dround's house there was a fresh little breeze from the lake, blowing the smoke away from the city and cooling the air after the warm day. It was quiet and peaceful on the broad avenue — a very different kind of place from the dirty Yards whence I had come. It made me feel all the more that Dround didn't belong in Packington.

I sat waiting some time for Mr. Dround, and was growing impatient when his wife came into the room.

"Mr. Dround is engaged with his doctor," she said. "Won't you step into the garden with me?"

Behind the house, hidden from a cross street by a brick wall, was a little green lawn with one old willow tree. It was a pretty, restful kind of place, hardly to be looked for so near the heart of the city. In one corner there was a stone bench and some chairs, and a table with books and tea things. Across the top of the wall one could see a line of gray where the horizon met the lake.

"Pleasant place!" I exclaimed, looking across the little garden out to the lake.

"Yes, it makes the city in summer tolerable."

Her eyes followed mine as they rested on a bit of marble, old and sculptured with yellow figures, that had been set into the wall.

"I brought that from Siena," she explained. "It was in an old wall there. It reminds me of Italy," she added, touching the marble lightly with her fingers.

Suddenly she turned to me with a swift question: —

"So you're to be our new Mr. Carmichael?"

It was not woman's mere haphazard quizzing: she demanded the truth.

"No," I replied gravely, after a moment's hesitation. "Mrs. Dround, I have come here to tell Mr. Dround that I must decline his offer. I have other —"

"You are going over to them!" she cried quickly. There was no reproach in her voice, but she gave me a keen look that read to the bottom of my mind. "You will be a tool for the Jew and the Irishman!" There was a smile on her lips and a touch of scorn in her voice. "Tell me, why?"

And I told her, as I might a man whom I trusted, just what the situation was — how disastrous had been the row with Carmichael, and how foolish the cause, as I thought. She listened

without questions, and I went on to cover the whole matter —
to tell of the large plans that our great rival undoubtedly had
in view, plans which meant ultimately the consolidation of the
entire business in some great corporation under his control.
It was as clear to me as handwriting what he was aiming for —
the entire food-products business of the country; and it would
take a stronger man than Henry I. Dround to stand against
him.

"So, Mrs. Dround," I concluded, "the best thing you and I
can do for Mr. Dround is to advise him to retire, to sell out —"

"He would never do that," she interrupted me quietly.

"You must make him see it," I urged.

"There are some things I cannot do. You will not understand; I cannot tell you — it is not my right. Only he will go
on to the bitter end."

I bowed. There was nothing further to be said, and we sat
silently for a few minutes.

"But are you sure," she began again, "that that would be
the best way? Is it best to run to your enemy, crying for quarter?"

"Not if you can put up a good fight."

She drew her fingers caressingly over the outlines of the old
marble.

"I think you could put up the right kind of a fight," she remarked quietly. "Suppose that you saw your way clear to
go in — to fight — what would you do?"

"The first thing," I said, smiling, "would be to hit Strauss
between the eyes."

"Just how?"

"Do what he is doing, if I could: get together all the independent concerns that could be bought or persuaded into join-
ing. Then you would be in a position to make terms with the
railroads and force agreements from the big fellows. And I

shouldn't let my scruples stand in the way, either," I added hardily.

"Naturally not — if the others were the same kind!"

"And if your husband were made like you," I thought to myself, "the chance would be worth the trying." "If," I continued aloud, "you could get the Jevons Brothers, the E. H. Harris Company, Griscom, in Omaha, and two or three others, there would be a beginning. And there is this London and Chicago concern, which could be had cheap," I mused half to myself, remembering Carmichael's words.

"I was sure you knew what must be done," she took me up in the same cool, assured tone. "You aren't the man to follow in the traces. You are the kind that leads, that builds. And this is building! What is the first step?"

I looked at her, but this time I did not laugh. She had risen from the stone bench and stood gazing out across the quiet sward to the blue lake beyond. Her dark features were alight with enthusiasm. Then she looked over at me inquiringly, expecting me to take her lead, to walk on boldly with her.

And there of a sudden — for until that moment there was nothing in my mind but to tell Mr. Dround that I was to leave him — there shot into my head a plan of how this thing might be handled, the sketch of a great campaign. All the seeds of thought, the full years' schemings, the knowledge and experience of life I had been getting — everything that was within me came surging up into one grand purpose. How it came to me of a sudden, born of a few words this woman had spoken here in the garden by the blue lake, is beyond my explanation. Suddenly I saw a way, clear and broad ahead — the way for me to travel.

"You will have to take the first steps by yourself — manage this London and Chicago Company affair on your own responsibility." Mrs. Dround's voice was now matter-of-fact, as though the time for clear thinking had come. "Then, when you have your plans ready — know just what must be done — you will have the necessary help. I can promise that!"

I understood what she meant — that Mr. Dround was not to be approached until the scheme was ripe. Then she would swing him to a decision. That was the wise way.

"You are right," I agreed. "It would be useless to trouble him until the land is mapped. When it comes to forming the company —"

"Yes, then," she interrupted, seeing my point. "Then I shall be of use."

"My, — but it's a big gamble!" I said low to myself.

"That is the only kind worth making!" she flashed.

It struck the right note in my heart. She held out her hand, and I took it in mine.

"We're partners on this thing!" I smiled.

"Yes — to the end. Now, shall we go to Mr. Dround?"

Here was a woman who should have headed a regiment, or run a railroad, or sat at a game with a large stake!

Mr. Dround opened the door on the veranda and came forward, walking feebly.

"How do you do, Harrington?" He greeted me, giving me a thin, feverish hand. "The doctor's been gone a good while, Jane," he added querulously. "I have been waiting for you in the library."

Mrs. Dround moved away while we discussed some matters of urgency, and then Mr. Dround said hesitantly: "I hope you see your way clear, Harrington, to accepting my offer. It promises a great future for a man as young as you, with your energy," he added a trifle pompously.

"It is pretty late to talk of that to-night," I replied, evasively.

Mrs. Dround was walking slowly toward us; she stopped by the marble piece in the wall and seemed to be examining it. But I knew that she was listening.

"There are some plans I want to talk over with you first. If they prove satisfactory to you, we could make an arrangement, perhaps."

Mrs. Dround turned her head and looked at us inquiringly.

"Oh, very well; I expect to be at the office to-morrow. This Commission for the Exposition takes a great deal of my time and energy just now." (It was the year before the great Fair, and Mr. Dround was one of the Commissioners for that enterprise.) "But we will take up your plans at once," he concluded graciously, giving me his hand.

There was a family party at my house that evening. Will had arrived from Texas, where he had been to look over the field for me, and May was visiting us with her children. As I walked up the path to the house on my return from Mr. Dround's, I could hear Sarah's low laugh. She and May were rocking back and forth behind the vines of the piazza, watching the children at their supper. May was looking almost plump and had a pleasant flush on either cheek; for good times had made her blossom out. But Sarah was the handsomer woman, with her wavy, rich brown hair and soft profile. Instead of May's prim little mouth, her lips were always half open, ready to smile. As I kissed her, she exclaimed: —

"Where have you been, Van?"

"Seeing some one."

"I know," she said with a pout. "You have been with that horrid Irishman. Well, I hope you made him give you just loads of money."

"But suppose I haven't been to see John?" I asked laughingly, thinking she would be delighted to find out I was to keep on with Dround. "Suppose I took your advice?"

"What! Are you going to stay with Mr. Dround, after all? And all that money you were telling me about — millions!" she drawled in her soft voice like a disappointed child.

She seemed troubled to know that after all I had given up my chance to make money with Strauss and Carmichael.

"I guess we shan't starve, Sarah," I laughed back.

"You must do what you think best," she said finally, and repeated her favorite maxim, "I don't believe in a woman's interfering in a man's business."

After supper, as we sat out in the warm night, Will talked of his trip through the Southwest.

"It's a mighty big country down there, and not touched. You folks up North here haven't begun to see what is coming to that country. It's the new promised land!"

And he went raving on in the style I love to hear, with the sunshine of great lands on his face and the wind from the prairies blowing low in his voice. It was like music that set my thoughts in flow, and I began to see my scheme unfold, stretch out, embrace this new fertile country, reach on to foreign shores. . . . Then my thoughts went back to the garden by the lake, with the piece of yellow marble in the wall.

"That's a pretty little place the Drounds have behind their house," I remarked vaguely to Sarah in a pause of Will's enthusiasm.

"What were you doing in the Drounds' garden?" Sarah asked quickly.

"Oh, talking business!"

"It's a queer place to talk business."

"It's a pretty place, and there's a piece of marble in the wall they got in Italy — Siena, or some such place."

"So you were talking business with Jane?" Sarah persisted.

"Well, you can call it that. Tell me more about that country, Will. Maybe the future will take us there."

In the warm, peaceful evening, with a good cigar, anything seemed possible. While the women talked of schools and the children's clothes, I saw visions of the coming year — of the great gamble!

CHAPTER XIV

THE FIRST MOVE

---

*The Chicago and London Packing Company — Bidding for bonds
— A man named Lokes — A consideration for services performed
— Bribery — A sheriff's sale — We take the trick — The tail of a
snake — Not a gospel game*

SLOCUM had been after the bondholders' protective committee
of the London and Chicago Company. There were only a
million and a half of bonds out, which, before their smash,
could be picked up for less than twenty. Lately, on the rumor
that one of the strong Chicago houses was bidding for them,
their price had risen somewhat. The hand of Carmichael working through one of the smaller corporations controlled by
Strauss was plain enough to one who watched, and I resolved
as the first step in my campaign to outwit my old boss in this
little deal. From the price of the bonds it was evident that
Carmichael was offering the bondholders about twenty-five
for the control. I told Slocum to give forty and then arrange
to bid the property in at the sheriff's sale.

The lawyer reported that two of the bondholders' committee were favorable to our terms: they hated the Strauss
crowd, and they were afraid to wait for better terms, as money
was hardening all the time. But the third man, who had been
the treasurer of the defunct corporation, held out for a higher
figure. Slocum thought that this man, whose name was Lokes,
might be dickering with Carmichael secretly to secure some
favors for himself in the deal. This Lokes was not unknown to

me, and I considered Slocum's suspicions well founded. He had left behind him in Kansas City a bad name, and here in Chicago he ran with a set of small politicians, serving as a middleman between them and the financial powers who used them. In short, I knew of but one way to deal with a gentleman like Mr. Lokes, and I had made up my mind to use that way.

Slocum made an appointment with Lokes in his office, and I went there to meet him and arrange to get the London and Chicago outfit with as little delay as possible. Lokes was a small, smooth-shaven fellow, very well dressed, with something the air of a horsy gentleman. First he gave us a lot of talk about the value of the London and Chicago properties, and the duty of his committee to the bondholders. He and his associates had no mind to let the property go for a song. I made up my mind just what inducement would reach him, while he and Slocum argued about the price of the bonds. When Lokes began to throw out Carmichael at us, I broke in: —

"Mr. Lokes, you know there isn't much in this deal for that crowd. But I don't mind telling you frankly that it is of prime importance to the interests we represent."

Slocum looked up at me, mystified, but I went on: —

"We propose to form a large packing company, into which we shall take a number of concerns on which we have options. We want this property first. When our company is formed we might make it very well worth your while having been friendly to us in this transaction."

Lokes didn't move a muscle: this was the talk he had been waiting for, but he wanted to hear the figures. I told him enough of our plans to let him see that we had good backing and to whet his appetite.

"Now we have offered your committee forty cents on the dollar for your bonds, which is fifteen more than the other crowd will give you. If you will induce your associates to take bonds in our corporation, we will give you fifty, instead of forty — and," I concluded slowly, "there will be fifty thousand dollars of preferred stock for your services."

At the word "services" Slocum jumped up from the table where he had been seated and walked over to the window, then came back to the table, and tried to attract my attention. But I kept my eyes on Lokes.

"What will you do for the others?" Lokes asked significantly, meaning his two associates on the committee.

"Nothing!" I said shortly. "You will look after them. They will do what you say. That is what we pay for."

It was plain enough that I was offering him a good-sized bribe for his services in turning over to us the assets of the London and Chicago concern rather than to our rivals, and for bonds in the prospective company instead of cash. That did not trouble him: he was aware that he had not been asked to meet me to talk of the health of the bankrupt company of which he had been the treasurer. Lokes thought awhile, asked some more questions about our company, and finally hinted at his preference for cash for his services.

"Either forty cash with no bonus for your services, or fifty in bonds with the preferred stock for you," I answered shortly.

Pretty soon he took his hat and said he was going to see his associates on the committee, and would be back in the course of the afternoon.

"He's gone over to Carmichael," I remarked to Slocum, when he had closed the office door behind Mr. Lokes. "But John won't touch him — he won't believe his story. He doesn't think I've got the cash or the nerve to play this game. We'll see him back in an hour or two."

"Do you know, Van, what you are doing?" Slocum asked sombrely, instead of replying to my remark. "You have bribed that man to betray his trust."

"I guess that was what he came here for, Sloco. But we are offering them a good price for their goods. This man Lokes happens to be a rascal. If he had been straight, we could have saved that preferred stock. That's all there is to it."

But Slocum still shook his head.

"It's a bad business."

"Well, it costs money. But I mean to put this thing through, and you know at the best I may lose every cent I have made in twelve years. It's no time to be squeamish, Slocum."

"I wish —" he began, and paused.

"You wish, if there is any more of this kind of thing, I would get some one else to do my business? But I can't! I must have a man I can rely upon."

It meant a good reward for him, too, if we carried through my great plan. But Slocum was not the one to be reached in that way. He needed the money, and wanted it badly, but money alone wouldn't make him stick by me. I knew that.

"We'll hope this is the last," I said, after a time. "And, besides, I take the risk. I want you, and you won't go back on me. I need you, Slo!"

He made no reply.

Sure enough, late that afternoon Slocum telephoned me that Lokes had come back and signified his consent and that of his associates to our terms. The bondholders would take notes, to be converted later into bonds of the new company at fifty cents on the dollar. Lokes asked for some kind of agreement about the stock he was to get for his "services," which I refused to give him, on Slocum's advice. He had to content himself with Slocum's statement that he was dealing with gentlemen.

The next step in the proceedings was the sheriff's sale of the defunct corporation's effects, which was ordered by the court for the following Monday. That comedy took place on the court-house steps according to law. The sheriff read the decree of court to an audience of hoboes, who were roosting on the steps, and some passers-by halted to see the proceedings. When the sheriff asked for bids, a little Jew lawyer in a shiny silk hat stepped forward out of the crowd and made his bid. This was Marx, the junior member of a firm employed by Strauss. Just as the sheriff was about to nod to the Jew, Slocum stepped forward with a certified check in his hand and bid in the property for seven hundred and fifty thousand dollars.

There was nothing for Marx to do; Carmichael had given him no instructions for this contingency. He had his orders, and he stood there with his jaw hanging, while Slocum handed in the certified check and completed the formality of the sale.

"It is fraud!" Marx shouted, shaking his fist in my face as we left.

Perhaps he was right; but whatever fraud there was in the transaction did not concern Marx or the men he represented. They had been euchred at their own game. And they knew it: we never heard anything more from the Strauss crowd about the London and Chicago bonds.

"Well, you've got it," Slocum said, as we came away from the sale. "I hope we won't have trouble with Lokes."

"That's all right," I replied. "We've got him where he can't make trouble."

"There's usually a tail to this kind of thing — you never can tell when you have reached the end."

But I was too jubilant to take gloomy views. The skirmish was over, and we were a step nearer my goal.

A few days after that I ran across John Carmichael as I was picking my way in the muck out of the Yards. He was driving in a little red-wheeled road wagan such as the local agents use for running about the city. He called out: —

"Hey, Van Harrington! Come over here!"

"Can't Strauss do any better by you than that? Or maybe you have gone back to collecting again?" I asked.

The Irishman grunted his acknowledgment of my joke, and we talked about one thing and another, both knowing perfectly well what there was between us. Finally he said it: —

"So you thought you could do better by sticking with the old man?"

I nodded.

"How long do you think he'll keep goin'?"

"About as long as I stay with him, John."

"And you put him up to buying that junk at the auction the other day?" he added.

"I bought it for myself," I replied promptly.

"The h—l you did! Say, kid, this ain't any gospel game you are in. You needn't look for favors from our crowd."

"We aren't asking any just now. When we want them, I guess we'll get all that we need."

"You will, will you?" Big John raised his whip and hit his horse as if he meant to lay the same lash on me one of these days. The red-wheeled cart disappeared down the road, the figure of the burly Irishman leaning forward and flecking the horse with his lash.

CHAPTER XV

THE ATLAS ON THE FLOOR

A tell-tale portrait — When the fire of life has gone — The guiding hand — A woman who understands — The highroads of commerce — The great Southwest — Dreams — The art of life — "No one asks, if you succeed"

MR. DROUND's illness kept him away from business for a month or more. He had always been in delicate health, and this worry over the loss of Carmichael and the bad outlook in his affairs was too much for him. His absence gave me the opportunity to form my plans undisturbed by his timidity and doubts. After he recovered, his time was much absorbed by the preparations for the Fair, in which he was much interested. In all this I could see a deft hand guiding and restraining — giving me my rein. At last, when I was ready to lay my plans before Mr. Dround, I made an appointment with him at his house.

He was sitting alone in his great library, looking at a picture which one of the artists attracted to the city by the Fair was painting of him. When he heard my step he got up sheepishly and hung a bit of cloth over the portrait, but not before I had seen the cruel truth the painter had been telling his patron. For the face on the canvas was old and gray; the daring and spirit to fight, whatever the man had been born with, had gone out of it. I pitied him as he stood there by his picture, his thin lips trembling with nervousness. He seemed to shrink from me as though afraid of something. We sat down, and after the first words of politeness neither of us spoke. Finally he asked: —

"Well, Harrington, how do you find matters now that you have had time to look into the situation?"

"Very much as I expected to find them," I replied bluntly. "And that is as bad as could be. Something must be done at once, and I have come to you to-day to settle what that shall be."

He flushed a little proudly at my words, but I plunged in and sketched the situation to him as it had become familiar to me. At first he was inclined to interrupt and question my statements, but he saw that I had my facts. As I went on, showing him how his big rivals had taken his markets — how his business had fallen so that he could no longer get those special rates he had been too virtuous to accept — he seemed to slink into his chair. It was like an operation; but there was no use in wasting time in pity. His mind must be opened. Toward the end he closed his eyes and looked so weak that once I stopped. But he motioned to me to go on.

"And what do you advise?" he asked weakly at the end.

"I have already begun to act," I replied with a smile, and outlined what had been done.

He shook his head.

"That has been tried before. All such combinations have failed. Strauss, or one of the others, will split it up."

I did not believe that the combination which I had to propose would be so easily disturbed. In the midst of our argument some one came into the room behind us and paused, listening. I stopped.

"What is it, my dear?" Mr. Dround said, looking up. "We are talking business."

"Yes," she said slowly. She was in street clothes, with hat, and she began to draw off her gloves slowly. "Shall I disturb you?"

"Why, no," he answered indifferently, and I resumed my

argument. Mrs. Dround sat down behind the table and opened some letters, busying herself there. But I felt her eyes on my words. Unconsciously I addressed the rest of my argument to her. When I had finished, Mr. Dround leaned back wearily in his seat and sighed: —

"Yours is a very bold plan, Mr. Harrington. It might succeed if we could get the necessary financial support. But, as you know well enough, this is hardly the time to provide money for any venture. The banks would not look favorably upon such a speculative suggestion. We shall have to wait until better times."

"We can't wait," I said brusquely. "Bad times or not, we must act."

"Well, well, I will think it over. It is time for my medicine, isn't it, Jane?" he said, looking fretfully at his wife.

It was a broad hint for me to take myself off, and my wild schemes with me. For a moment I felt disgusted with myself for believing that anything could be accomplished with this failing reed. Mrs. Dround came softly up to her husband's chair and leaned over him.

"You are too tired for more business to-day, dear. Come — let me get your medicine."

She took his arm and with all the gentleness in the world led him from the room, motioning to me with one hand to keep my seat. When they had gone I removed the cloth from the portrait on the easel and took a good look at it. It was the picture of a gentleman, surely. While I was looking at it, and wondering about the man, Mrs. Dround came back into the room and stood at my side.

"It is good, isn't it?"

"Yes," I admitted reluctantly, thinking it was only too good. As I replaced the cloth over the picture, I noticed that her lips were drawn tight as if she suffered. I had read a part of their story in that pathetic little way in which she had led her husband from the room.

"So you have started," she said soon, turning away from the picture. "How are you getting on? Tell me everything!"

When she had the situation before her, she remarked: —

"Now is the time to take the next step, and for that you need Mr. Dround's help."

"Exactly. These separate plants must be taken over, a holding company incorporated, and the whole financed. It can be done if —"

"If Mr. Dround will consent," she finished my sentence, "and give his aid in raising the money?"

Her shrewdness, immediate comprehension, roused my admiration. But what was her interest in the scheme? As Sarah had told me, it was generally believed that Jane Dround had a large fortune in her own right. Why should she bother with the packing business? She might spend her time more agreeably picking up Italian marbles. Her next words partly answered my wonder: —

"Of course, he will see this, and will consent; or prepare to lose everything."

I nodded.

"I don't like to pull out of things," she said slowly.

"Mr. Dround is in such poor health," I objected.

"This is not his fight: it is yours. All that he can do is to give you your first support. Leave that to me. Tell me what you will do with this corporation — what next?"

She was seated in a little chair, resting her dark head upon her hands. Her eyes read my face as I spoke. Again, as the other time when we had spoken in the garden, I felt as though lifted suddenly on the wings of a strong will. At a bound my mind swept up to meet her mind. On the shelf near by there was a large atlas. I took it down, and placing it on the rug at our feet, turned the leaves until I came to the plate of the United States.

"Come here. Look there!" I said, indicating the entire eastern third of the map with a sweep of my hand. "There is nothing for us that way to be had. We could never get to the seaboard. The others own that territory."

The map was streaked with lines of railroad running like the currents of a great river from the broad prairies of the Dakotas, across the upper Mississippi Valley, around the curve of the Great Lakes, eastward to the Atlantic seaboard.

"Those are the old highroads," I went on, following the lines of trade with my finger. "And those are the old markets. We must find a new territory, make it, create the roads. And it must be a territory that is waiting, fertile, unexplored! Here it is!"

My hand ran down the map southwestward, crossing Kansas, Nebraska, Oklahoma, Indian Territory, resting on the broad tract marked Texas.

"For us that will be what the Northwest has been for our fathers. There lies the future — our future!"

"Our future," she repeated slowly, with pleasure in the words. "You plan to feed this land?"

"Settlers are pouring in there, now, like vermin. The railroads are following, and already there are the only strong markets we have to-day — those I have been building up for five years."

We sat there on the floor before the atlas, and the bigness of the idea got hold of both of us. I pointed out the great currents of world trade, and plotted a new current, to rise from that same wheat land of the Dakotas, flowing southward to the ports of the Gulf. Already, as I knew, the wheat and corn and meat of this Western land had begun to turn southward, avoiding the gate of Chicago with its heavy tolls, to flow by the path of least resistance out through the ports of the Gulf to Europe and Asia.

"This is but the beginning, then — this packing company?" she questioned slowly, putting her finger on the inner truth, as was her wont.

"Perhaps!" I laughed back in the recklessness of large plans. "The meat business is nothing to what's coming. We shall have a charter that will let us build elevators, railroads, own ports, run steamship lines — everything that has to do with the handling of food stuffs. Some day that canal will be dug, and then, then" . . .

I can't say how long we were there on our knees before that atlas. It may all seem childish, but the most astonishing thing is that most of what we imagined then has come true in one way or another. And faster even than my expectation.

At last we looked up, at the same moment, and our eyes rested on the portrait above us. The cloth had slipped from the canvas, and there was the speaking face, old and saddened — the face without hope, without desire. It seemed the face of despair, chiding us for our thoughts of youth and hope. Mrs. Dround arose from the floor and hung the cloth in its place, touching the portrait softly here and there. Then she stood, resting her hands on the frame, absorbed in thought. A kind of gloom had come over her features.

"This — this scheme you have plotted, is life! It is imagination!" She drew a long breath as though to shake off the lethargy of years. "That art," she pointed to the picture of a pale, ghostly woman's face, hanging near by us on the wall — "that is a mere plaything beside yours."

"I don't know much about art: that is the work of a man's own two hands. But mine is the work of thousands and thousands, hands and brains. And it can be ruined by a trick of fate."

"No, never! You shall have your chance — I promise it — I know! Sit down here and let us go back to the first steps and work it out again carefully."

So there in the fading twilight of the afternoon was formed the American Meat Products Company. Again and again we went over the companies to be included, the sources of credit, the men to interest, the bankers from whom money might be had.

"It is here we must have Mr. Dround's help," I pointed out significantly.

She nodded.

"When this step is taken, I think he ought to go abroad — he needs the rest. He could leave all else to you, I think."

I understood; the corporation once formed, he would drop out.

"There might be matters to which he would object —"

She translated my vague words.

"No one asks, if you *succeed*," she answered tranquilly.

And with that observation were settled those troublesome questions of morality which worried Mr. Dround so deeply.

As I left I said in homage: —

"If this thing is pulled off, it will be *yours!*"

"Oh, no! Mr. Dround doesn't like women to meddle with business. It is all yours, all yours — and I am glad to have it so."

Her eyes came back to mine, and she smiled in dismissal.

CHAPTER XVI

THE STRUGGLE

Hard times — How to make something out of nothing — The problem of finance — Getting help — Cousin Farson — A trip down the coast — Paternal admonition — The beautiful city beside the lake — The last ditch — A strong woman's nonsense — The Drounds sail for Europe — I am in command

IT is not my purpose to recall all the details of the crowded years that followed. From the autumn of '92, when the events that I have just related occurred, through the period of deepening depression in all business and the succeeding era of prosperity, I can do little more than touch here and there upon more vital events. Suffice it to say that we were met at the start with hard times, a period of tight money, which prevented the quick realization of my plan to incorporate the properties that had been gathered together. One way and another the companies were carried along, by issuing notes and securing what financial help could be got, waiting for the favorable time to launch our enterprise. Here Mr. Dround was a strong help: once committed to the undertaking, he persuaded others and used his credit generously. Sometimes he looked back, seeking to retreat from the positions to which he was being forced; but he saw only ruin behind him, and perforce went ahead.

Strange to say, we met at first little or no opposition from our strong rivals. Whether it was that Strauss and his crowd were willing to let the mice foregather into one trap before showing their claws, or that they despised us as weaklings, no one could say. We were able, even, to join the great packers in one of those private agreements that made it possible for us to secure our share of the home trade. Mr. Dround was aware of this fact, but averted his eyes. Necessity knows little squeamishness. It must have filled John Carmichael with unholy joy to know that Dround had come to this compromise with his virtue.

So, in spite of the hard times, we pushed on, branching out here and there as the chance offered, building a plant in Texas, where Will was sent to take charge, and making a deal with a car line that had been started by some Boston men. But the time came when we had to have more money, and have it at once. There was none to be raised in Chicago, where the frost of the panic had settled first and hardest. Slocum, who was my right hand all these months, suggested that the money might be had from the Boston men who owned the car line. So in July, '93, we made a hurried trip to the East. They were frightened in Boston, and we met with little but disappointment. Men were waiting for Congress to repeal the silver law, or do something else to make it pleasant, and wouldn't listen to putting out another dollar in a Chicago enterprise. Then it occurred to Slocum that we might interest a man he knew named Farson, the rich man of his old home, Portland.

Farson, we found, was down the coast somewhere on his vacation, and we followed after him. It was the first time I had ever been in that part of the country, and the look of it was queer to me — a lot of scrawny, rocky fields and wooden-built towns. When we failed to find Farson in Portland, it did not seem to me worth while to go on — I doubted if there was as much money in the whole town as we had to have; but Sloco was strongly of the opinion that these Maine people had fortunes tucked away in their old stockings. So we kept on down the coast, and found our man at his summer cottage, on a little rocky island.

This Mr. Farson was a short, wiry, little man, almost sixty years old, with a close-cropped gray mustache, and looked for all the world like a retired school-teacher. He received us on his front piazza, and it took him and Slocum half an hour to establish just the degree of cousinship they were to each other. I wanted to laugh and to put in: "We've come to make your fortune, cousin. It don't make any difference whether you are third once removed or second twice removed." But I thought it likely that Slocum knew his business best with these people and kept quiet.

When Slocum got around to saying that we were interested in various Western enterprises, the weather seemed to grow cool all of a sudden. But Cousin Farson listened politely and asked some good questions at the end. Then he let us go all the way across the harbor to the hotel where we had put up, to get our dinner. I thought we had lost him, but Slocum thought not. For Cousin Farson had asked us to go fishing with him in the afternoon.

"He might have given us a sandwich," I growled to Slocum. "That place of his looks as if he could afford it."

Slocum smiled at my irritation.

"He did not ask you down here. He doesn't feel responsible for your coming. Probably Cousin Susan would need a warning before inviting two strangers to dinner."

Well, the little old schoolmaster came over in the afternoon with a very pretty steam launch. The fishing was not all a pretence. He liked to fish; but I never saw a man who listened as keenly as that man did. And I did the talking. I let him see that we were engaged on a big work; that in putting his dollars into our packing-houses he wasn't just taking a flyer, way off at the end of the earth. I had had some experience in dealing with men by this time; it was no raw young schemer who came to this party. And I had observed that what men want when they are thinking of putting their money into a new enterprise is to have confidence in the men who will spend their dollars. My experience has shown me that the cheapest thing to get in this world is money. If you have the ideas, the money will flow like water downhill. At any rate, that was the way it worked with good Mr. Farson.

We stayed there in Deer Isle three days, and had one simple meal in the banker's house after Cousin Susan had been duly warned. At the end of the time Farson thought he would give us a couple of hundred thousand dollars and take some of our bonds, and he thought maybe his brother-in-law would take a few more, and also his brother-in-law's brother. In short, Mr. Farson was the first one in a long row of bricks. He went up with us on the Boston boat, when we started back, to secure the others. It was a glorious night early in August, and, after Slocum had gone to bed, the old banker and I sat up there on the deck watching the coast fade away in the moon-light. I had never seen anything like it before in my life — the black rocks starting right out of the water, the stiff little fir trees, the steep hills rolling back from the sea.

"This is the prettiest thing I have ever seen!" I exclaimed. "My wife must come down here next summer."

"Yes," the old gentleman replied, with evident pleasure in my praise of his native rocks. "I can tell you that there is very little in the world to compare with the charm of this coast."

Then he began to talk of other lands, and I found that he had been all over the earth. He talked of Italy, and India, and Japan, and parts of Russia. After a time he began to ask me questions about myself, and being an easy talker, and happy over the success we had had, I told him a good deal of my story, and how I had come to enter the present undertaking.

It was easy to tell him things — he had quick sympathy and was as keen as a boy. He seemed to approve of my general plan, but advised patience.

"This silver trouble will lead to a period of bad times," he remarked.

"The very time to prepare," I retorted.

"True," he laughed, "when you have the faith and energy. But I am an old man. I wish to live in peace the rest of my life. Young man, I have been through two panics and the war. I lost a son while I was in the Wilderness. He would have been about your age," he added, in a far-away tone.

That switched the talk from business, and we sat there on deck until nearly dawn, discussing religion all the time. As he bade me good-by at the Boston station the next evening, I remember his saying to me with one of the pleasantest smiles I ever saw on a man's face: —

"Now, Mr. Harrington, I can see that yours will be a busy life. Success will come not merely in these matters, but in many others." He wagged his head confidently. "I don't make many mistakes in men. But if you ever want to have such pleasant talks as we had last night, when you get to be an old man like me, you must see to it that your hands are kept clean. Remember that, my boy!" And he patted my shoulder like a father.

It was a queer thing for one man to say to another at the end of a business day. I had occasion to think of it later, although at the time I put it down to the old gentleman's eccentricity. We parted very cordially. I felt that a valuable ally had been secured — one who had it in his power to bring others with him to our aid, — and I liked the old boy himself.

Among other things, Mr. Farson had asked me casually about a little line of Missouri railroad — the St. Louis Great Southern, it was called. He and his friends were pretty well loaded with the securities of this bankrupt little road, and the banker wanted me to look into it and advise him what to do with the property. Thus it happened that the St. Louis Great Southern became another link in my plan of conquest. Altogether it was a most important connection, that between us and Farson's crowd, and it was fortunate that Slocum thought of Cousin Farson in our hour of need.

All this time there had been building the beautiful city of white palaces on the lake, and it was now open for the world to see what Chicago had dreamed and created. Although it had made me impatient to have Mr. Dround spend on it his energy that was needed in his own business, now that it was accomplished, in all its beauty and grandeur, it filled me with admiration.

There were few hours that I could spend in its enjoyment, but I remember one evening after my return from the East when we had a family party at the Fair. May and Will were spending his vacation with us during the hot weather, and the four of us, having had our dinner, took an electric launch and glided through the lagoons beneath the lofty peristyle out to the lake, which was as quiet as a pond. The long lines of white buildings were ablaze with countless lights; the music from the bands scattered over the grounds floated softly out upon the water; all else was silent and dark. In that lovely hour, soft and gentle as was ever a summer night, the toil and trouble of men, the fear that was gripping men's hearts in the market, fell away from me, and in its place came Faith. The people who could dream this vision and make it real, those people from all parts of the land who thronged here day after day — their sturdy wills and strong hearts would rise above failure, would press on to greater victories than this triumph of beauty — victories greater than the world had yet witnessed!

Nevertheless, in spite of hopeful thoughts like these, none knew better than I the skeleton that lay at the feast, the dread of want and failure that was stealing over all business. But for that night we were happy and without fear. . . .

As our launch drew up at the landing beside the great fountain, another launch glided by our side, holding a number of the Commissioners and some guests of distinction. Among them were the Drounds, who had entertained liberally all this season. The two boat parties came to shore together, and stood looking at the display of fireworks. The Court of Honor was thronged with thousands and thousands; the great fountain rippled in a blaze of light; the dark peristyle glowed for a moment in the fantastic flame from the fireworks. I turned and caught the light of the illumination in the dark face of Jane Dround. She bowed and smiled.

"In your honor!" she murmured half mockingly, as a rocket burst into a shower of fiery spray in the heavens above. "I hear that you return from Boston victor. You should hear Henry! He has no doubts now." She laughed in high spirits, and we stood there awhile gazing.

"To-night I have no doubts; but to-morrow — who knows?"

Her brows contracted seriously.

"You need, my friend, one great quality, and you must get it somehow — patience!"

"That is true, but —"

"Patience!" she repeated slowly; "the patience that covers years. Perhaps you think that is a woman's virtue, but men, too, must have it if they are to endure. Remember — patience! Now, before any one comes, let me tell you: we are to leave for Europe as soon as the Fair closes. Do you think that it will be all right by that time? Say yes or no," she added, as we were approached by May and Sarah.

"Yes," I answered with a strange feeling of sadness.

Once more, before we left the grounds, I caught a moment of talk with Mrs. Dround.

"To you the game — the great game!" she exclaimed softly. "And to me the waiting. But remember, one useless woman is watching across the water every move you make, and when the time comes that you want help, when you cannot go on alone —"

It sounded like woman's sentiment, and I interrupted jokingly: —

"When I am in the last ditch, cable you?"

"Don't laugh at me! I am more earnest than you know. If that time comes — if you don't know which way to turn for help, if you have done *all*, and still —"

We were standing beside a bandstand, and at that moment the music crashed out, flooding us with deafening sound.

She pressed my hand, smiled, and turned away. I thought no more of her words then. But some weeks later, before the Drounds sailed for Europe, there came in my mail an envelope addressed in a woman's hand. Inside there was only another envelope, marked: —

"For the last ditch!"

I tossed it into a drawer, rather annoyed by the silliness of it all. It was the first evidence of weakness I had ever detected in this intelligent woman.

CHAPTER XVII

NO GOSPEL GAME

Elementary lessons in finance — What is a panic? — The snake begins to show signs of life — An injunction of the court — Inquiries — Ed Hostetter knows our man — How to deal with a political judge — Slocum objects — My will prevails — The injunction is dissolved

---

SARAH and I were sitting over our coffee one morning, six months after the Fair had closed its gates for the last time. Our second child, a little girl, was but a few weeks old, and this was the first morning that Sarah had breakfasted with me for some weeks. She had been glancing at the morning paper, and suddenly she looked up from it with wonder on her face.

"The Tenth National Bank has failed. Isn't that Mr. Cross's bank?"

I nodded.

"Will the Crosses lose all their money?"

"It's likely enough — what's left of it — all his and her folks', too."

"Yesterday some one told me the Kentons were trying to sell their place at the lake. What does it mean? Why are people growing poor?"

"It's the panic," I answered briefly. "Business has been getting worse and worse ever since the Fair. Some think it started with the Fair, but the trouble goes back of that."

She put aside the paper and looked at me seriously.

"Van, what is a panic?"

It seemed strange that she should ask such a question in a simple, childish way. But she had been shut away from people and things of late, and it was not her nature to explore what was not right in her path.

"A panic," I replied, finishing my coffee, "is hell! Now I must run and see what has happened to us."

She looked at me in round-mouthed astonishment, and when I bent over to kiss her good-by, she said reprovingly:

"You don't mean it could touch us, Van?"

"It might," I smiled, thinking of the troubled waters where I was swimming.

"We must trust Providence —"

"And me."

"Van!" she kissed me with a bit of reproof. "I wish you would be more religious."

My wife had been growing very serious of late. Under May's example she had taken to church work and attended religious classes. She and May had discovered lately a new preacher, who seemed a very earnest young man. The Bible class he had formed sometimes met at our house, and Sarah preferred to go to his church, which was a long way from our house, to the church near by where we had a pew. It made little difference where I was taken to church, and I was glad to have Sarah pleased with her young preacher. So I kissed my wife good-by and hurried off, half an hour late as it was.

There was trouble brewing. It had shown a hand some months back, darkly and mysteriously. One day, while I was East, a man had walked into Slocum's office, introduced himself as Henry A. Frost, and said that he represented some minority bondholders of the defunct London and Chicago Company. We knew that there were a few scattered bonds outstanding, not more than forty thousand dollars all told, but we had never looked for trouble from them. Mr. Frost represented to Slocum that his "syndicate" did not wish to make us trouble, but that before the property of the London and Chicago concern was finally turned over to our corporation he wished to effect a settlement. Slocum asked him his figure for the bonds held by his "syndicate," believing at the worst that Frost would demand little more than the cash price of fifty. To his astonishment the man wanted par and interest, and when Slocum laughed at his proposal, he threw out hints of trouble that might come if his "syndicate" were not satisfied.

Slocum referred the matter to me, and advised me to seek some compromise with Frost. "For," he said, "our record is not altogether clear in that transaction," referring to the sum we had paid for services to the treasurer of the bankrupt corporation. This move on the part of Frost and his associates was blackmail, of course, but the lawyer advised compromise. It would have been the wise thing to do; but having succeeded so far, I felt my oats too much to be held up in this fashion. I refused peremptorily to deal with the man, and Slocum intimated to him, when he called for a reply, that we would not consider giving him more than the other bondholders had received; namely, fifty per cent of the par value of the bonds he held in new bonds. Frost went off, and we had heard nothing more from him.

Meanwhile we had gone our way, making ready to turn over our properties, rounding up this matter and that, guarding against the tight money market, and quietly getting things in order for putting out our securities. Then one day had come, like a thunderbolt from an open sky, an injunction, restraining the American Meat Products Company from taking over the properties of the London and Chicago Company, the petitioners alleging that they held bonds of the latter concern, and that the sale of its properties to the representatives of the

American Meat Products Company had been tainted with fraud. A Judge Garretson, of the Circuit Court, had granted the temporary injunction one night at his house, and the argument for the permanent decree was set for April 10, a fortnight later. The names of the petitioners, all but Frost's, were unknown to us.

"There is the trail of the snake!" Slocum muttered when he had read the injunction. "We had better find Lokes. This will be in the papers to-night, and in the Eastern papers to-morrow morning — you will hear from it all over."

Sure enough, the next noon I had a telegram from Farson in Boston: —

"Papers print injunction A. M. P. Co.; charge fraud. Wire explanation."

"Cousin John didn't let the grass grow under him," Slocum grimly remarked when I handed him this telegram at luncheon. "You had better let me answer him. Now for Lokes: he denies all knowledge, and it's plain enough that he isn't interested in having this matter aired. But some one must have found out pretty accurately what has happened. Perhaps Lokes when he was drunk let out what he had got from us. Anyhow, it's blackmail, and the question is what are we going to do about it. It will cost us a pretty penny to settle now!"

The situation was alarming. Unless we could get that injunction dissolved, and speedily, our project faced serious danger. The banker Farson's telegram was only the first. The banks and our backers East and West would soon call us to account.

"It *is* blackmail," I said to Slocum, "and if there is a way out we will not pay those rats. Find out what you can about them."

In a day or two he came over to me with the information he had obtained. The "syndicate" consisted of three or four cheap fellows, hangers-on of a broker's office. One of them happened to be a relative of Judge Garretson, who had issued the midnight injunction.

"I got that last from Ed Hostetter," Slocum explained. "I met him on the street as I was coming over here. Having heard that this Lucas Smith lived out Ed's way, in May Park, I asked him if he knew anything about the man. He said at once: 'You mean the jedge's brother-in-law? He's a political feller.' Of course this Smith is a bum like the rest."

So we had in Ed, who had come back to work for me, having failed in a market where I had started him after the sausage plant was sold.

"Ed," I said to him, "we want you to find out all you can about this brother-in-law of Judge Garretson's. See if you can learn how many of those London and Chicago bonds he holds."

The next morning Ed brought us the information that Lucas Smith was willing enough to talk, boasting that he and his friends were going "to tune up those packers in good style." Ed thought they had got their tip from one of Lokes's pals. It seems that Smith owned, nominally, only two of the bonds. And there we were! Slocum rubbed his chin, trying to see light in a dark place.

"What sort of a man is this Judge Garretson?" I asked the lawyer.

"Good enough for a political judge, I guess. He's up for re-election this fall. There was some talk about his attitude in traction cases, but nothing positive against him."

"See here, Ed!" — I turned to Hostetter abruptly — "I want you to go straight out to this Lucas Smith's place and find him. Tell him you know where he can get twenty-five thousand dollars for those two bonds of his the day Judge Garretson dissolves that injunction."

"Hold on, Van!" Slocum interposed. "That is too strong! I stuck by you last time, but I won't stand for this!"

"Go on, Ed!" I called out to Hostetter peremptorily. "Tell him just that — the day the injunction is dissolved he gets twenty-five thousand dollars for his bonds, and the other rats don't get a cent!"

Slocum rose without a word and put on his hat. I put my hand on his shoulder and pushed him back into his chair.

"You aren't going to quit like that, Sloco, after all these years! Think it over. What else is there for us to do? Can we have this business aired in court? What will Farson say to that story of Lokes's? Do you think we could buy the bonds from those *rats* for any likely figure? — for any figure, if Carmichael is waiting around the corner to pick up our cake when we are forced to drop it?"

He sank into the chair rather limp, and we looked at each other for a minute or two.

"Well," he said slowly, "it might as well come out now as later."

"You have got to sit in the boat with me, Sloco! I need you." I leaned across the table and looked into his eyes. Slowly, after a time, he nodded, and gave himself up to me to do my will. In the heat of my trouble, I scarce realized what that acquiescence cost him: he never gave another sign. But it cost him, one way and another, more than I ever could repay, — and now I know it.

We walked out together, and as I turned in the direction of home I said cheerfully: —

"Once out of this mess, old man, we shall be on easy street, and you can buy a block of those old brick shanties back in Portland!"

The lawyer smiled at my speech, but turned away without another word.

Judge Garretson dissolved the injunction in due course. What is more, he roasted the petitioning parties who had entered his court "with flimsy and fraudulent pretexts." There was a righteous flavor to his eloquence that would have been worthy of a better cause. Nevertheless, that same evening Lucas Smith collected his price from Ed and delivered his bonds.

I turned to Slocum, who was with me in court when the decision was handed down, and said jubilantly: —

"That worked. They can't touch us now! I guess we've seen the end of this business."

Slocum demurred still.

"Maybe, but I doubt it. You don't think that Frost and his pals are going to sit quiet after such a roast? They will nose around to find out who sold them out."

But I did not pay much heed to the lawyer's fears.

CHAPTER XVIII

THE STRIKE

The labor question from the inside — A talk with strikers — Tit for tat all round — A ticklish place for an argument — My anarchist — Bluff — It works — We call it square

MEANTIME, for a little entertainment, we had a strike in one of our Indiana plants. At first it didn't make much difference: all the packers had been shutting down here and there during the cold months, and we were ready to close that particular plant.

But as the severe winter of '94 passed, and the men saw that we were in no hurry to start work until better times, they began to get ugly, to set fire to the buildings, and do other injuries. There was no police protection to amount to anything in any of these country places, and it would cost too much to keep a sufficient force of hired detectives to guard the property.

It got on toward spring and we wanted to open the place for a short run, but I was determined not to give in to the union, especially since they had taken to hurting the property. There had been a number of strikes that year, notably the great one at Pullman, followed by the railroad trouble. It was a most senseless time for any man with a job to quit work, and the employers were feeling pretty set about not giving in.

I remember that about this time some of the preachers in the city, and among them the Reverend Mr. Hardman, Sarah's young man, got loose on the strike question and preached sermons that were printed in the newspapers. Hardman's ideas were called "Christian Socialism," and it all sounded pretty, but wouldn't work twenty-four hours in Chicago. I wanted Sarah to try a new minister, who had sense enough to stick to his Bible, but she was loyal to Hardman, and even thought there might be something in his ideas.

Well, it got along into July, and I concluded to run down to our Indiana plant and see what could be done with the situation. There was a committee of the union waiting for me in the superintendent's office. We talked back and forth a considerable time, and finally I said: —

"See here, boys, I want you to come over the plant with me and let me show you what some of you strikers have done, and what it will cost us before we can open up."

So I tramped over the place with the men, and I pointed out damages to the property that would cost the company over ten thousand dollars to repair.

"Now, go home and ask your union if they will stand for that bill?"

They thought it was my little joke. They could not understand that a union, if it is to have the power to force a rise in wages, must be responsible also for the damage done by its members. Nor could they see that if the company wasn't making money, they could not make more money out of the company.

At last, after talking with the lot of obstinate Poles for three hours, I turned them all away, with the suggestion that they might see a trainload of men coming in from the South in about a week if they didn't come back — for we were going to open on the first of the month. They trotted off to a saloon to talk it over. The superintendent shook his head and talked about a riot if we should try getting in new men. Then he and I went over the place together to see about improvements, and spent another hour looking into every corner of the building.

He left me up in the loft of the main building, while he went back for some plans that were in the office. I poked about here and there in the dusty, cobwebbed place. There was only rough scantling for a floor, and below my feet I could see the gaping mouths of the great vats, still filled with dirty, slimy water. Pretty soon I heard the tread of feet coming up the stairs. It didn't sound like the superintendent. He was a light man, and this was a heavy person. I called out to the man to take care, as the light was none too good, and a tumble to the floor below into one of those vats would be no joke. He did not reply, and I was bending over looking down between the boards and trying to make out who it was, when suddenly I felt myself grasped by the neck. I straightened up, and both of us came near tumbling over backward through the loose boarding.

"Quit your fooling!" I cried, wondering what had got into the fellow.

Then I threw him off a bit and could see that I had to do with one of those men who had been talking with me down below in the office.

"So you get some other help, you do, you do?" he began to spit at me. "I know you! I know you!"

There was very little light in that loft, for the day was pretty well over. All that could be seen by me was a stocky, short man, with a face covered by a heavy beard. I remembered that I had seen him in the office with the other men, though he had not done any talking.

"Well," I said, "what are *you* after, John?"

Considering my position, I thought it was as well to speak good-naturedly. It wasn't just the place for a wrestling match.

"I know you!" He came forward again and shook his fist

in my face. "You are one of the men who murdered my friends. Yes, you did murder them!"

"You're drunk, John," I said as coolly as I could.

"Yes, you do know. Seven, eight year ago. At the trial!"

"So you are an anarchist! Those were your friends, were they?"

"And this time yust look out for yourself!"

He made a grab for me, and I jumped out of his reach. In doing so, I slipped on one of the boards, and went through part way. In the distance below me I could see those tough-looking vats.

It was only a question now of how soon the superintendent would come. I could not hear the sound of his steps below. Perhaps my anarchist had settled him first. In that case there was little help for me. If I should struggle, he could kick me over the edge as easily as you could brush off a fly from the side of a bowl. So, to gain time, I thought I would try to make the man talk. Then, at the last, I could grab him by the legs and fight it out in that way, or pull him down with me.

"So you think you'll get even by killing me! What is the good of that? You'll be caught the first thing, and you and your mates won't get one cent more for your day's work than you've had before. I don't count for so much. Some one else will take my place in this business, and you will have the same trick to play over again. He will boss you, and you will work for him."

My theory of life seemed to amuse my earnest friend, for he undertook to give me a lesson then and there on the rights of the anarchist.

"Maybe all the others like you will get killed some day," he concluded.

"Perhaps, John," I answered. "But you'll never kill us all. That's one sure thing. And if by any luck you should do away with all my kind, your own men would take to robbing you on a big scale as they do now on a small one. Here, give me your hand and help me out."

Very likely his answer to my bluff would be my end. But I was tired out, holding my two hundred pounds there in the air with my elbows. Strangely enough, while I watched him, waiting for him to act, and expecting the last blow, I did not seem to care half as much as I should have expected to. I thought of Sarah and the children; I hated to leave the job I had set myself half-done, with a lot of loose ends for other folks to bungle over; and it didn't look inviting down there below. But the fall alone would probably do for me at once, and, personally, my life didn't seem to be of much consequence.

But my anarchist friend made no move. It seemed to trouble him, the way I took his attack. So I gave a great heave, raised myself half up to the girder where he stood, and held out my hand.

He took it! A moment more I found myself standing upright beside my anarchist. The next thing was to induce him to continue the discussion a few floors lower down, where there would be less likelihood of losing our balance in the course of a heated argument. But I sat down, friendly-like, on one of the cross-beams, and began to talk.

"So you are an anarchist? Yes, I helped to hang your friends. I had some doubts about the matter then. But just here, now, after my experience with you, I haven't any at all."

I gave him a good sermon — the gospel of man against man, as I knew it, as I had learned it in my struggles for fortune. I showed him how I was more bound than he, — bound hand and foot, for he could run away, and I couldn't. At bottom he wasn't a bad sort of fellow, only easily excited and loose-minded. In conclusion I said: —

"Now we'll just step down. I am going home to get some supper."

I started, and he followed on meekly after me. It was a

rather creepy feeling I had, going over those stairs! They were perfectly dark by this time, and steep.

"You'll try to fix me for this?" the fellow said, when we reached the first floor, and I had started toward the office.

"I guess we'll call this square," I replied, "and forget it. Good night."

He made a line for the gate, and that was the last I ever saw of him. I found the superintendent locked in the office. He had been spending his time telephoning to the nearest town for help.

Then I took the train for Chicago. That experience was the greatest bracer I had ever had in my life. Hanging there with the expectation every minute of dropping into the vats below had steadied my nerves for a good long haul. And I needed it, too.

CHAPTER XIX

DENOUNCED

The snake lifts its head — My picture gets into the newspaper — The Reverend Mr. Hardman in his church — The opinions of ministers — Mr. Hardman points his finger at me — I reply — A scene — The real blow — May has her say — Women, religion, and this earth

---

IT was the Saturday after my little adventure in Indiana. As I was riding downtown in a street car, my eye was caught by a coarse cut in the newspaper that the man opposite me was reading. The picture seemed in a general way familiar. Underneath it ran these flaring head-lines: —

BRIBERY OF A JUDGE!

OFFICIAL IN PACKING CONCERN IMPLICATED!

EXCLUSIVE STORY IN THE NATIONALIST!

I bought a copy of the paper, and when I reached my office I read the article. It was sprung, plainly enough, to hit Garretson, who was up for reëlection, and, in the main, they had a straight story, — Lokes, Frost, the judge's brother-in-law, and all. And the right figures, too! The reference to Slocum and me was vague, and Ed was left out altogether. My picture was put in alongside of the judge's and labelled "Vice-President and General Manager of the American Meat Products Company." The inference was plain, and the paper wouldn't have dared to go so far, I judged, if they hadn't their facts where they could produce them. There was no word of the story in the other morning papers. I folded up the article and put it away in my desk, then telegraphed Slocum, who had gone to St. Louis on some railroad business for Farson and me.

Luckily, the *Nationalist* was not a sheet that ever found its way into my house, but that evening I looked apprehensively at Sarah. She was pale and quiet, — she had been downtown all day shopping, — but she said nothing to indicate that she was specially disturbed. The next day was Sunday, and though Mr. Hardman's preaching was not much to my liking, I drove over with Sarah to the little church on the North Side where he held forth. There was a pretty large congregation that morning, mostly women and poor people of the neighborhood, with a few North Side men whom I knew in a business way.

The Reverend Mr. Hardman never preached a good sermon that he had written out beforehand. He was one of those Episcopal preachers who come out in front of the chancel rail, cross their hands, look down on the floor, and meditate a few minutes to get their ideas in flow. Then they raise their eyes in a truly soulful manner and begin. But to-day, for some reason, Mr. Hardman didn't go through his trick. He marched out as if he had something on his mind to get rid of quick, and shot out his text: —

"What shall it profit a man if he gain all and lose his own soul?"

Then he began talking very distinctly, pausing every now and then after he had delivered a sentence. He said that we had fallen on evil days; that corruption was abroad in the land, polluting the springs of our national life. And the law breakers came and went boldly in our midst, the rich and powerful, the most envied and socially respected. Every one knows the style of his remarks from that introduction. Most preachers nowadays feel that they must say this sort of thing once or twice a year, or their people won't believe they read the papers. So long as he kept out in the open I had no objection to his volleys. I had heard it all before, and in the main I agreed with him — only he saw but a little way into the truth.

Suddenly his right arm, which had been hanging limp by his side, shot out, and as we were sitting pretty well up front on the main aisle it *seemed* to point at us. Sarah gave a little start, and her cheeks flushed red.

"And I say," the minister thundered, "that when such men come into our churches, when they have the effrontery to mingle with God-fearing people, and, unrepentant of their crimes, desecrate this sanctuary, yea, partake of the Holy Body, I say it is worse for them than if they were mere common thieves and robbers! I tell you, my people, that here in our very midst one of them comes — a man who has defied the laws of man and God, the most sacred; who has corrupted the source of justice; who has bought that which the law denied him! This man has used . . ."

I had been getting angry, and was looking the minister in the eye pretty fiercely. At that moment Sarah gave a little groan. She was very white.

"Come!" I whispered to her, getting up. "Come. It's time you got out of this."

At first she shook her head, but as I refused to sit down she rose to follow me. I had stepped to the aisle and turned to give Sarah my arm when she fainted — just sank down with a groan in my arms.

"So this is the gospel you preach!" I called out to the minister, who had paused and now stepped forward to help me raise Sarah. "Let her alone! You have hit her hard enough already. Another time when you undertake this kind of business, you had better know what you are talking about."

He stepped back to his desk and kept silent, while I and

one of the ushers who had come forward to help me lifted Sarah and carried her to the door. When we got to the end of the aisle Sarah opened her eyes and stood up.

"I have had enough of *your* gospel, my friend!" I called back. "I am going where I shall hear religion and not newspaper scandal."

Sarah groaned and pulled gently at my arm. Once in the carriage, she turned her face to the window and looked out as if she were still shocked and sick. I tried to say something to comfort, but I could only think of curses for that meddlesome Pharisee, who thought it was his duty to judge his flock.

"Don't talk about it!" Sarah exclaimed, as if my words gave her pain.

So we rode home in silence all the way. At the end she turned to me: —

"Just say it isn't true, Van!"

I began to say a few words of explanation.

"No, just say it isn't true!" she interrupted. "I can't understand all that you are saying. Just say that you haven't done anything wrong. That's all I want."

"Some people would think it was wrong, Sarah," I had to say after a while.

She gave a little groan and shut her lips tight. When we entered the house May was there, with her children.

"Why, my land!" she exclaimed on seeing us. "What brings you people back so soon? Sarah looks sick!"

Sarah was ready to faint again. May helped her up to her room, and I went into my study. Pretty soon May came down to me.

"What's the matter with Sarah, Van?" she asked sharply. "She seems all queer and out of her head."

Then I told her what had happened.

"Did you see the piece in the paper?" I asked at the end.

May shook her head. "But I shouldn't wonder if Sarah had seen it."

"Why do you think so?" I asked.

"Why, she seemed troubled about something yesterday when she came into the house after she had been downtown shopping. She asked me whether I generally believed the things I saw in the papers. I asked her what kind of things, and she said, — 'Scandals about people in business.' I thought it was queer at the time."

"She won't talk to me about it," I said.

May didn't make any reply to this, and we sat there some time without talking. Then May asked in a queer little voice: —

"Tell me, Van, is there anything in that story? Is it true in the least way?"

"I'll tell you just how it was," I answered.

May was not the kind of person that could be put off with a general answer, and I was glad to give her the inside story. So I told her the circumstances of the case. "It was blackmail and robbery — the judge was waiting to be bought. These rats stood between us and what we had a perfect right to do. There's hardly a business man in this city who, under the circumstances, would not have done what we did!"

"I don't believe that!" May exclaimed in her sharp, decisive little way.

She sat looking at me rather sternly with the same look on her face that I had remembered for twenty years. And the next thing that she said was pretty much what I thought she was going to say: —

"Van, you are always a great hand to think what you want to believe is the only thing to believe! You know that!"

She smiled unconsciously, with the little ironical ripple which

I knew so well, and I smiled, too. I couldn't help myself. We both seemed to have gone back to the old boy and girl days. But I was angry, as well, and began to defend myself.

"No," she interrupted. "It isn't a mite of use for you to bluster and get angry, Van. I don't trust you! I haven't for some time. I have been worried for Will. Don't you let him mix himself up in your ways of doing things, Van Harrington!"

"If he is so terribly precious," I said hotly, "I guess you had better take him back to Jasonville."

"Maybe I shall," she answered quietly. "I'd take him to the meanest little place in creation rather than know he had done any such thing as you say you have done!"

We were both pretty angry by this time, and yet we both smiled. She was such a snappy, strong little woman — I admired her all the time she was making me angry! Somehow it brought back all that time long ago when I had thought the world began and ended with her. We had never been so near each other since. And I think she felt somewhat in the same way.

"Well," I said at last, "I am not going to fight this thing out with you, May, or with any other woman. I have too much else on hand. I am answerable for all I do or have done. If you and Will don't like my company, why, we have got to do without you."

I wished I hadn't been so small as to make that fling. She flashed a look at me out of her eyes that brought me to my senses in a moment. I took her by the shoulders. "See here, May, we mustn't quarrel. Let's all hang together in this, as in other things. You women don't know what business means."

She smiled back into my eyes and retorted, "It seems to be just as well we don't!" In a moment more she added: "But you mustn't think that I can make up like this. You and I don't look at things in the same way."

"Never did!" I said dryly. "At any rate, you had better go up now and look after Sarah. She can't keep on this way. She's got to look at this more sensibly. She isn't like you, May!"

"No," May retorted, "she isn't! But this hurts her, too. Perhaps she cares more what folks *say* than I do. And she believes in her religion, Van."

"That's all right. Her religion tells her to forgive, and not to judge, and a few other sensible truths, which that minister seemed to forget to-day."

"I never expected to see you, Van Harrington, asking for quarter in that way!" she flashed.

Then she went back to Sarah. What my sister-in-law said set me to thinking queer thoughts. I admired the way she took the matter, though it made me pretty angry at the time. It seemed straight and courageous, like her. If we had married, down there at home in the years past, there would have been some pretty lively times between us. I could never have got her to look at things my way, and I don't see how I could have come to see things her way. For in spite of all the preacher and May had to say, my feeling was unchanged: women and clergy, they were both alike, made for some other kind of earth than this. I was made for just this earth, good and bad as it is, — and I must go my way to my end.

TREACHERY

THE Monday morning after Mr. Hardman's outbreak, Slocum was waiting for me at my office. In reply to my telegram he had come back from St. Louis, where he had been attending to some business in connection with Farson's railroad.

"They got it pretty straight this time," was all he said as a greeting, with a car-worn sort of smile.

"They can't prove it! We'll bring suit for libel. I must put myself straight — for family reasons."

But the lawyer shook his head doubtfully.

"That wouldn't be safe, Van! It's too close a guess. I rather think they've got all the proof they want."

"Where did they get it, then? Not out of Lokes. He hasn't any reason to squeal. Nor the judge, nor his brother-in-law!"

"Of course not; but how about Frost? This is the way I figure it out: when those rats were euchred in their hold-up game by Garretson's dismissing his injunction, they were mad enough and determined to find out who sold them. It didn't take them long to see that the judge had been fixed in some way. They nosed around, and spotted the judge's brother-in-law as the one who made the trade. Then they started out to get proof."

"Well?"

Slocum looked at me shrewdly.

"I have been thinking about that all the way back from St. Louis. There is only one man left in the combination."

We stared at each other for a minute.

"You don't mean *him!*" I gasped.

"Who else?"

"Not Hostetter — not Ed!"

"Send for him, and we'll find out," he answered shortly.

I telephoned out to our office in the Yards to send Hostetter to the city, and while we waited we discussed the story in all its bearings.

"We've got the trick," Slocum commented in reply to my desire for action. "And Marx, who managed this business for Carmichael, is shrewd enough to see it. *They* won't bother us."

There was some comfort in that reflection: no matter what the scandal might be, we had the London and Chicago properties in our possession, and nothing short of a long fight in court could wrest them from our control.

"The only thing to do," the lawyer continued, "is to keep quiet. The papers will bark while the election is on, and it looks mighty bad for Garretson. But out here most people forget easily."

It was queer to hear old Slocum talking in that cynical tone, as if, having accepted the side that was not to his taste, he took pleasure in pointing out its safety.

"Well," I grumbled, thinking of May and Sarah, "it's mighty uncomfortable to be held up by rats like Lokes, Frost, and company, and then be branded as a briber!"

"What do you care?" Slocum asked harshly. "It won't hurt *you* much. You'll make money just the same, and there aren't many who would lay this up against you. Of course, there are always a few who are shrewd enough to guess just about what has happened, and remember, — yes, remember a story for years! But you don't care for their opinion!"

I knew that he was thinking of the honest men in his own profession, the honorable men at the head of the bar, who would mark him henceforth as my hired man.

Hostetter arrived soon, a shifty look in his eyes. He had changed a good deal since that time he had slept out on the lake front. He was a heavy man, now, with a fleshy face, and his dress showed a queer love for loud finery. He wore a heavy seal ring, and a paste diamond in his tie, which was none too clean. His sandy mustache dropped tight over his mouth. Yet in spite of his dress and his jewellery, he was plainly enough the countryman still.

"Ed," I said at once, "have you been talking to any one about that matter of the bonds — the deal with Lucas Smith?"

He glanced at Slocum and then at me. One look at his face was enough: the story was there.

"You low dog!" I broke out.

Slocum tried to hush me. Hostetter muttered something about not knowing what we were talking about.

"You're lying, Ed! Tell me the whole truth. Did you sell what you knew to the *Nationalist*, or to Frost and his crowd?"

He became stubborn all at once, and refused to answer. I turned to the lawyer: —

"See that man! I picked him out of the bankruptcy court two years ago, after giving him his third start in business. Last winter I sent his wife South and kept her there six months so that she could get well."

I turned to Ed.

"Whose bread are you eating now, to-day?"

He picked up his hat and started for the door. But I called him back. It came over me all at once what we had been through together, and I couldn't let him leave that way, sneak out of my sight for good and all.

"Tell me, Ed," I asked, more miserable than he, "are you going over to Carmichael to get some more pay for this?"

"Maybe, if I did," he replied sullenly, "it'd be some better than it is working for you."

"I don't think so — not long. Folks like you aren't worth much. Come, Ed! Did I ever do a mean thing to you? Didn't I give fifteen cents when we hadn't but twenty between us? What were you thinking when you did this dirty piece of business? Just tell me you were drunk when you did it. I would have given you ten times as much as you ever got from them to know you couldn't do it!"

Then he began to go to pieces and cry, and he told me all I wanted to know. It was a plain case of the poison of envy. I was rich and on top, and he was working for thirty dollars a week for me. His wife, who had always kept a grudge against me for not making up to her in the old days, had taunted him for taking his wages from me. She kept telling him that I did nothing for him, and when she found out about his dealing with Lucas Smith for me, she saw her chance. Somehow Frost got on his track, and evidently they thought his information was worth paying something for. That was the whole story.

While we were talking, Slocum slipped out of the room. It was a pitiful scene.

"Ed," I said finally, "you must go back to the country. That is the only place for you. You'll grow worse in the city the longer you stay. Your belly's got bigger than your brain, and your heart is tainted at the core. I will start you on a ranch I've got in Texas. Think it over and get out of this place as soon as you can. I'm sorry for you, Ed. For you have done something the taste of which will never get out of your mouth."

He left my office without a word, and that was the last I ever saw of him. When he had gone Slocum came back and sat down.

"It was a pretty tough thing for Ed to do," he remarked calmly, looking out into the muddy street, where men were hurrying along the pavements. I made no remark, and he added in the same far-off tone of voice: "That's the worst of any piece of crooked business: it breaks up the man you work with. Ed is a rascal now — and he was never that before!"

"That's true enough," I assented gloomily.

Slocum advised me to leave the city for a while, because should the *Nationalist* charges be investigated by the Grand Jury, it might be awkward for me. But I refused to leave the city: no matter what happened, I was not the man to run and hide. The Democratic papers made all they could out of the affair, and then after the election it died away. Garretson was reëlected, and that was a kind of vindication for him.

But the insiders in the city knew that something had been wrong, and, as Slocum said, the scandal connected with quashing that injunction followed us for many years. It was of less importance to me than to Slocum; for the men with whom I dealt were used to stories like mine. They believed what they had a mind to, and did business. But for Slocum it was more serious.

The worst of it for me was at home. Sarah brooded over the newspaper talk until she was morbid, refusing to go almost anywhere she would be likely to meet people she knew. The Bible classes had been given up, and, naturally enough, we never went back to Mr. Hardman's church, nor returned to our old church. Sarah and I talked about it once or twice, but we got nowhere.

"I should think you would care for the children!" she would cry, persisting in considering me as a criminal.

"You'll see that it won't make the smallest difference to any one a year hence, if you'll only hold up your head!"

"Well, I don't understand business, but May thinks it pretty bad, I know, because she doesn't come to the house any more when you are at home."

"She has no reason to act that way. And I don't mean to have you or May or any other woman holding me up with your notions of what's right and wrong, just because the newspapers make a lot of talk."

That ended the matter between us; but for a long time Sarah avoided our old friends, and the house was unusually quiet.

What troubled me more than the racket in Chicago was the way that Dround and Farson and a few other of our backers might take the story. The Drounds were in Egypt, but they would hear the news quickly enough. Mr. Dround was the president of our corporation, and the most influential single stockholder. With his ideas, he might become a nuisance, or draw out altogether, which would be awkward in the present condition of the company.

As for Farson, I always counted a good deal on that crusty bit of rock, and he had never failed me yet. One thing after another had come up in the last four years, and he and his friends had backed me solidly. We were pretty deep in other enterprises than this packing business — railroads and land in that Southwest where I had set my eyes. While the scandal was the worst we never heard a word from Farson, and I was congratulating myself that he had overlooked the matter, when one morning I received a despatch: "Meet me Union Station twelve to-morrow. FARSON." That was all.

When he got out of the sleeper that noon I missed his usual warm smile. He refused my invitation to lunch at the City Club, and led the way into the fly-specked, smelly restaurant at the station. We ate our miserable meal, and he said little while I talked to him about our affairs. It was like talking to a blank wall: he listened but said nothing. After a while he interrupted me in a kind of thin whisper, as if his mind had been absent all the time: —

"What about this Judge Garretson? It isn't true?"

"You mean what the papers say?"

The old gentleman didn't like newspapers. But he waived that aside with a frown.

"The facts!" he whispered across the table. "I should not have mentioned it had it not been for a conversation which I had the other day in New York with Judge Sloan, of the Chicago bar. He tells me that it is generally believed to be true that this Garretson was bribed, and that my old friend Jeff Slocum was mixed up in it. He says that Slocum has lost his reputation among the best men of the profession on account of his connection with this scandal. What are the facts?"

"This is hardly the place to go into all that," I replied somewhat tartly.

"I don't know but that the place is good enough," the banker observed dryly, "provided you have the right things to say." But he took the frost out of his severe tone by one of his most genial smiles, and added more gently: —

"Perhaps you young men don't realize how serious it is to have such rumors get around about your reputation. Why, my boy, it puts you in another class! You are no longer gentlemen, who can be trusted with honest people's money and confidence."

Farson would be a hard man to bring to my point of view! I said by way of allegory: —

"When a man comes out of the alley and puts a pistol in your face, and asks for all the money you have on you, you don't wait to see where you hit him, do you? We don't here in Chicago. The men who are making all this talk were the hold-ups, and they did not get our money." I laughed.

But he did not laugh with me — instead, he shut up like a

clam all at once. He finished his corned beef hash and tea, making a few remarks about the train service on the road he had come over. I asked him some questions about our railroad matters, but he merely mumbled "Um, um" to all I had to say. Finally he said with his usual calm courtesy that he had some letters to write, and as the train for the West he was to take did not leave for some time he would not detain me, but would go upstairs to the waiting-room and write his letters. So he seized his worn old grip and marched off.

"Cursed old Maine Yankee," I said to myself, and I repeated the remark over the telephone to Slocum, telling him the result of my luncheon with the banker.

"Maybe so," the lawyer telephoned back. "But we can't afford to let him get his back up."

"It's up already — he's been talking with Sloan, and I gather the judge didn't speak highly of you or me."

"I suppose not," came the answer over the wire, and Slocum's voice sounded dreary. "That kind of thing dies hard."

It *was* dying hard, and no doubt about it!

CHAPTER XXI

A SQUEEZE

The great fit of dumps — Keeping afloat — Interest on bonds — A sudden financial frost — Strauss shows his hand — I heard the lion in his den — He soars — I give him food for thought — The thermometer rises once more — They treat me with consideration at the bank

---

As every one knows, the recovery of business from that awful fit of depression which followed '93 was slow. At times it would seem that the country was ready to throw off its fit of sickness and begin to grow again. Then there would come along some new set-back, and we were all in the dumps once more.

It had been a great fight to keep the Meat Products Company afloat during these hard times. It was all we could do to pay our fixed charges, which were heavy, as most of the concerns that formed the corporation had demanded bonds in payment for their properties before they would consent to join us. There was also, of course, a big issue of stock, preferred and common, which, by a mutual agreement, was not to be marketed for three years. We had not yet come in sight of a dividend on this stock; hence there were signs of dissatisfaction among the little fellows, who had expected wonders of the company. And the time was fast approaching when they would be at liberty to dump their stock on the market for what they could get for it.

The Strauss crowd, since their secret attempt through the tool Frost and his "syndicate" to thwart our plans, had kept their hands off us. They knew well enough what was our financial condition, and were biding their time to strike. But so far, clear down to the winter of '96, we had been able to meet all interest charges promptly, and had thus kept the corporation from foreclosure. That year as the time approached for the March payment of interest on the bonds and sinking-fund requirement, it became evident that our treasury would not be able to meet the sum required, and that it would be necessary for us to borrow for the immediate emergency. We already had a good deal of our paper out in Chicago, and so Slocum and I went East to raise what we needed. That was not so easy as it would have been in the days when we could rely on Farson's aid. But after considerable efforts we got together in New York what was needed for the emergency, and I left for home. That was the fourteenth of February. I congratulated myself that the danger was past, for I was sure that, with the opening of our new plant in Kansas City, and the constant improvement in our business, we ought to be beyond attack when the next payment was due in the fall. After that period we should be on the road to dividends.

I had been at home a couple of days, my attention given to other matters of importance, when one morning notice came from the Mercantile National Bank, where we did most of our business, that some large notes were called. We had over two hundred and fifty thousand dollars in "call" loans due that bank, and though, during these uncertain times, we could not get any long paper, the management of the Mercantile had been friendly to us from the start, and I had no reason to anticipate trouble in that quarter. But when I went over to see the Mercantile people I met with only a polite and cool reception. The loans were called; they must be paid; money was hardening, and so on. It was a granite wall, with just as much human consideration in it as stone and steel — and back I went to my office to think.

There was more than the ordinary bankers' caution in this

sudden financial frost; and, whatever was the power working against us, it was strong enough to close the doors of credit throughout the city. Wherever I went those dreary two days, from bank to bank, I was met with the same refusal: money was not to be had on any terms. The word had gone out that we were a doomed ship, and not a bank would touch our paper. After a second sleepless night I made up my mind to a desperate step, with the feeling that if it failed the game was up.

As soon as I reached my office on the last day of grace I got old Strauss himself on the telephone and asked for an appointment. He was gracious enough when I reached his office; it was the cordiality of a hungry eater before a good meal.

"What can I do for you, Mr. Harrington?" he purred.

I cut into the meat of the matter at once.

"What are your terms?"

"Do you mean that you wish to sell your property?" he asked indifferently.

"Not a bit of it."

"Then how can I help you, Mr. Harrington?" he inquired blandly.

"You can take your hand off the banks, and let us get a living."

He shrugged his shoulders deprecatingly, as if I gave him credit for too much power, and we had it out at some length. He had no interest in the Meat Products Company. If the corporation went into the hands of a receiver, he and his friends might consider buying it up, and he was willing to discuss terms if we wished to deal in a friendly manner before it reached the courts. I rose from my chair as if to go.

"Very well, Mr. Strauss," I said dryly. "You have made it impossible for us to get any money in Chicago, but you don't own the earth. There is money in New York — about four hundred thousand dollars lying there for me at this moment."

"To pay the interest on your bonds!" he shot back, showing how closely he had followed us.

"Yes," I admitted, "to meet our March interest and sinking fund. But I am going across the street to the telegraph office to wire it out here and take up our paper."

He looked at me inquiringly, waiting for the next move.

"And the March interest?" he suggested.

"We shall default."

The old dog raised his eyebrows, as if to say that was what he had been waiting for all along.

"Of course," I went on, "that is what you have been working for, and that is why the Mercantile people come down on us at this moment. You think you have got us where you can squeeze the life out of us. Well, you have."

"You are a smart young man, Harrington," the great packer replied genially. "But you have got into a big game. You'd much better have listened to Carmichael when he offered you a chance with us."

"Thanks!" I said glumly.

"Now, why can't we avoid a fight and settle this matter between ourselves? There might be something good in it for you."

"I know the way you settle such matters."

"According to your own talk, there isn't much left for you folks."

"Only this," I said slowly, and I walked back to his desk and leaned over it: "I don't sell out to you. We default. The bonds will be foreclosed, and maybe your crowd will hold the majority of 'em. But when we get into the courts, Mr. Strauss, on a receivership, I go before the judge and tell the story. I have the papers, too. And part of that story will have to do with certain agreements which our company has made with you and the other packers. And more than that, behind these arrangements there are a lot more of the same kind in our safe that we got from Dround and others. Now, if you want the whole story of the packing business aired in court and in the papers throughout the country, you'll have your wish."

"Pshaw!" he said coolly, "you don't suppose that bluff counts! They can't do a thing to us."

"Maybe not," I replied. "Nothing more than a congressional investigation, perhaps. And that might block your little game."

"Go on, young feller!" he exclaimed contemptuously.

"That's all. I want you to know that I am in this fight to the end, and if it ruins me and my friends, I will see that it hurts you. Now, if you want to fight, let the bank call this money."

We had some more talk on the same subject, and, though the great packer maintained an air of indifference, I thought I had made some impression on him. Then we parted, and the old fellow paid me the compliment of seeing me as far as the door of his office.

From Strauss's place I went to the telegraph office, wired for the money in New York, and in due time presented myself at the Mercantile Bank ready to take up the notes, as I had told Strauss. The president of the bank was waiting for me with a flurried look on his face.

"You have come in to renew your paper, Mr. Harrington?" he remarked, as if there had been no trouble between us.

"No," I said; "I have come to pay what we owe. I don't do any more business with you."

"We have reconsidered the matter, and we shall be very glad to renew your paper."

Strauss had seen the point to my remarks, and concluded to retreat!

"Thank you, I don't care to get any more call money from you fellows," I said placidly. "You make too much trouble."

Well, when I left the president's room I had arranged for a

loan of four hundred thousand dollars for six months. I had measured myself against the great Strauss, and never again would the big fellow seem to me so terrible. I judged that, for a time, the American Meat Products Company would be left to do business undisturbed. . . .

On my desk, when I returned from the bank that afternoon, was a telegram from Mr. Dround from New York: "We arrived to-day — leaving for Chicago."

For once, Mr. Dround had made up his mind in a hurry.

JUDGMENTS

"In Rome you must do as the Romans, or be done!" I quoted jocularly.

Mrs. Dround smiled appreciatively.

"From all accounts you have been a tremendous Roman!"

"Well, at least I haven't been done — not yet."

Jane Dround smiled again and turned her face from the window of the library, through which could be seen dots of ice and snow sailing out on the blue lake. The years she had been gone in Europe had dealt lightly with her. She had grown a trifle stouter, and looked splendidly well — dark, and strong, and full of life.

"I did my best," she continued half humorously. "I tried to get lost in darkest Africa beyond the reach of telegrams and newspapers. But a party of Chicago people coming up the Nile crossed the path of our dahabiyeh, recognized us, came aboard — and brought the story. Cables wouldn't hold him then! We came as the crow flies; it was no use to plead sickness — he was ready to leave me behind in Paris!"

She laughed again genially.

"It was nothing much to get excited about," I replied a little impatiently; "and it has passed now, anyway, like a winter snow in the city — slush, water, nothing!"

"But the principle! You forget the principle!" she remonstrated dryly.

"I know — and he's going to resign from the presidency — that ought to satisfy his principle — but we must keep him on the board."

"It was a judge, too! A sworn officer of the law!" Mrs. Dround interrupted, quoting demurely from Henry I's remarks about the injunction scandal.

"Very well, he can make over his stock to you, then! It won't trouble you, and you can draw the big dividends we are going to pay soon. I don't want him to get out now, when the fruit is almost ripe to shake."

"Is that the only reason?" Mrs. Dround asked quickly.

"Of course, we don't want his stock coming on the market in a big block. It would break us all up. And it might easily get into the wrong hands."

For Mr. Dround, in the brief interview that we had had on his return, had intimated his desire not only to withdraw from the presidency of the corporation, which had been merely a nominal office, but to dispose of his stock as soon as the agreement expired in the fall, suggesting that I had best find some friendly hands to take his big holding. In his gentlemanly way he had told me that he had had enough of me and was quite ready to snow me under, if it could be done in a polite and friendly fashion.

"So you want him to wait?" Mrs. Dround suggested indifferently.

"Yes, until I am ready!"

She made no reply to this remark, and after a moment I said more lightly: —

"But I came to welcome you home, — I want you still to be my friend, my partner!"

"They say you are a dangerous partner," she retorted, looking closely at me, — "deep in all sorts of speculative schemes, and likely to slip. They say you are un — scrupulous" — she drawled the word mockingly — "and a lot more bad things. Do you think that is the right kind of partner for a simple woman?"

"If you've got the nerve!"

"Well, let me show you some of the new pictures we have bought." And she turned me off with a lot of talk about pictures and stuffs and stones, until I arose to leave.

Shortly afterwards my carriage took me back to the city, where I had to meet some gentlemen who were interested in my schemes for the development of the new Southwest. As I rode through the windy, dusty streets, my thoughts went back over the years since that time when at the suggestion of this woman I had just left, I had put my hand to building something large out of Henry I. Dround's tottering estate.

In a busy life like mine, one event shades into another. Each path to which a man sets his feet leads to some cross-roads, and from there any one of the branches will lead on to its own cross-roads. While the adventurer is on his way it is hard to tell why he takes one turning and not another, why he lays his course here and not there. Years later he may see it plotted plain, as I do to-day — plotted as on a map. Then the wanderer may try to explain what made him move this way or that. Yet the little determining causes that turned his mind at the moment of choice are forever forgotten. The big, permanent motive remains: there is the broad highroad — but why was it left, why this turn and double across the main track?

So it was with me. The main highroad of my ambition was almost lost in the thickets in which I found myself. Struggling day by day against the forces that opposed me, I had lost sight of direction. The words with Jane Dround, the flash of her dark eyes, pierced my obscurity, gave me again a view of the destiny to which I had set myself. Some fire in her fed me with courage, and made my spirit lighter than it had been for months. . . .

When I reached home in the evening, I found Sarah ill with a nervous headache.

"Will is back!" she exclaimed on seeing me, and her tone scarcely concealed a meaning beyond her words.

"What's that? He didn't send me word that he was coming."

"May telephoned — he's just got in."

Something unexpected must have brought him suddenly all the way from Texas, where he was looking after our interests. The news was disturbing.

"I saw Jane Dround this afternoon," I remarked idly. "She's looking fine — never saw her better."

"Jane!" my wife said slowly. "So she's back once more." Then after a pause she exclaimed: —

"I don't like her!"

Sarah, who rarely said a bitter word about any one, spoke this harshly, and I looked at her in surprise.

"I don't trust that woman, Van! She is secret. And I believe she influenced you — that time about the judge."

It was the first time for months that Sarah had referred to this matter.

"I'll go and ring up May," I said, not caring to refute this wild accusation, "and ask them to come over tonight."

"I asked them for dinner, but she wouldn't come," Sarah remarked gloomily. "No one wants to come here but people like the Webbs and Coopers — people who think they can make something out of your schemes."

"Oh, I guess they aren't the only ones who are willing to come. And what's the matter with the Webbs and the Coopers? If the rest of your friends don't like us, we can get along without their society. I guess New York will stand us, and that's where we shall be before many years, if all goes well. This place is only a gossipy old village."

"I don't want to go to New York!" Sarah wailed.

When I had May at the telephone, she answered my invitation in a dry little voice: —

"Yes, we are coming over to see you about a matter. Will has something important to say to you."

By the tone of May's voice I judged that we should have a rather lively family party, and I was not mistaken. Sarah was still lying on the lounge in my study when Will and May came in after dinner. There was battle in May's eyes and in her tight-shut lips. It had been a long time since she had come to the house when I was at home. And to-night Will, too, was looking very pale and troubled.

"May," I said, "you look as if you had a gun trained on me. Fire away, only make it something new. I am tired of that old matter about the judge. 'Most everybody has forgotten all about that except you and Sarah."

"It's something new, fast enough, Van; but it isn't any better," she retorted. "Couldn't you find any one else to do your dirty work but your own brother?"

"What's the matter now?"

"Show him the article, Will."

Will unbuttoned his coat and reached for his inner pocket. From it he hauled out a bulky newspaper, which he handed me. It was a copy of the Sunday *Texas World*, and a front page article was heavily pencilled.

"That's too much, Van," he protested solemnly, handing me the paper. "Read it."

"Yes, read it all!" May added. The three were silent while I ran through the article. It was the usual exaggerated sort of newspaper stuff purporting to describe the means used to secure a piece of railroad legislation, in which I and some New York men were interested. The sting lay in the last paragraph: —

"It is commonly understood that the lobby which has been working for the past winter in the interest of this rotten bill is maintained by a group of powerful capitalists, dominated by the head of a large Chicago packing company. This gentleman, who suddenly shot into publicity the past winter as the result of an unusually brazen attempt to corrupt a Chicago judge, has opened his office not three blocks from the state Capitol, and has put his brother in charge of the corruptionist forces. . . . The deserving legislators of our state may soon expect to reap a rich harvest!"

A few more generalities wound up the article. I folded the paper and handed it back to Will. No one said a word for a few moments, and then Will observed: —

"That isn't pleasant reading for an honorable man!"

"I don't see how it should trouble you, Will. You are down there to look after our interests in a legitimate way enough. If you don't like the job, though, I can get another man to take your place."

"Van," May interrupted, "don't try to squirm! You know that's true — what's written there! You didn't ask Will to use the bribe money, because you knew he wouldn't do anything dishonorable. But you let him take the blame, and sent some one else with the money, no doubt. What was that partner of Mr. Slocum's sent down there for?"

"Will," — I turned to my brother, — "let us settle this by ourselves. It's a man's business, and the women won't help us."

"No, Van," May replied. "I guess we women are as much

concerned as anybody. Where there's a question of my husband's honor, it's my business, too. I stay."

"Well, then, stay! And try to understand. This bill the paper rips up is all right. We must have it to put our road through to the Gulf, and if it were not for the money the Pacific Western road, which owns the state, is putting up against us we shouldn't have any trouble. They want to keep us out, and Strauss and his crowd want to keep us out, too, so that they can have all the pie to themselves. I have been working at this thing for years in order that we can get an outlet to the seaboard, untouched by our rivals. They think to block us just at the end, but I guess they will find out they are mistaken when the line-up comes next month. That's all!"

"Do you think that explanation is satisfactory? Of course, Van, you want the bill passed!" May said ironically.

"What does it mean — what has Van been doing?" Sarah asked for the first time, sitting up and looking from one to another in a puzzled way.

None of us answered, and finally Will said: —

"I guess, Van, you and I don't see things quite the same way. I know you wouldn't ask me to do what you thought was bad, but all the same there's too much that's true in that piece in the paper, and I don't want to have it said — there's things going on down there that aren't right — and May feels — I feel myself, that it ain't right. We don't think the same way, you and I. So we had better part now, before we have any bad feeling."

"All right! Did you come over here to-night to tell me that?"

"No, Van," May put in hastily, her voice trembling with feeling. "That wasn't all. Will and I came to ask you to give up the sort of business you are doing down there. We want you to turn back into the right road before it is too late. If you don't land in the penitentiary, Van Harrington, your money will do you no good. It will taste bad all your life!"

We were all pretty well stirred up by this time. I was weary of meeting these charges of dishonesty on all sides. This last was too much — to have my family accuse me of a crime, when I did not feel guilty, not for a minute!

"I don't see why you should say that, May!" Sarah suddenly bridled. "After all, it's only the newspapers, and no one believes them to-day."

This unexpected defence from Sarah aroused May afresh.

"Oh, he don't deny it! He can't. First it was a judge — he bought a judge and paid for him, and he never came out and denied it! Now it's worse even than that. It's the people of a whole state he's trying to buy through their representatives."

"Who are there for sale," I laughed.

"Does that make it any better?" she turned on me. "Seems to me, Van, you don't know any longer the difference between black and white!"

"We've got a perfect right to build that road, and build it we will — that's all there is to that matter!"

And so we argued for hours, May and I doing most of the talking. For I wanted her to understand just how the matter lay. No business in this large, modern world could be done on her plan of life. That beautiful scheme of things which the fathers of our country drew up in the stage-coach days had proved itself inadequate in a short century. We had to get along with it the best we could. But we men who did the work of the world, who developed the country, who were the life and force of the times, could not be held back by the swaddling-clothes of any political or moral theory. Results we must have: good results; and we worked with the tools we found at hand.

"It's no use your saying any more!" May exclaimed at last. "I understand just what you mean, Van Harrington. It's the same way it was with the judge's peaches. You wanted 'em, and you took 'em! What you want you think is good for every one, especially for Van Harrington. And you are so wise and strong you think you can break through all laws because laws are made for small people, like Will and me, and you and your kind are Napoleons. You talk as if you were a part of God's destiny. And I say" — here her voice broke for a moment — "I say, Van, you are the devil's instrument! You and those like you — and there are a good many of them — are just plain big rascals, only the laws can't get hold of you."

Her lips trembled and at the end broke into that little ironical smile which I knew so well, the smile she had when I used to get into some boyish scrape, and she was looking through me for the truth. But for all her hot words, I knew she had kindly feeling for me somewhere in her heart. Nevertheless, Sarah, who had been following our talk as well as she could, fired up at her accusations.

"I think, May," she remonstrated with all her dignity, "that you cannot say any more such things in my husband's house."

"Yes," I added, "we have had too much talk all around. You can't change my character any more than you can make wheat grow in Arizona or sugar-cane in Dakota. And I don't want to change your views, either, May."

For though she made me pretty angry, I admired the way she stood to her guns. She was a fighter! And Will must act as she decided. Whoever travelled with her would have to travel by her star.

"Yes," my brother replied, "it's gone too far now to change. Words don't do any good. Come, wife, let us go."

"I am sorry for Sarah!" May said, taking Sarah's hands in hers. "She suffers for you, Van, and she will suffer for this all her life. But I am sorrier for you, Van, for you have gone too far to suffer!"

Thereupon she swept out of the room, her little figure swelling with dignity; and Will followed her, as the needle swings to its magnet, pausing only long enough to reach for my hand and press it. When the front door shut upon them the house seemed suddenly cold and empty. Sarah had slipped back to the lounge, and was staring up at the ceiling, a tear trickling across her face.

"I suppose May won't ever come back again. And we were planning to take that cottage this summer so that the children could be together."

That detail didn't seem to me very important, but it was the one that showed to Sarah the gulf which had opened between us. Sarah's little world, by that token, had suffered an earthquake.

"Oh," I said, trying to comfort her, "like as not this will blow over! May has disapproved of me before this."

But in my heart I felt there wasn't much likelihood that this breach would be healed. Knowing May as I did, I had no idea that she would let Will continue with me, even in another position. No compromise for her! To-morrow or next day Will would come into the office to take his leave. . . .

"I guess, Van, I'll go to bed."

It was the first word Sarah had spoken for half an hour. The tears had dried on her face. She gave me a light kiss, and left me. . . .

The house seemed cold and desolate, as if the pleasant kindliness of life had gone out of it when my brother and his wife had left. I made up the fire, lighted a fresh cigar, and sat down to think. Somehow years had gone by in that evening; I was heavy with the heaviness of middle life.

To take the other road, her road — that was what May demanded of me. How little she knew the situation! That would mean immediate ruin for me and mine, and for those men who had trusted me with their money. The world that I had been building all these years would crumble and vanish like smoke into the void out of which I had made it! Not that May's talk had meaning or sense to it, either. Nor do men made as I am alter at the sound of words. We are as we are, and we grow with the power to do that which we must do. May was merely an unreasonable and narrow woman, who saw but one kind of good.

In all the forty years of my life there had been no evil as I know evil. No man could say that he had harm from me — unless it might be poor Ed Hostetter — and for thousands of such workers as live from day to day, depending on men like me to give them their chance to earn bread for their wives and children, I had made the world better rather than worse. Unthinking thousands lived and had children and got what good there was in life because of me and my will.

But to the others, the good ones, to Farson and Dround and May, I was but a common thief, a criminal, who fattened on the evil of the world. What had they done to make life? What was their virtue good for? They took the dainty paths and kept their clothes from the soil of the road. Yes, and what then? A renewed sense of irritation rose within me. Why should I be pestered like this, why should I lose my brother and May, why should Sarah be hurt, because they were too good to do as I had done?

So my brother and May went their way. They left me lonely. For the first time since the day, many years before, when I walked out of the police station alone into the city, the loneliness of life came over me. To-morrow, in the daylight, in the fierce fight of the day, that weakness would go; but to-night there was no hand to reach, no voice to speak, from the multitude of the world. One person only of all would know, would place big and little side by side and reckon them rightly — would understand the ways I had followed to get my ends. Jane Dround would throw them all a smile of contempt, the little ones who weigh and hesitate!

There was the soul of the fighter.

CHAPTER XXIII

HAPPINESS

I learn of Mr. Dround's intentions — A plea for myself — Despots — A woman's heart — The two in the world that are most near — Sarah's cry — Jane defends herself — To go away forever — Vows renewed

---

"Henry is simply furious — thinks his name has been involved — and he means to sell every share of stock he holds as soon as the agreement expires."

"I knew that he would do just that!"

Mrs. Dround threw back her coat and looked up with a mischievous smile on her face. She was a very handsome woman these days, not a month older than when I saw her first. She had reached that point where Nature, having done her best for a woman, pauses before beginning the work of destruction.

She had come this afternoon to call on Sarah, and, having failed to find her at home, was writing a note at her desk, when I came in from the day's business, a little earlier than was my wont.

"It isn't just that matter of the injunction. You know, my friend, people here in the city — Henry's friends — say that you are engaged in dangerous enterprises — that you are a desperate man yourself! Are you?"

"You know better than most!" I answered lightly. "But I am getting tired of all this talk. I had a dose of it in the family the last time."

She nodded as I briefly related what had happened with Will and May.

"And, of course, Sarah feels pretty badly," I concluded.

"Poor child!" she murmured. "I wondered what was the matter with her these days. She will feel differently later. But your brother, that is another question."

"He and his wife will never feel differently."

She tossed aside the pen she held and rose to her feet.

"Never mind! I know you don't mind really — only it is too bad to have this annoyance just now, when you have much on your shoulders. I wish I could *do* something! A woman's hands are always tied!"

She could say no more, and we sat for some time without further talk. I was thinking what would happen when Mr. Dround's stock was dumped on the market, to be snapped up by my enemies. Our company was very near the point of paying dividends, and with a friendly line of railroad giving us an outlet into the Southwest, the struggling venture would be in a powerful position.

"If he would wait but six months more!" I broke out at last.

She shook her head.

"Where a question of principle is involved, —"

Her lips curved ironically.

"What would *you* do, tell me, if a parcel of scamps were holding you up for the benefit of your enemies? Suppose you had a perfect right to do the business you had in hand. Would you put tail between legs and get out and leave your bone to the other dog?"

"If I wanted to starve, yes! I should deserve to."

"You and I think surprisingly alike very often!"

"I always liked despots," she replied. "And, as a matter of fact, despots — the strong ones — have always really done things. They do to-day — only we make a fuss about it and get preachy. No, my friend, don't hesitate! The scrupulous ones will bow to you in time."

"You would have made something of a man!"

She bowed her head mockingly.

"That is man's best compliment to poor, weak woman. But I am content, when I touch the driving hand, now and then."

After a time she added: —

"You will find the way. It is not the last ditch, far from it. A man like you cannot be killed with one blow!"

She had given the warning, done what she could, and now she trusted me to do the rest. Her will, her sympathy, were strong behind me. So when this moment was over, when she went her way and I mine, out into the world of cares and struggle, I might carry with me this bit of her courage, her sureness. I felt that, and I wanted to say it to her, to let her see that it was more herself than her good will or her help that I valued. But it was an awkward thing to say.

Her hands lay upon the desk between us. They were not beautiful hands, merely strong, close-knit — hands to hold with a grip of death. I looked at them, thinking that in her hands was the sign of her character. She raised her eyes and gazed at me steadily for several moments.

"You know how I feel?"

I nodded.

"You don't need a woman's sympathy — but I want you to know how I feel — for my own sake."

"Thank you for it. In this life a man must stand pretty much alone, win or lose. I have always found it so — except when you and I have talked things over. That hasn't been often. This is a tight place I find myself in now. But there is a way out, or if there isn't — well, I have played the game better than most."

"Even that thought doesn't give happiness," she mused. "I

know, because, my friend, I, too, have stood alone all my life."
She gave me this confidence simply, as a man might.

"I suppose a woman counts on happiness," I said awkwardly
in response. "But I have never counted much on that. There
have always been many things to do, and I have done them,
well or ill I can't say. But I have done them somehow."

It was a clumsy answer, but I could find no proper words
for what I felt. Such things are not to be said. There followed
another of those full silences which counted with this woman
for so much more than words. Again it was she who broke
it: —

"For once, only once, I want to speak out plainly! You are
younger than I, my friend, — not so much in years as in other
things. Enough, so that I can look at you as — a friend. You
understand?"

She spoke gently, with a little smile, as if, after all, all this
must be taken between us for a joke.

"From the beginning, when you and Sarah first came into
our lives, I saw the kind of man you were, and I admired you.
I wanted to help you — yes, to help you."

"And that you did!"

"Not really. Perhaps no one could really help you. No one
helps or hinders. You work out your fate from the inside,
like all the powerful ones. You do what is in you to do, and
never question. But I longed for the woman's satisfaction of
being something to you, — of holding the sponge, as the boys
say. But a mere woman, poor, weak creature, is tied with a
short rope — do you know what that means? So the next best
thing, if one can't live one's self, is to live in another — some
strong one. When you are a woman and have reached my age,
you know that you can't live for yourself. That chance has
gone."

"I don't believe it," I protested. "You are just ready to live."

She gave me a smile for my compliment, and shook her head. "No, I don't deceive myself. Most women do. I know when I have reached the end of my chapter. . . . So I have followed you, step by step — oh, you don't know how closely! And I have sucked in all the joy of your success, of your power, of you — a man! I have lived a man's life."

"But you went away?" I said accusingly.

"Yes, I went away — because that would help! It was the only thing I could do — I could go away."

For the first time her voice shook with passion. I was answered.

"Now I have come back to find that my hands are tied more than ever. I can help you no more. Believe me, that is the hardest thing yet. I can help you no more! My husband — you understand? No, you need not understand. A woman is bound back and across by a thousand threads, which do not always show to the eye. . . . I may yet keep my husband from throwing you over, but that is no matter — the truth is I count no longer to you. If the world had been other than it is, my friend, I should have been by your side, fighting it out daily for you, with you. As it is —"

She threw up her arms in a gesture of disgust and remained silent, brooding. It was not necessary to complete the words. Nor could I speak. Something very wonderful and precious was passing before my eyes for the last time, something that had been near was floating off, would never come back. And life was so made that it was vain, useless, to try to hold it, to cry out, to do anything except to be still and feel the loss. My hands fell beside hers upon the polished surface of the desk, and we sat looking into one another's eyes, without fear. She was feeling what I was feeling, but she was looking deeper into fate than I could look. For she was wiser as a woman than I was as a man. We were the two in the world most near, and between us there was a gulf that could not be crossed. The years that are to come, my heart said to me then, will be longer than those that have passed.

"Listen," she whispered, as though she were reading my thoughts. "We shall never need more than this. Remember! Nothing more than this. For I should be a hindrance, then, not a help. And that would be the end of me, indeed. You have your will to work, which is more than any woman could give you. And I have the thought of you. Now I must go away again — we have to live that way. It makes no difference: you and I think the same thoughts in the same way. What separation does a little distance put between you and me? I shall follow after you step by step, and when you have mounted to the broad level that comes after accomplishment, you will be glad that it has been as I say, not different. It is I that must long. For you need no woman to comfort and love you!"

It was finished, and we sat in the deepening twilight beyond words. The truth of what she had spoken filled my mind. There was nothing else for us two but what we had had: we had come to the top of ourselves to know this, to look it in the face, and to put it aside. . . .

The twilight silence was broken sharp in two by a cry that rang across the room. We started from our dream together and looked around. Sarah was standing midway in the long room, steadying herself by a hand reached out to a chair. I ran to hold her from falling. She grasped my arm and walked on unsteadily toward Jane.

"I knew it! I knew it always!" she cried harshly. "You tortuous woman — you are taking him from me! You did it from the first day! How I hate you!"

She dropped into a chair and sobbed. Jane knelt down by her side and, grasping her hands, spoke to her in low, pleading words: —

"No, child, you are wrong! You wrong *him*. He is not such a man. There is no truth in your cruel words."

"Yes, you have made him do dishonorable things. He has acted so his own family have left him. I know it is *you!*" she sobbed. "He has done what you would have him do."

"Child, child!" Jane exclaimed impatiently, shaking gently the hands she held. "What do you mean by saying such a thing?"

"Hasn't he done all those bad things? He never denied it, not when he was accused in church before every one. And May said it was true."

She looked resentfully at Jane through her tears. The older woman still smiled at her and stroked her hands.

"But even if it were true, *you* mustn't take the part of his accusers! That isn't for a woman who loves him to do. You must trust him to the end."

Sarah looked at her and then at me. She pushed Jane from her quickly.

"Don't you defend him to me! You have stolen him! He loves you. I saw it once before, and I see it on your face now. I know it!"

"Come!" I said, taking Sarah by the arm and leading her away. "You don't know what you say."

"Yes, I do! You treat me like a child, Van! Why did you have to take him?" she turned and flamed out to Jane. "You have always had everything."

"Have I had everything?" the other woman questioned slowly, quietly, as if musing to herself. "Everything? Do you know all, child? Let me tell you one thing. Once I had a child — a son. One child! And he was born blind. He lived four months. Those were the only months I think I have ever lived. Do you think that I have had *all* the joy?"

She was stirred, at last, passionate, ironic, and Sarah looked at her with wondering surprise, with awe.

"You grudge me the three or four hours your husband has given me out of the ten years you have lived with him! You hate me because he has talked to me as he would talk to himself — as he would talk to you each day, if you could read the first letter of his mind. And if I love him? If he loves me? Would you deny yourself the little I have taken from you, his wife, if it were yours to take and *mine* to lose? But be content! Not one word of what you call love has passed between us, or ever will. Is that enough?"

They looked at each other with hate plainly written on their faces.

"You are a bad woman!" Sarah exclaimed brokenly.

"Am I? Think of this, then. I could take your husband — I could from this hour! But for his sake, for *his* sake, I will not. *I will not!*"

Sarah groaned, covering her eyes, while Jane walked rapidly out of the room. In a moment the carriage door clicked outside, and we were alone.

"You love that woman, Van!" Sarah's voice broke the silence between us with an accusing moan.

"Why say that —" I began, and stopped; for, after this hour, I knew what it was for one person to be close to another. However, it seemed a foolish thing to be talking about. There would be no gain in going deeper into our hearts.

"There has never been a word between us that you should not hear," I replied; "and now let us say no more."

But Sarah shook her head, unconvinced.

"It is two years or more since I have seen Jane," I added.

"That makes no difference. Jane was right! You love her!" she repeated helplessly. "What shall we do?"

"Nothing!" I took her cold hands and sat down opposite her, drawing her nearer me. "Don't fear, my wife. They are going away again, I understand. She will go out of our life for always."

"I have my children," Sarah mused after a pause.

"We have *our* children," I corrected. "And it's best to think of them before ourselves."

"Oh, if we could take them and go away to some little place, to live like my people down in Kentucky — you and me and the children!"

I smiled to myself at the thought. To run away was not just to pack a trunk, as Sarah thought!

"It would be impossible. Everything would go to pieces. I should lose pretty much all that we have — not only that, but a great many other people who have trusted me with their money would lose. I must work at least until there is no chance of loss for them."

"But aren't you a very rich man, Van?"

"Not so rich as I shall be some day! But I might make out to live in Kentucky, all the same."

"You think I must have a great deal of money?"

"I always want you to have all that money can get."

"To make up for what I can't have!" She burst into sobs. "I am so wretched, Van! Everything seems strange. I have tried to do what is right. But God must be displeased with me: He has taken from me the one thing I wanted."

That was a bitter thought to lie between husband and wife. I took her in my arms and comforted her, and together we saw that a way lay clear before us, doing our duty by one another and by our children, and in the end all would come out well. As we sat there together, it seemed to me as though there could be two loves in a man's life, — the love for the

woman and her children, who are his to protect; and the
hunger love at the bottom of the heart, which with most is
never satisfied, and maybe never can be satisfied in this life.

So she was comforted and after a little time went to her
room, more calm in spirit. Then I called my secretary, and
we worked together until a late hour. When my mind came
back to the personal question of living, the fire on the hearth
had died into cold ashes and the house was still with the still-
ness of early morning. For the moment it came over me that
the fight I was waging with fortune was as cold as these ashes
and doomed to failure. And the end, what was it?

Upstairs, Sarah lay half dressed on the lounge in my room,
asleep. The tears had dried where they had fallen on her
cheeks and neck. Her hair hung down loosely as though she
had not the will to put it up for the night. As she lay there
asleep, in the disorder of her grief, I knew that the real sorrow
of life was hers, not mine. The memory of that day of our
engagement came back to me — when I had wished to protect and cover her from the hard things of life. And again, as
that time, I longed to take her, the gentle heart so easily hurt,
and save her from this sorrow, the worst that can come to a
loving woman. As I kissed the stained face, she awoke and
looked at me wonderingly, murmuring half asleep: —

"What is it, Van? What has happened? It is time for you
to go to bed. I remember — something bad has happened.
What is it, Van? Oh, I know now!"

She shuddered as I lifted her from the lounge.

"I remember now what it is. You love that woman, but I
can't let you go. I can't bear it. I can't live without you!"

"That will never come so long as there is life for us both,"
I promised.

She drew her arm tight about my neck.

"Yes! You must love me a little always."

CHAPTER XXIV

WAR

Wall street and the people of the country — Collateral — I decide to go home — Slocum finds that I am a patriot — I plan to enlist — Hardman once more — Claims — A midnight problem — The telegram

---

WAR! That was what was in the air those days. It had muttered on for months, giving our politicians at Washington something to mouth about in their less serious hours. Then came the sinking of the *Maine* in Havana Harbor, and even Wall Street could see that the country was drifting fast into war. And in their jackal fashion, the men of Wall Street were trying to make money out of this crisis of their country, starting rumors from those high in authority to run the prices of their goods up and down. To those men who had honest interests at stake it was a terrible time for panic, for uncertainty. One could never guess what might happen over night.

But throughout the land, among the common people, the question at issue had been heard and judged. The farmer on his ranch, the laborer in his factory, the hand on the railroad — the men of the land up and down the States — had judged this question. When the time came their judgment got itself recorded; for any big question is settled just that way by those men, not at Washington or in Wall Street.

The sick spirit of our nation needed just this tonic of a generous war, fought not for our own profit. It would do us good to give ourselves for those poor Cuban dogs. The

Jew spirit of Wall Street doesn't rule this country, after all, and Wall Street doesn't understand that the millions in the land long to hustle sometimes for something besides their own bellies. So, although Wall Street groaned, I had a kind of faith that war would be a good thing, cost what it might.

And it might cost me the work of my life. Latterly, with the revival of trade, my enterprises had been prospering, and were emerging from that doubtful state where they were blown upon by every wind of the market. For the American Meat Products Company had kept its promise and was earning dividends. It had paid, in the past year, six per cent on the preferred stock, and, what with the big contracts we were getting from the Government just now, it would earn something on the common. So far very little of our stock had come upon the market, although the period covered by the agreement among the stockholders not to sell their holdings had passed. In spite of Mr. Dround's threats, there was no evidence that he had disposed of his stock up to this time. It was probable that when he saw what a good earner the company had proved to be, he had reconsidered his scruples, as he had done years before in the matter of private agreements and rebates.

And that rag of a railroad out of Kansas City, which Farson and his friends found left on their hands in the panic times of '93, now reached all the way to the Gulf and was spreading fast into a respectable system. After Farson had withdrawn his help at the time of our disagreement, we had interested a firm of bankers in New York, and, one way and another, had built and equipped the road. A few years of good times, and all this network of enterprises would be beyond attack. Meanwhile, I was loaded down to the water's edge with the securities of these new companies, and had borrowed heavily at home and in the East in the effort to push through my plans.

This was my situation on that eventful day when the news

of the sinking of the *Maine* was telegraphed over the country, and even gilt-edged securities began to tumble, to slide downhill in a mad whirl. In such times collateral shrank like snow before a south wind.

All the morning I had sat in my office with a telephone at my ear, and it seemed to me that but one word came from it — Collateral! collateral! Where was it to be had? Finally, I hung up the receiver of my telephone and leaned back in my chair, dazed by the mad whirl along which I was being carried. My secretary opened the door and asked if I would see So-and-so and the next man. A broker was clamoring to get at me. They all wanted one thing — money. Their demands came home to me faintly, like the noise of rain on a window.

"Jim," I said to the man," I am tired. I am going home."

"Going home?" he gasped, not believing his ears.

"Tell 'em all I am going home! Tell 'em anything you want to."

While the young man was still staring at me, Slocum burst past him into the room. Even his impassive face was twisted into a scowl of fear.

"Harris is out there," he said hurriedly. "He says some one is selling Meat Products common and preferred. Big chunks of it are coming on the market, and the price has dropped fifteen points during the morning."

I said nothing. Anything was to be expected in this whirlwind.

"Do you suppose it's Dround's stock?" he asked.

"Perhaps," I nodded. "It don't make much difference to us whose it is."

"We can't let this go on."

"I guess it will have to go on," I replied listlessly.

Slocum looked at me wonderingly. He had seen me crawl out of a good many small holes, and he was waiting for the word of action now.

"Well?" he asked at last.

"I am going home." I got up and took his arm. "Come along with me, old man. I want to get out of this noise."

The elevator dropped us into the hurly-burly of the street. Men were hurrying in and out of the brokers' offices, where the last reports for the day were coming in.

"D—n this war!" Slocum swore, as I paused to buy a paper.

"Don't say that, Slo!" I protested. "This war is a great thing, and every decent American ought to be proud of his country, by thunder! I am."

The lawyer looked at me as if my head had suddenly gone back on me.

"I mean it. I tell you, Slo, nations are like men. They have their work to do in this life. When it comes to an issue like this, they can't shirk any more than a man can. If they do, it will be worse for them. This war will do us good, will clean us and cure us for a good long time of this cussed, little peevish distemper we have been through since '93. That was just selfish introspection. This fight for Cuba will bring us all together. We'll work for something better than our bellies. There's nothing so good as a dose of real patriotism once in a while."

"Van, you ought to be in the Senate!" he jeered.

"Perhaps I shall be there one of these days, when I have finished this other job."

The idea seemed to strike him humorously.

"You think it might be hard work for me to prove my patriotism to the people? Don't you believe it. The people don't remember slander long. And those things you and I have done which have set the newspapers talking don't worry anybody. They are just the tricks of the game."

So we sauntered on through the streets that March afternoon, discussing, like two schoolboys, patriotism and government; while back in the office we had left white-faced men

were clamoring for a word with me, seeking to find out
whether I was to go under at last.

"Well," Slocum finally asked, as he was leaving me, "what
are you going to do about this pinch?"

"There's nothing to be done to-night. I'm going to read the
papers and see what they say about the war. I am going home.
Perhaps to-morrow it will be all over. Lordy! We'll make a
tolerable big smash when we go down!"

"Get some sleep!" was Slocum's advice.

The papers were red-hot with the war spirit, and they did
me good. Somehow, I was filled with a strange gladness because of the war. Pride in the people of my country, who
could sacrifice themselves for another people, swelled my heart.
Where could you read of a finer thing in all history than the
way the people's wrath had compelled the corrupt, self-seek-
ing politicians in Washington to do their will — to strike an
honest blow, to redeem a suffering people! It comes not often
in any man's life to feel himself one of a great nation when
it arises in a righteous cause with all the passion of its seventy
millions. Let the panic wipe out my little pile of money. Let
the war break up the dreams of my best years — I would not
for that selfish cause stay its course. It made a man feel clean
to think there was something greater in life than himself and
his schemes.

I walked on and on in the March twilight, leaving behind me
the noisy city, and the struggle of the market. Why not go
myself — why not enlist? I suddenly asked of myself. The
very thought of it made me throw up my head. Slocum could
gather up the fragments as well as I, and there would be enough
left in any case for the children and Sarah. Better that fight
than this! When the President issued a call for volunteers,
maybe I could raise a regiment from our men.

The street was shadowed by the solid houses of the rich, the respectable stone and brick palaces of the "captains of industry," each big enough to house a dozen Jasonville families. I looked at them with the eyes of a stranger, as I had the day when I roamed Chicago in search of a job. Perhaps I had envied these men then; but small comfort had I ever had from all the wealth I had got out of the city. Food and drink, a place to sleep in, some clothes — comfort for my wife and children — what else? To-day I should like to slip back once more to the bum that landed in Chicago, — unattached, unburdened, unbound. . . .

I let myself into the silent house. Sarah and the children were at our place in Vermilion County, where I had a house and two thousand acres of good land, to which I escaped for a few days now and then. I had my dinner and was smoking a cigar when a servant brought me word that a man was waiting to see me below. When I went into the hall I saw a figure standing by the door, holding his hat in his hands. In the dim light I could not make out his face and asked him to step into the library, where I turned on the light. It was the preacher Hardman.

"What do you want?" I asked in some surprise.

"I suppose I ought not to trouble you here at this hour, Mr. Harrington," he said timidly. "But I am much worried. You remember that investment you were kind enough to make for me a few years ago?"

His question recalled to my mind the fact that he had given me a little inheritance which had come to his wife, asking me to invest it for him. I had put it into some construction bonds.

"What about it?" I asked.

He stammered out his story. Some one had told him that I was in bad shape; he had also read a piece in the paper about the road, and he had become scared. It had not occurred to him to sell his bonds before he preached that little sermon at me; but, now that my sins were apparently about to overtake me, he wished to save his little property from destruction.

"Why don't you sell?" I asked.

"I have tried to," he admitted, "but the price offered me is very low."

I laughed at the fellow's simple egotism.

"So you thought I might take your bonds off your hands? Got them there?"

"My wife thought, as your —" he stammered. I waived his excuse aside.

He drew the bonds from his coat pocket. As I sat down to write a check I said jokingly: —

"Better hustle round to the bank to-morrow and get your cash."

"I trust you are not seriously incommoded by this panic," he remarked inquiringly.

"Gold's the thing these days!" I laughed.

(The cashier at the bank told me afterward that Hardman made such a fuss when he went to cash his check that they actually had to hand him out six thousand dollars in gold coin.)

The preacher man had no more than crawled out with profuse words of thanks than I had another caller. This time it was a young doctor of my acquaintance. He was trying to put on an indifferent air, as if he had been used to financial crises all his life. He had his doubts in his eyes, however, and I took him into my confidence.

"If you possibly can, stick to what you have got. It may take a long time for prices to get back to the right place, but this tumble is only temporary. Have faith — faith in your judgment, faith in your country!"

I knew something of his story, of the hard fight he had made to get his education, of his marriage and his wife's sickness, with success always put off into the future. He had brought me his scrapings and savings, and I had made the most of them.

When at last the doctor had gone away somewhat reassured, I sat down to think. There were a good many others like these two — little people or well-to-do, who had put their faith in me and had trusted their money to my enterprises. Not much, each one; but in every case a cruel sum to lose. They had brought me their savings, their legacies, because they knew me or had heard that I had made money rapidly. Could I leave them now?

I might be willing to go off to Cuba and see my own fortune fade into smoke. But how about their money? No — it was not a simple thing just to go broke by one's self. To-morrow my office would be crowded by these followers, and there would be letters and telegrams from those who couldn't get there. So back to the old problem! I rested my head on my hands and went over in my mind the situation, the amount of my loans, the eternal question of credit — where to get a handhold to stay me while the whirlwind passed, as I knew it must pass.

Hour after hour I wrestled with myself. Ordinarily I could close my eyes on any danger and get the sleep that Nature owes every hard-working sinner. But not to-night. I sat with my hands locked, thinking. Along about midnight there sounded in the silent house a ring at the door-bell: it was a messenger boy with a delayed telegram. I tore it open and read: —

"Remember my letter." It was dated from Washington, and was not signed.

CHAPTER XXV

THE LAST DITCH

Romantic folly — The impulse that comes from beyond our sight — I go to seek Mr. Carboner — An unpromising location for a banker — I receive advice and help — Dickie Pierson gets an order from me — What is Strauss's game?

The yellow paper lay in my hand, and, with a flash, my memory went back to that mysterious note which Jane Dround had sent on the eve of her departure for Europe. It lay undisturbed in a drawer of my office desk. I smiled impatiently at the woman's folly — of the letter, the telegram. And yet it warmed my heart that she should be thinking of me this day, that she should divine my troubles. And I seemed to see her dark eyebrows arched with scorn at my weakness, her thin lips curl disdainfully, as if to say: "Was this to be your finish? Have I helped you, believed in you, all these years, to have you fall now?" So she had spoken.

But still I was unconvinced, and in this state of mind I went back to bed, knowing that I should need on the morrow what sleep I could get. But sleep did not come: instead, my mind busied itself with Jane Dround's letter — with the woman herself. As the night grew toward morning I arose, dressed myself, and left the house. The letter in my office pulled me like a thread of fate; and I obeyed its call like a child. In the lightening dawn I hurried through the streets to the lofty building where the Products Company had its offices, and groped my way up the long flights of stairs. As I sat down at my desk and unlocked the drawers, the morning sun shot in from the lake over the smoky buildings beneath me. After some hunting I found the letter. Mrs. Dround wrote a peculiar hand — firm, clear, unchangeable, but with curious tiny flourishes about the *r*'s and *s*'s.

As I glanced at it, the woman herself rose before my eyes, and she sat across the desk from me, looking into my face. "Yes, I need you," I found myself muttering; "not any letter, but *you*, with your will and your courage, now, if ever. For this is the last ditch, sure enough!"

The letter shook in my hand and beat against the desk. It was a silly thing to leave my bed and come chasing down here at five in the morning to get hold of a romantic woman's letter! My nerves were wrong. Something in me revolted from going any further with this weakness, and I still hesitated to tear open the envelope. The other battles of my life I had won unaided.

At the bottom of our hearts there is a feeling which we do not understand, a respect for the unknown. Terror, fear, — call it what you will, — sometime in life every one is made to feel it. All my life has been given to practical facts, yet I know that at the end of all things there are no facts. In the silence and gray light of that morning I felt the strong presence of my friend, holding out to me a hand. . . . I tore open the letter. Inside was another little envelope, which contained a visiting-card. On it was written: "Mr. J. Carboner, 230 West Lake Street," and beneath, in fine script, this one sentence: "*Mr. Carboner is a good adviser — see him!*"

This was fit pay for my folly. Of all the sentimental nonsense, an adviser! What was wanted was better than a million dollars of ready cash — within three hours. It was now half-past six o'clock, and I had left until half-past nine to find an ordinary, practical way out of my present difficulties. Then the banks would be open; the great wheel of business would begin to revolve, with its sure, merciless motion. Nevertheless, in spite of my scepticism, my eyes wandered to a map of the city that hung on the wall, and I made out the location of the address given on the card. It was a bare half-mile across the roofs from where I sat, in a quarter of the city lying along the river, given up to brick warehouses, factories, and freight yards. Small likelihood that a man with a million to spare in his pocket was to be found over there!

In this mood of depression and disgust I left my office, to get shaved. "Street floor, sir," the elevator boy called out to wake me from my preoccupation. As I stood on the curb in the same will-less daze, a cab came prowling down the street, crossed to my side, and the disreputable-looking driver touched his dirty hat with his whip: —

"Cab, sir?"

"Two-thirty West Lake," I said to him mechanically, and plunged into his carriage.

The cab finally drew up beside a low, grimy brick building that looked as if it might have survived the fire. There was a flight of dirty stairs leading from the street to the office floor, and over the small, old-fashioned windows a faded sign read "Jules Carboner." In response to my knock an old man opened the locked door a crack and looked out at me. When I asked to see Mr. Carboner, he admitted me suspiciously to a little room, which was divided in two by a high iron screen. On the inner side of the screen there was a battered desk, a few chairs, and a row of leather-backed folios that might have been in use since the founding of the city. A small coal fire was burning dully in the grate. As I stood waiting for Mr. Carboner, a barge laden with lumber cast its shadow through the dirty windows. . . .

"And what may you want of me?"

The words were uttered like a cough. The one who spoke them had entered the inner office so noiselessly that I had not heard him. He had a white head of hair, and jet-black eyes. I handed him my card with Mrs. Dround's note.

"I was expecting you," the old gentleman remarked, glancing indifferently at my card. He unlocked the door of the iron grating and held it open, pointing to a chair in front of the fire. Mr. Carboner was short and round, with swarthy, full-blooded cheeks. Evidently he was some sort of foreigner, but I could not place him among the types of men I knew.

"What do you want of me?" he demanded briskly.

"Oh, just a lot of money, first and last!" I laughed.

This announcement didn't seem to trouble him; he waited for my explanation. And remembering that I was to look to him for advice as well as cash, I proceeded to explain briefly the situation that I found myself in. He listened without comment.

"Finally," I said rather wearily, "just now, when I am in deep water with this railroad and all the rest, and the banks calling my loans, some fellows are selling their Meat Products stock. It will all go to my enemies — to Strauss and his crowd, and I shall find myself presently kicked out of the company. I suppose it's Mr. Dround's stock that's coming on the market. It's like him to sell when prices are going down."

The little old fellow shook his head.

"It is not Mr. Dround's stock," he said. "Most of that is over there." He nodded his head in the direction of a small safe which stood in one corner of the room.

"How did you get it?" I exclaimed in my astonishment, jumping to my feet.

"Never mind how — we have had it three months," he replied with a smile. "You need not fear that it will come on the market just now."

My heart gave a great bound upward: with this block of

stock locked up I could do what I would with Meat Products. Strauss could never put his hands on it. Jane Dround must have worked this stroke; but how she did it was a mystery. I walked back and forth in my excitement, and when I sat down once more Mr. Carboner began a neat little summary of my situation: —

"You are engaged in many ventures. Some are strong." He named all the good ones as if he were quoting from a carefully drawn report. "Some are weak." He named the others. "Now, you are trying to hold the weak with the strong. It is like a carrying a basket of eggs on your head. All goes well until some one runs against you. Then bum, biff! — you have the beginning of an omelet."

His way of putting it made me laugh.

"And the omelet is about ready to cook in an hour or two!" I added.

"We shall see presently. You want to sell out this packing business, some day, eh? To Strauss! You take big chances. You are a new man. They suspect you. They call your loans. They think that you are thin in the waist? You have to borrow a great deal of money and pay high for it?"

"You have sized me up, Mr. Carboner."

"And after you have sold to Strauss there will be railroads — ah, that is more difficult! And then many other things — always ventures, risks, schemes, plans, great plans! For you are very bold."

"Well, what will you do for me?" I asked bluntly.

"I think we can carry you over this river, Mr. Harrington," he replied, looking at me with a very amiable air, as if he were my schoolmaster and had decided to give me a holiday and some spending money. Who made up the "we" in this firm of Rip Van Winkle bankers? Carboner seemed to divine my doubts; for he smiled as he reached for a pad of paper and began to write in a close, crabbed hand.

"Take that to Mr. Bates," he directed. "You know him, eh?"
Did I know Orlando Bates! If I had been to him once at the
Tenth National, of which he was president, I had been to him
fifty times, with varying results. I knew every wrinkle in his
parchment-covered face.

"He will give you what you want," the old man added.

I still hesitated, holding Carboner's scrawl in my hand.

"You think it no good?" He motioned to the sheet of coarse
paper. "Try it!"

"Don't you want a receipt?" I stammered.

"What for? Do you think I am a pawnbroker?"

The mystery grew. Suppose I should take this old fellow's
scrawl over to Orlando Bates, and the president of the Tenth
National should ask me what it meant?

"It is good," Carboner said impressively.

"Whose is it?" The words escaped me unconsciously. "I
want to know whose money I am taking."

"I hope it will be no one's," he answered imperturbably,
"except the bank's. You come to me wanting money, credit.
I give it to you. I ask no questions. Why should you?"

Was it a woman's money I was taking to play out my game.
I recalled the story Sarah had told me years ago about Jane
Dround's father and his fortune. He was a rich old half-breed
trader, and it was gossiped that he had left behind him a pile of
gold. Perhaps this Mr. Carboner was some French-Canadian
friend or business partner of Jane's father, who had charge of
her affairs. As Sarah had said, Jane Dround was always secret
and uncommunicative about herself. My faith in the piece of
paper was growing, but I still waited.

"If you lay these matters down now," Carboner observed
coldly, poking the fire with an old pair of tongs, "they will
be glass. If you grasp them in a strong hand, they will become
diamonds."

But to take a woman's money! I thought for a moment — and

then dismissed the scruple as swiftly as it had come. This woman was a good gambler!

"All right!" I exclaimed, drawing on my overcoat, which I had laid aside.

"Good! Don't worry about anything. Make your trees bear fruit. That is what you can do, young man." Old Carboner patted me on the back in a fatherly fashion. "Now we will have some coffee together. There is yet time."

The man who had opened the door for me brought in two cups of strong coffee, and I drank mine standing while Carboner sipped his and talked.

"This disturbance will be over soon," he said sagely. "Then we shall have such times of wealth and speculation as the world has never seen. Great things will be done in a few years, and you will do some of them. There are those who have confidence in you, my son. And confidence is worth many millions in gold."

He gave me his hand in dismissal.

"Come to see me again, and we will talk," he added sociably.

On the ground floor of my building there was a broker's office. It was a new firm of young men, without much backing. My old friend, Dickie Pierson, was one of them, and on his account I had given the firm some business now and then. This morning, as I was hurrying back to my office, I ran into Dick standing in the door of his place. He beckoned me into the room where the New York quotations were beginning to go up on the board. He pointed to the local list of the day before; Meat Products stretched in a long string of quotations across the board, mute evidence of yesterday's slaughter.

"What's wrong with your concern?" Dick asked anxiously. "Some one is pounding it for all he is worth."

"Who were selling yesterday?"

"Stearns & Harris," he answered. (They were brokers that Strauss's crowd were known to use.)

There was a mystery here somewhere. For there could not be any considerable amount of the stock loose, now that Dround's block was locked up in Jules Carboner's safe. Yet did the Strauss crowd dare to sell it short in this brazen way? They must think it would be cheap enough soon, or they knew where they could get some stock when they wanted it.

"What's up?" Dick asked again, hovering at my elbow. I judged that he had gone into Meat Products on his own account, and wanted to know which way to jump.

"It looks bad for us," I said confidentially to Dickie. "You needn't publish this on the street." (I reckoned that the tip would be on the ticker before noon.) "But Dround has gone over to the other crowd. And probably some of our people are squeezed just now so they can't hold their Meat Products." I added some yarn about a lawsuit to make doubly sure of Dickie, and ordered him to sell a few hundred shares on my own account as a clincher.

When I reached my telephone I called up some brokers that I trusted and told them to watch the market for Meat Products stock, and pick it up quietly, leading on the gang that was pounding our issues all they could. An hour later, on my way back from the Tenth National, where I had had a most satisfactory interview with Mr. Orlando Bates, I dropped in at Dickie Pierson's place. Meat Products shares were active, and in full retreat across the broad board.

"I guess you had better sell some more for me," I said to Dickie. "Sell a thousand to-morrow."

CHAPTER XXVI

VICTORY

The shorts are caught — Big John comes to my office to get terms — An exchange of opinions — An alliance proposed — I reject it — My enemies are flattering — I have arrived

---

THEY sent old John Carmichael around to treat with me. He had to come to the office the same as any other man who had a favor to ask. Slocum and I and two or three others who were close to us were there waiting for him, and discussing the terms we should give.

"They must be short in the neighborhood of fifteen thousand shares common and preferred the best we can make out," Slocum reported, after conferring with our brokers. "How did you have the nerve, Van, to run this corner when you knew Dround's stock was loose?"

"It isn't loose," I answered.

"Where is it, then? We know pretty well where every other share is, but his block has dropped out of the market. It was transferred to some New York parties last October."

I smiled tranquilly. There had been no leak in our barrel. Slocum and I had been around to all the other large holders of Meat Products, and I knew they would not go back on us. The Strauss crowd would find the corner invulnerable.

When Carmichael came in he nodded to me familiarly, just as he used to at Dround's when he had been away on a trip to New York or some place, and called out gruffly: —

"Say! I told them you were a bad one to go up against.

Say, Harrington, do you remember how you scalped poor old McGee back in the days when you were doing odd jobs at Dround's? Well, I came over here to see what you want for your old sausage shop, anyway."

With that gibe at my start in the packing business he settled back in his chair and pulled out a cigar.

"I don't know that we are anxious to sell, John," I replied.

"What? That talk don't go. I know you want to get out mighty bad. What's your figure?"

"You fellows have given us a lot of trouble, first and last," I mused tranquilly. "There was that injunction business over the London and Chicago Company, and the squeeze by the banks. You have tried every dirty little game you knew."

Carmichael grinned and smoked.

"I suppose you want our outfit to turn out some more rotten canned stuff for the Government. What you sold them isn't fit for a Chinaman to eat, John." Thereupon I reached into a drawer of my desk and brought out a tin of army beef marked with the well-known brand of the great Strauss. I proceeded to open it, and as soon as the cover was removed a foul odor offended our nostrils. "Here's a choice specimen one of our boys got for me."

Carmichael smoked on placidly.

"That is something we have never done, though we couldn't make anything on our contract at the figures you people set. And little of the business we got, anyway! Strauss ought to be put where he'd have to feed off his own rations."

So we sat and scored one another comfortably for a time, and then came to business. The terms that Slocum and I had figured out were that Strauss and his crowd should pay us in round numbers two hundred dollars per share preferred and common alike, allowing every shareholder the same terms. Carmichael leaped to his feet when he heard the figures.

"You're crazy mad, Van," he swore volubly. Then he stated his plan, which was, in brief, that we should make an alliance with the great Strauss and sell him at "reasonable figures" an interest in our company.

"And let you and Strauss freeze out my friends? Not for one minute! Go back and tell your boss to find that stock he's short of."

Carmichael threw us an amused glance.

"Do you think that's worrying us? If you want a fight, I guess we can give you some trouble."

It seems that they had another club behind their backs, and that was a suit, which they were instigating the Attorney-general to bring against the Meat Products Company for infringing the Illinois anti-trust act. The impudence and boldness of this suggestion angered me.

"All right," I said. "You have our figure, John."

He left us that day, but he came the next morning with new proposals from his master. They were anxious to have a peaceable settlement. I had known for some time that these men were preparing for an astonishing move, which was nothing less than a gigantic combination of all the large food-product industries of the country, and they could not leave us as a thorn in their side. They must annex us, cost what it might.

So now they talked of my ability, of what I had done in making a great business out of a lot of remnants, and they wanted to buy me as well as our company, offering me some strong inducements to join them. But I told Carmichael shortly: —

"I will never work with Strauss in this life. It's no use your talking, John. There isn't enough money coined to bring me to him. You must buy our stock outright — and be quick about it, too."

He could not understand my feeling, and it was not reasonable. But all these years of desperate fight there had grown up in my heart a hatred of my enemy beyond the usual cold passions of business. I hated him as machine, as a man, — as a cruel, treacherous, selfish, unpatriotic maker of dollars.

So in the end they came to my terms, and the lawyers set to work on the papers. The Strauss interest were to take over the Meat Products stock at our figure, and also the Empress Line, our private-car enterprise, and two or three smaller matters that had grown up in connection with the packing business. When Slocum and I went on to New York to finish the transaction, Sarah and the girls accompanied us, on their way to Europe, where they were going for a pleasure trip.

Thus in a few months my labors came to flower, and suddenly the map of my life changed completely. The end was not yet, but no longer was I the needy adventurer besieging men of means to join me in my enterprises, dodging daily blows in a hand-to-hand scrimmage — a struggling packer! I had brought Strauss to my own terms. And when the proud firm of Morris Brothers, the great bankers, invited me to confer with them in regard to our railroad properties in the Southwest, and to take part in one of those deals which in a day transform the industrial map of the country, I felt that I had come out upon the level plateau of power.

DOUBTS

IT was that autumn of jubilation after the Spanish War. The morning when I drove through the city to the bankers' office, workmen were putting up a great arch across the avenue for the coming day of celebration. Our people had shown the nations of the world the might and the glory in us. Forgotten now was the miserable mismanagement of our brave men, the shame of rotten rations, the fraud of politicians — all but the pride of our strength! A new spirit had come over our country during these months — a spirit of daring and adventure, of readiness for vast enterprises. That business world of which I was a part was boiling with activities. The great things that had been done in the past in the light of the present seemed but the deeds of babes. And every man who had his touch upon affairs felt the madness of the times.

Among the gentlemen gathered in the bankers' office that morning was my old friend Farson. I had not seen him since our unpleasant luncheon at the railroad station. He greeted me courteously enough, as if he had once been acquainted with somebody by my name. It was apparent that he had come there to represent what was left of the old New England interests in the railroad properties; but he did not count in that gathering. The men at Morris Brothers listened to me most of the time that morning!

As we broke up for luncheon Farson congratulated me dryly on the success I had met with in the negotiations.

"I hope, then, we shall have your support," I remarked, forgetting our past dispute.

"I am here to see that my friends are taken care of," he replied grimly; "all we hope is to get our money back from the properties. My people do not understand you and your generation. We are better apart."

"I am sorry you think so," I said, understanding well enough what he meant.

"I am sorry, too: sorry for you and for our country in the years to come. For she it is who suffers most by such ideals as you stand for."

"I think that you are mistaken there," I answered peaceably. "We are the ones who are making this country great. If it weren't for men like me, you good people wouldn't be doing any business to speak of. There wouldn't be much to be done!"

"Our fathers found enough to do," he retorted dryly, "and they did not buy judges nor maintain lobbies in the legislature."

"There wasn't any money in it those days!" I laughed.

Talking thus we reached the place where I was to lunch with some others, and I asked him to join the party. The uncompromising old duck refused; he wouldn't even break bread with me at a hotel table.

"I am sorry you won't eat with me, Mr. Farson. I don't hope to convert you to my way of thinking and feeling. But you were good to me and saved my life when I was in a tight place, and I am glad to think that no loss ever come to you or your friends through me. I have made money for you all. And I wish you would stay with me and let me make a lot more for you in this new deal we are putting through."

"Thank you," he said with a dry little smile, "but I and my friends will be content with getting back the money we have spent. Mr. Harrington, there is one thing that you Western gentlemen — no! it is unfair to cast that slur on one section of the country, and I have met honorable gentlemen West as well as East — but there is one thing that you gentlemen of finance to-day fail to understand — there is always a greater rascal than any one of you somewhere, and it is usually only a question of time when you will meet him. When that time comes, he will pick the flesh from your bones, and no one will care very much what happens to you then! And one thing more: to one who has lived life, and knows what it is, there is mighty little happiness in a million dollars! Good morning, sir."

He was a lovable old fool, though! All through luncheon and the business talk that followed in the afternoon the old gentleman's remarks kept coming back to me in a queer, persistent way. Feeling my oats as I did, in the full flood of my success, there was yet something unsatisfied about my heart. My brain was busy with the plans of the Morris Brothers, but nothing more.

After the work of the day was over, Sarah and I drove up to the Park to see the parade of fine horses and carriages and smart-looking folks who were out taking their airing. It was a beautiful, warm October day, and Sarah took considerable interest in the show. The faces of those in the carriages were not much to look at, take them by and large. They were the faces of men and women who ate and drank and enjoyed themselves too much. They were the faces of the people who lived in the rich hotels, who made and spent the money of our country. And as I looked at them, Farson's last words came back to my thoughts: —

"There's mighty little happiness in a million dollars."

"Van," Sarah said after a time, "let us drive over the avenue. I want to look at that house the Rainbows spoke to us about."

So we turned out of the Park toward the house on the avenue which we thought of buying; for we had been talking somewhat of moving to New York to live after this year.

As we got out of our carriage in front of the lofty gray stone house, a man and a woman came toward us on the walk. The man seemed old and moved heavily, and the woman's face was bent to one side to him. Sarah glanced at them and stood still.

"Van," she whispered, "there are Mr. and Mrs. Dround!"

She hesitated a moment, and then, as the two came nearer, she stepped forward to meet them, and Jane looked up at us. The two women glanced at each other, then spoke. Mrs. Dround said something to her husband, and he gave me a slow look of returning recognition, as if my face recalled vague memories.

"Mr. Harrington?" he said questioningly, taking my hand in a hesitating way, as though he were not quite sure about me yet. "Oh, yes! I am glad to see you again. How is Mr. Carmichael? Well, I hope, and prospering?"

The man's mind was a blank!

"Yes, Mrs. Dround and I have been abroad this winter," he continued, "but we have come back to live here. America is the proper place for Americans, I have always believed. I have no patience with those people who expatriate themselves. Yes, Mrs. Dround wanted me to take a place in Kent, but I would not listen to it. I know where my duty lies," — he straightened himself with slow pompousness, — "How are the children? All well, I hope?"

Jane was talking with Sarah, and the four of us after a while entered the house, which was just being finished by the contractor. In the hall Mr. Dround turned to Sarah and made some remark about the house, and the agent, who happened to be there, led them upstairs. Jane and I followed.

"So you have come home to live?" I asked.

"Yes!" She sank down on a workman's bench, with a sigh of weariness. As I looked at her more closely, it seemed to me that at last age had touched her. There were white strands in her black hair, and there were deep circles beneath the dark eyes — eyes that were dull from looking without seeing anything in particular.

"It was best for Henry," she added quietly. "He is restless over there. You see, he forgets everything so quickly now. It had been so for nearly a year."

There was the story of her days — the watcher and keeper of this childish man, whose mind was fading away before its time. With a sense of the cruelty in it, I turned away from her hastily and looked out of the window.

"I do not mind, most times," she said gently, as in answer to my action. "It is easier to bear than some things of life."

"Shame!" I muttered.

"But there are days," she burst out more like her old self, "when I simply cannot stand it! But let us not waste these precious minutes with my troubles. Let us talk of *you*. You are still young in spite of —"

"The gray hair and the two hundred and forty pounds? I don't feel so young as I might, Jane!"

She colored at the sound of her name.

"But you have got much for your gray hairs — you have lived more than most men!"

"Tell me," I demanded suddenly, — "I know it was your hand that pulled me from the last hole. It was your money that Carboner risked? I knew it. Old Carboner wouldn't tell, but I knew it!"

"And you were on the point of refusing my help," she

added with an accusing smile. "I should have scorned you, if you had gone away without it!"

"Oh, I didn't hesitate long! And I am glad now it was yours, in more ways than one," I added quickly. "It was a profitable deal, — Carboner wrote you the terms?"

"Yes, but it would have made no difference if it had come out badly — you can't know what it meant to me to do that! To work with you with all my strength! It was the first real joy I ever got from my money, and perhaps the last, too. For you are beyond my help now."

"How did Carboner get hold of your husband's stock?" I persisted curiously.

"That is my secret!" she smiled back with a look of her old self. "Why should you want to know? That is so like a man! Always wanting to know why. Believe in the fairies for once!"

"It was a mighty clever fairy this time. She had lots of power. Do you see that, after all, in spite of all the talk about genius and destiny and being self-made and all that, I did not win the game by myself? I would have been broke now, a discredited gambler, if it hadn't been for your helping hand. It was you! And I guess, Jane, we all have to have some help."

"You don't begrudge me the little help I gave you — the small share I had in your fortune?"

"No, I don't mind. I am glad of it."

That was sincere enough. I had come to see that no man can stand alone, and I was not ashamed to have taken my help from the hand of a woman.

"But suppose I had gambled with your money and lost it? I might have easily enough."

"Do you think I should have cared?"

"No, Jane, I guess not. But I should have!"

"It's been the joy of these terrible years, knowing that you were here in the world accomplishing what you were born to do! And that I had a little — oh, such a little! — share in helping you do it. Poor I, who have never done anything worth while!"

"It seems queer that a woman should set so much store on what a man does."

"It's beyond a man's power to know that! But try to think what you would be if you were a helpless cripple, tied to your chair. Don't you suppose that when some strong, handsome athlete came your way with all his health, you would admire him, get interested in him, and like to watch those muscles at work, just the muscles you couldn't use? I think so. And if a good fate put it in your power to help him — you, the poor cripple in your chair — help him to win his race, wouldn't you be thankful? I can tell you that one cripple blesses you because you are you — a man!"

The excitement of her feelings brought back the dark glow to her face, and made her beautiful once more. Ideas seemed to burn away the faded look and gave her the power that passion gives ordinary women.

"You and I think alike, I love to believe. Start us from the two Poles, and we would meet midway. We are not little people, thank God, you and I. We did not make a mess of our lives! My friend, it is good to know that," she ended softly.

"Yes," I admitted, understanding what she meant. "We parted."

"We parted! We lived a thousand miles from one another. What matters it? I said to myself each day: 'Out there, in the world, lives a man who thinks and acts and feels as I would have a man think and act and feel. He is not far away.' "

She laid a hand lightly on my arm and smiled. And we were silent until the voices of the others in the hall above reminded us of the present. Jane rose, and her face had faded once more into its usual calm.

"You are thinking of moving to New York? What for?"

I spoke of my new work — the checker-board that had been under discussion all day at the bankers'.

"You are rich enough," she remarked. "That means so many millions more to your account."

"No, not just that," I protested. "It's the solution to the little puzzle you and I were working at over the atlas in your library that day years ago. It is like a problem in human physics: there were obstacles in the way, but the result was sure from the start."

"But you are near the end of it — and then what?"

"I suppose there will be others!" After a time I added, half to myself: "But there's no happiness in it. There is no happiness."

"Do you look for happiness? That is for children!"

"Then what is the end of it?"

For of a sudden the spring of my energies was slackened within me, and the work that I was doing seemed senseless. Somehow a man's happiness had slipped past me on the road, and now I missed it. There was the joy we might have had, she and I, and we had not taken it. Had we been fools to put it aside? She answered my thoughts.

"We did not want it! Remember we did not want that! Don't let me think that, after all, you regret! I could not stand that — no woman could bear it."

Her voice was like a cry to my soul. On the stairs above Mr. Dround was saying to Sarah: —

"No, I much prefer our Chicago style of building, with large lots, where you can get sunshine on all four sides. It is more healthy, don't you think, Mrs. Harrington?"

And Sarah answered: —

"Yes, I quite agree with you, Mr. Dround. I don't like this house at all — it's too dark. We shall have to look farther, I guess."

Jane turned her face to mine. Her eyes were filled with tears, and her mouth trembled. "Don't regret — anything," she whispered. "We have had so much!"

"Van," Sarah called from the stairs, "you haven't seen the house! But it isn't worth while. I am sure we shouldn't like it."

"You mustn't look for your Chicago garden on Fifth Avenue," Mrs. Dround laughed.

As we left the house, Sarah turned to Jane and asked her to come back with us to the hotel for dinner. But the Drounds had an engagement for the evening, and so an appointment was made for the day following to dine together. When we had said good-by and were in the carriage, Sarah remarked reflectively: —

"Jane looks like an old woman — don't you think so, Van?"

CHAPTER XXVIII

A NEW AMBITION

Jane Dround points the way again — The shoes of Parkinson and the senatorial toga — Strauss is dead — Business or politics? — A dream of wealth — The family sail for Europe

---

"I AM writing Sarah that after all we cannot dine with you. My husband is restless and feels that we must leave for the West to-night. It was very sweet of Sarah to want us, but after all perhaps it is just as well. We shall see you both soon, I am sure. . . .

"But there is something I want to say to you — something that has been on my mind all the long hours since our meeting. Those brief moments yesterday I felt that all was not well with you, my friend. Your eyes had a restless demand that I never saw in them before. I suspect that you are beginning to know that Success is nothing but a mirage, fading before our eyes from stage to stage. You have accomplished all and more than you planned that afternoon when we hung over the atlas together. You are rich now, very rich. You are a Power, in the world, — yes, you are, — not yet a very great planet, but one that is rapidly swinging higher into the zenith. You must be reckoned with! My good Jules keeps me informed, you see. If you keep your hold in these new enterprises, you will double your fortune many times, and before long you will be one of the masters — one of the little group who really control our times, our country. Yet — I wonder — yes, my doubt has grown so large since I saw you that it moves me to write all this. . . . Will *that* be enough? Mere wealth, mere power of that kind, will it satisfy? . . . It is hard enough to tell what *will satisfy*; but there are other things — other worlds than your world of money power. But I take your time with my woman's nonsense — forgive me!

"I hear from a good authority in Washington that our old Senator Parkinson is really on his last legs. That illness of his this spring, which they tried to keep quiet, was really a stroke, and it will be a miracle if he lasts another winter. Did you know him? He was a queer old farmer sort of politician. His successor, I fancy, will be some one quite different. That type of statesman has had its day! *There* is a career, now, if a man wanted it! . . . Why not think of it?

"Good-by, my friend. I had almost forgotten, as I forgot yesterday, to thank you for making me so rich! Mr. Carboner cabled me the terms of your settlement with Strauss. They were wicked!

"JANE DROUND.

"It would not be the most difficult thing in the world to capture Parkinson's seat — if one were willing to pay the price!"

The idea of slipping into old Parkinson's shoes made me laugh. It was a bit of feminine extravagance. Nevertheless this letter gave me food for thought. Jane was right enough in saying that my wonderful success had not brought me all the satisfaction that it should. Now that the problems I had labored over were working themselves out to the plain solution of dollars and cents, the zest of the matter was oozing away. To be sure, there was prospect of some excitement to be had in the railroad enterprises of the Morris Brothers, although it was merest flattery to say that my position counted for much as yet in that mighty game. Did I want to make it count?

I sipped my morning coffee and listened to Sarah's talk. Beyond business, what was there for me? There was our place down in Vermilion County, Illinois. But stock-farming was an old man's recreation. I might become a collector like Mr. Dround, roaming about Europe, buying old stuff to put in a house or give to a museum. But I was too ignorant for that kind of play. And philanthropy? Well, in time, perhaps when I knew what was best to give folks, which isn't as simple as it might seem.

"I am sorry the Drounds couldn't come," Sarah was saying, glancing at Jane's note to her. "I liked Jane better yesterday than ever before — she looked so worn and kind of miserable. I don't believe she can be happy, Van."

"Well, she didn't say so!" I replied. . . .

Yes, I knew Senator Parkinson — a sly, tricky politician, for all his simple farmer ways. He was not what is called a railroad Senator, but the railroads never had much trouble with him. . . .

Before we had finished our breakfast Carmichael sent up word that he must see me, and I hurried down to the lobby of the hotel. He met me at the elevator and drew me aside, saying abruptly: —

"The old man is dead! Just got a wire from Chicago — apoplexy. I must get back there at once."

Strauss dead! The news did not come home to me all at once. His was not just like any other death. From the day when the old packer had first come within my sight he had loomed big and savage on my horizon, and around him, somehow, my life had revolved for years. I hated him. I hated his tricky, wolfish ways, his hog-it-all policy; I despised his mean, unpatriotic character. Yet his going was like the breaking of some great wheel at the centre of industry.

I had hated him, and for that reason I had refused all offers to settle on anything but a cash basis for my interests in the companies he was buying from us. Carmichael and some others had urged me again and again to go in with them and help them build the great merger, but I had steadily refused to work with Strauss. "I cannot make a good servant," I had said to John, "and I don't want a knife in my side. The country is big enough for Strauss and me. I'll give him his side of the pasture."

But now he was dead, and already, somehow, my hate was fading from my heart. The great Strauss was but another man like myself, who had done his work in his own way. Carmichael, who was a good deal worked up, exclaimed: —

"This won't make any hitch in our negotiations, Harrington. Everything will go right on just as before. The old man's plans were laid pretty deep, and this deal with you is one of the first of them. His brother Joe will take his place, maybe, and if he can't fill the shoes, why, young Jenks, who seems to be a smart young man, or I will take the reins."

(Old Strauss had been married three times, but his children had all died. There was no one of his own to take the ball of money he had made and roll it larger; no one of his own blood to grasp the reins of his power and drive on in the old man's way!)

"Say, Van," the Irishman continued, "why don't you think it over once more, and see your way to join us? You didn't care for the old man. But you and I and Jenks could swing things all right. And we could keep Joe Strauss in his place between us. God, kid, the four of us could make a clean job of this thing — there's no limit to what we could do!" As he uttered this last, he grasped me by the arms and shook me.

I knew what he meant — that with the return of prosperity, with vast capital ready for investment, with the control of the packing and food-products transportation business — which we packers had been organizing into a compact machine — there was no limit to the reach of our power in this land, in the world. (And I was of his way of thinking, then, not believing that a power existed which could check our operations. And I do not believe it now, I may add; nor do I know a man conversant with the modern situation of capital who believes that with our present system of government any effective check upon the operations of capital can be devised.)

"Think it over," Carmichael urged, "and let me know when I return from Chicago the first of the week. You don't want to make the mistake of your life by dropping out just now."

But while he was talking to me, urging on me the greatness of the future, my thoughts went back to that letter of Jane Dround's. She had seen swiftly a truth that was coming to me slowly. There might be twenty, forty, sixty millions in the packers' deal, but the joy of the game had gone for me. All of those millions would not give me the joy I had when I sold that sausage plant to Strauss! I shook my head.

"No, I don't want it, John. But Strauss's death makes a big difference. I am willing to offer some kind of trade with you, — to let you have my stock on better terms, if your people will do what I want."

Carmichael waited for my proposal. I said: —

"Old Parkinson is pretty near his end, I hear. It's likely there will be a vacant seat in the Senate sometime soon."

The Irishman's eyes opened wide in astonishment.

"Strauss used to keep in touch with Springfield," I suggested. "He and Vitzer" (who was the great traction wolf in Chicago) "used to work pretty close together sometimes —"

"You want to go to the Senate, Van?"

Carmichael burst into a laugh that attracted the attention of the men sitting around us.

"It might work out that way," I admitted.

"And how about that judge business?" he inquired, still laughing. "The papers would make it some hot for you."

"No doubt. I don't expect I should be exactly a popular candidate, John. But I calculate I'd make as good a Senator as Jim Parkinson, and a deal more useful one."

Carmichael stopped laughing and began to think, seeing that their might be a business end to this proposition. The time was coming when he and his associates would need the services of an intelligent friend at Washington. He reckoned up his political hirelings in the state.

"It might be managed," he said after a while, "only our crowd would want to be sure we could count on you if we helped put you there. There's a lot of bum, cranky notions loose in Congress, and it's up to the Senate to see that the real interests of the country are protected."

"I ought to know by this time what the real interests are," I assured him, and when he rose to leave for his train I added pointedly: "In case we make this arrangement there's more stock than mine which you could count on for your deal. We'd all stay in with you."

For there was the stock Carboner had locked up in his safe, and Slocum's, and considerable more that would do as I said. If Carmichael and young Jenks put through their merger and swallowed the packing business whole, I knew that our money would be in good hands.

"Well, when Parkinson gets out we'll see what we can do," Carmichael concluded.

And thus the deal for Parkinson's seat was made right there. All that remained was for the old man to have his second stroke.

"You in the Senate — that's a good one!" John chuckled. "I suppose next you will be wanting to be made Secretary of the Treasury, or President, maybe!"

"I know my limit, John."

"D——d if I do! The old man would have enjoyed this. But,

Van, take my advice and stay out. There ain't much in that political business. Stay with us and make some money. Right now is coming the biggest time this country has ever seen. And we are the crowd that's got the combination to the safe. These New York financiers think they are pretty near the whole thing, but I reckon we are going to give even them a surprise."

With this final boast, he got into his cab and drove off.

The day was brilliantly sunny, and the street was alive with gay people. What the Irishman said was true — I felt it in the sunny air: the greatest period of prosperity this country had ever seen was just starting. It was the time when two or three good gamblers could pick up any kind of property, give it a fine name, print a lot of pretty stock certificates, and sell their gold brick to the first comer. The people were crazy to spend their money. It was a great time! Nevertheless, at the bottom of all this craze was a sure feeling that all was well with us — that ours was a mighty people. And that was about right.

Well, I loved my country in my own way; and I had all the money I knew what to do with. Why not take a seat in "the millionnaires' club," as the newspapers called that honorable body, the United States Senate?

Before I left for the West the family sailed for Europe. Little May and sister Sarah, as we called the girls, had persuaded their mother to take them over to Paris for a lark. May, who was thirteen, was running the party. She was a tall, lively girl, with black hair and eyes, and was thought to resemble me. The other was quieter in her ways, more like Sarah. We had lost one little boy the summer before, which was a great sorrow to us all. The older boy, who was at school preparing for college, took after his mother, too. He was a pleasant-mannered chap, with a liking for good clothes and other playthings. I did not reckon that he ever would be much of a business man.

The morning that the steamer sailed Sarah was nervous over starting, but May settled her in a corner of the deck and got her a wrap. Then the girls went to say good-by to some friends.

"Van," Sarah said to me when we were alone. She hesitated a moment, then went on timidly, "If anything should happen to us, Van, there's one thing —"

"Nothing is going to happen! Not unless you lose your letter of credit, or the girls run off with you," I joked.

"There's one thing I want to speak about seriously, Van. It's May and Will!" She paused timidly.

"Well?"

"Can't you do something to make them feel differently?"

"I guess not. I've tried my best!"

"I know they are poor, and Will's in bad health, too, — quite sick."

"How did you know that?"

"Oh, I saw May once before I left. They are in Chicago again."

After a time I said: —

"You know I would give half of my money not to have it so, but it's no use talking. They wouldn't take a cent from me."

Sarah sighed. "But couldn't you get Will a place somewhere without his knowing about how it came?"

"I'll try my best," I said sadly.

Then it was time to leave the steamer; the girls came and kissed me good-by, hanging about my neck and making me promise to write and to come over for them later. Sarah raised her veil as I leaned down to kiss her.

"Good-by, Van," she said without much spirit. "Be careful of yourself and come over if you can get away."

Of late years, especially since the boy's death, Sarah seemed to have lost her interest in things pretty much.

The trip might do her good.

CHAPTER XXIX

THE SENATORSHIP

The people's choice — What the legislature of a great state represents — The Strauss lobby — Public opinion, pro and con — An unflattering description of myself — Carboner's confidences — On the bill-boards — Popular oratory — I discover my brother in strange company — I do some talking on my own account — An organ of kick and criticism — Turned crank

JANE DROUND was right about old Senator Parkinson. He came home to die early in the fall, and faded away in a couple of months afterward. The political pot at the capital of the state then began to hum in a lively fashion. It was suspected that the Governor himself wanted to succeed the late Senator, and there were one or two Congressmen and a judge whose friends thought they were of senatorial size. That was the talk on the surface and in the papers. But the situation was very different underneath.

The legislature might be said, in a general way, to represent the people of the state of Illinois, but it represented also the railroad interests, the traction and gas interests, and the packers, and when it came to a matter of importance it pretty generally did what it was told by its real bosses. This time it was told to put me in the Senate in place of the late Senator, and it obeyed orders after a time. Carmichael was honest with me, and stuck to his agreement to use the Strauss lobby in the legislature in my behalf.

Of course the papers in Chicago howled, all those that hadn't their mouths stopped with the right cake. The three largest

244 · MEMOIRS OF AN AMERICAN CITIZEN

papers couldn't be reached by our friends in any way, but their scoring did little harm. They had up again the story of Judge Garretson and the bonds of the London and Chicago concern. But the story was getting a little hazy in men's memories, and that kind of talk is passed around so often when a man runs for office in our country that it hasn't much significance. We did not even think it worth while to answer it. Besides, to tell the truth, we had nothing much to say. Our policy was, of necessity, what Slocum sarcastically described as "dignified silence." When my name began to be heard at Springfield more and more insistently, the Chicago *Thunderer* came out with a terrific roast editorially: —

"Who is this fellow, E. V. Harrington, who has the presumption to look lustfully on the chair of our late honorable Senator? Eighteen years ago Harrington was driving a delivery wagon for a packing firm, and there are to-day on the West Side retail marketmen who remember his calls at their places. We believe that his first rise in fortune came when, in some tricky way, he got hold of a broken-down sausage plant, which he sold later to the redoubtable Strauss. But it was not until the year '95, when the notorious American Meat Products Company was launched, that Harrington emerged from the obscurity of the Stock Yards. That corporation, conceived in fraud, promoted by bribery, was the child of his fertile brain. Not content with this enterprise, he became involved in railroad promotion in the Southwest, and he and his man Friday, Slocum, were celebrated as the most skilful manipulators of legislative lobbies ever seen in the experienced state of Texas.

"What will Harrington represent in the Senate, assuming that he will be able to buy his way there? Will he represent the great state of Illinois, — the state of Lincoln, of Douglas, of Oglesby? He will represent the corrupt Vitzer and the traction interests of Chicago, the infamous Dosserand and the gas gang — above all, he will represent the packers' combine, — Joe Strauss, Jenks, 'big John' Carmichael. These citizens, who are secretly preparing to perpetrate the greatest piece of robbery this country has ever witnessed, propose to seat Harrington in the United States Senate as their personal representative. Can the degradation of that once honorable body be carried to a greater depth?"

It was not a flattering description of myself, but Tom Stevens, the proprietor of the *Thunderer*, always hated Strauss and his crowd, and the papers had to say something. To offset that dose, the *Vermilion County Herald* printed a pleasant eulogy describing me as a type of the energy and ability of our country, — "the young man of farmer stock who had entered the great city without a dollar and had fought his way up to leadership in the financial world by his will and genius for commerce. Such practical men, who have had training and experience in large affairs, are the suitable representatives of a great commercial people. The nation is to be congratulated on securing the services of men of Mr. Harrington's ability, who could with so much more profit to themselves continue in the career of high finance."

The only trouble with this puff was that it was composed in the office of my lawyers and paid for at high rates. But, so far as affecting the result, the *Thunderer* and the *Vermilion County Herald* were about on a par. The order had gone out from headquarters that I was to be sent to the Senate to take Parkinson's vacant seat, and, unless a cyclone swept the country members off their feet, to the Senate I should go. All that I had to do was to wait the final roll-call and pay the bills.

My old, tried counsellor, Jaffrey Slocum, was managing this campaign for me. We could not use him at Springfield, however; for by this time he was too well known as one of the shrewdest corporation lawyers in the West. He represented the United Metals Trust, among other corporations, and had done some lively lobbying for them of late. He was a rich man now, and weighed several stone more than he did when he and I were living at Ma Pierson's joint. He was married, and had a nice wife, an ambitious woman, who knew what her husband was worth. She might push him to New York or Washington before she was done. Meantime, it was settled that he should take care of the packers' merger, when that came off, and that business would mean another fortune for him.

One day, while the election was still pending, I went over to see Jules Carboner. The old fellow was cheery as ever, and as pleased to see me as if I had been a good boy just home from school. We had some of his strong coffee and talked things over.

"By the way," he said, as I was leaving, "let me tell you now how we happened to get hold of that block of Products' stock."

And he explained to me the mystery of that stock, which had saved my life, so to speak, at a critical time. It seems that about three months before the war scare, when there were bad rumors about Meat Products all over the city, Dround had placed his stock in the hands of a New York firm of bankers. I suppose he was ashamed to let me know that he was going to break his last promise to me. For if he didn't tell those bankers to offer Strauss his stock, he knew that was just what they would do. So much for the scrupulous Henry I! The bankers felt around and tried to strike a bargain with the great packer, and negotiations were under way for some time about the stock. That gave our enemies the confidence to sell us short. They thought that, in case the market went wrong, they could put their hand on Dround's stock. Just at this point Carboner received word where the stock was and orders to buy it. He went to New York the next day and bought it outright, paying all it was worth, naturally. . . .

I came back from Carboner's place through Newspaper Row. On the boards in front of the offices one could read in large red and blue letters: —

HARRINGTON SAID TO BE SLATED FOR THE SENATE
FINAL BALLOT TO-DAY

Men passing on their way home from their work paused to read the bulletin, and I stopped, too. A group of laboring men were gathered about the door of a building near by, and from the numbers entering and leaving the place I judged that some kind of meeting was in progress within. As I stood there my attention was caught by a man who went in with several others. Something about the man's back reminded me of my brother Will, and I followed into the building and upstairs to a smoky room, where the men were standing about in groups, talking together, only now and then paying any attention to the speaker on the platform. He was a fat, round little fellow, and he was shouting himself out of breath: —

"Yes! I tell you right here, you and your children are sold like so many hogs over at the Yards. Don't you believe it? What do you pay for meat? What do you pay for every basket of coal you put in your stoves? The millionnaires there at Washington make the laws of this free country, and who do they make them for? Don't you know? Do they make 'em for you, or for Joe Strauss? They are putting one of their kind in the Senate from this state right now!" . . .

So he rambled on, and having sampled his goods, and not seeing the face I was looking for, I was moving toward the door, when I was arrested by the voice of a man who began to speak over in one corner.

"That's so. I know him!" he shouted, and the attention of the room was his. The men around him moved back, and I could see that the speaker was Will. He was dressed in a long waterproof coat, and his hat was tipped back on his head. An untrimmed black beard covered the lower half of his face. "I can tell you all about him," he continued in a thin, high voice. "He's the man who got a bill through Congress giving himself and his partners a slice of land out of the Indian Territory. He's the man who kept the Texas legislature in his hire the same as a servant."

Generally when I hear this kind of sawing-air I go about my business. The discontented always growl at the other fellow's bone. Give them a chance at the meat, and see how many bites they would make! It's hopeless to try and winnow out the truth from the mass of lies they talk about the trusts, capital, the tariff, corruption, and the rest of it. But it hurt all the same to have Will say such things about me. . . .

"He's the man who sold scraps and offal to the Government for canned beef —"

"That's a lie!" I spoke out promptly.

"Don't I know what I am saying? Didn't I try to live on the rancid, rotten stuff? My God, I've got some home now I could show you!"

Will turned to see who had contradicted him, and recognized me.

"You ought to know better than that," I replied, directly to him. "Some of it was rotten, but not the Meat Products' goods. We lost on our contract, too, what's more."

Will was a little startled, but he steadied himself soon and said again: —

"That's the same thing. You were all the same crowd."

"No; that wasn't so," I remonstrated, "and you ought to know it."

The men in the room had stopped their talking and were craning their heads to look at us. Will and I eyed each other for a time; then I turned to the crowd and made the first and last real public speech of my life.

"That's all a d——d lie about the beef *we* sold the Government. I know it because I inspected it myself. And I gave my own money, too, to support men at the front, and that is more than any of you fellows ever did. And the rest of the talk these gentlemen have been giving you is just about as wrong, too. Let me tell you one thing: if you folks were honest, if you didn't send rascals to Springfield and to Congress, if you weren't ready to take a dollar and club a man if he didn't hand it over, there wouldn't be this bribery business. I know it, because I've got the club over and over again. And one thing more, it's no more use for you and I to kick about the men who put their money into trusts than it would be to try to swallow all the water in the lake. That's the way business has got to be done nowadays, and if it weren't done you folks would starve, and your wives and children would starve —"

"Who are you?" some began to shout, interrupting me.

"I am E. V. Harrington!" I called back.

Then they hooted: "Hello, Senator. Put him out!"

I turned toward Will, and called to him: —

"Come on! I want to have a word with you, Will."

He followed me downstairs into a saloon. Some of the loafers who had heard our talk upstairs came in and crowded up to the bar, and I set up the drinks all around several times. Will wouldn't take any whiskey. Then the bartender let us into a little room at the end of the bar, where we could be by ourselves.

"Will!" I exclaimed, "whatever has happened to you?"

It wrung my heart to see what a wreck he was. He had let

his beard grow to cover up his wasted face. His eyes were sunk and bloodshot. The old waterproof covered a thin flannel coat.

"I'm all right," he replied gloomily. "What do you want of me?"

"I want you to come out and get some dinner with me, first," I said.

But he shook his head, saying he must go home to May.

"It ain't no use, Van," he added, in a high, querulous voice. "We don't belong together. May and I are of the people — the people you fatten on."

"Quit that rot! I am one of the people, too."

"Oh, you're Senator, I expect, by this time," he sneered. "What did it cost you, Van?"

"I don't want to talk politics."

"That's all I care to talk. I want to get a chance to show you fellows up one of these days. I'm considering a proposition for part control of a paper — a labor weekly."

So he talked for a while about his scheme of getting hold of a little three-cent outfit and making it into an organ of kick and criticism. He had seen life from the inside during the war, he explained, and he wanted to give the public the benefit of his experience. He had a snarl for every conceivable thing that was, and he was eager to express it. When I showed him that such an attitude was dead against American feeling, he accused me of trying to suppress his enterprise because it was aimed at my friends, "the thieves and robbers." It was hopeless to argue with him, and the more we talked the worse I felt. He was just bitter and wild, and he kept saying: "You taught me what it meant! You showed me what it was to be rich!" The war had ruined his health and weakened his mind. The gentle, willing side in him had turned to fury. He was a plain crank now!

"I'll buy this paper for you — or I'll start a new one for you
to curse me and my friends with — if you'll just take May and
the children and go down to my farm in the country. There
are two thousand acres down there, Will, and you can do as
you please on the place. When you've got back your health,
then you can start in to baste me as good as you've a mind to."

But he refused to compromise his "cause." So we parted at
the door of the saloon, he buttoning up his old raincoat and
striding out for the West Side without a look back to me. And
as I hailed a cab to take me to the club I heard in my ears that
charge, "You taught me what it meant to be rich, Van!" It
made me mad, but it hurt just the same.

Though I knew perfectly well that I was not responsible
for his crankiness, yet I thought that if he could have kept on
at business under me he would have been all right, earning a
good living for his wife and children, and not taking up with
thoughts he hadn't the mind to think out. For Will was not one
to step safely out of the close ranks of men, but he was always
a mighty faithful worker wherever he was put. And now he was
just a crank — good for nothing.

CHAPTER XXX

THE COST

A dinner at the Metropolitan Club — Old friends and enemies — A conservative Senator — Pleasant speeches — A favor for Henry I — I plan a gift for a tried friend — I find that I have nothing to give — Slocum's confession — Aims in life — The Supreme Bench — What money can't buy — Slocum pays for both

---

A NUMBER of men gave me a dinner that evening at the Metropolitan Club. Steele, Lardner, Morrison (of the New York and Chicago Railway Company), Joe Strauss, Jenks, Carmichael, and Bates were there, among others — all leaders in the community in various enterprises. Not all these gentlemen had looked with favor on my political aspirations; but, when they saw that I could win this trick as I had others, they sidled up to me. After all, no matter what they might think of me personally, or of my methods, they felt that I belonged to their crowd and would be a safe enough man to have in the Senate.

Just as we sat down, Slocum, who had been called to the telephone, came up to me, a smile on his wrinkled face, and said, raising his right hand: —

"Gentlemen, the legislature at Springfield has elected Mr. Harrington to fill the unexpired term of the late Senator Parkinson. Gentlemen, three cheers for Senator Harrington!"

As the men raised their champagne glasses to drink to me, Slocum shook me warmly by the hand, a smile broadening over his face. Although, as I told them, it had never been my part to talk, I said a few words, thanking them for their good-will, and promising them that I should do my best to serve the interests of the country we all believed was the greatest nation that had ever been. My old friend Orlando Bates, the president of the Tenth National, replied to my talk, expressing the confidence my associates had in me. In the course of his graceful speech he said, "Mr. Harrington is so closely identified with the conservative interests of the country that we can feel assured he will stand as a bulwark against the populistic clamor so rife in the nation at the present time." And young Harvey Sturm, also a bank president, who followed him with a glowing speech, made flattering references to the work I had done "in upbuilding our glorious commonwealth." After deprecating the growth of socialistic sentiments and condemning the unrestricted criticism of the press in regard to capital, he closed with a special tribute: "Such men as Edward Harrington are the brains and the will of the nation. On their strong shoulders rests the progress of America. Were it not for their God-given energy, their will, their genius for organization, our broad prairies, our great forests, our vast mines, would cease to give forth their wealth!"

There was more of the same sort of talk before we broke up. Afterward, as the theatres and the opera closed, men dropped in to hear the news, and many of them came up to congratulate me. Among others old Dround wandered into the club in the course of the evening, and, some one having told him that I had been elected Senator, he came up to the corner where I was standing with a group of men, and hovered around for a time, trying to get a word with me. After a while I stepped out and shook hands with him.

"I am very glad to hear this, Mr. Harrington," he said slowly, pressing my hand in his trembling fist. "I have always believed that our best men should take an interest in the government of their country."

His eyes had a wandering expression, as if he were trying in vain to remember something out of the past, and he continued to deliver his little speech, drawing me to one side out of hearing of the men who were standing there. "I thought once to enter public life myself," he said, "but heavy business responsibilities demanded all my attention. I wonder," he lowered his voice confidentially, "if you will not find it possible to further the claims of my old friend Paxton's son. He desires to secure a diplomatic post. I have urged his merits on the President, and secured assurance of his good-will; but nothing has yet been done. I cannot understand it."

Eri Paxton was a dissipated, no-account sort of fellow, but I assured Henry I. Dround that I would do my best for him. That was the least that the past demanded of me!

So it went on until past midnight, and the club began to empty, and I was left with a few friends about me. When they went I took Slocum up to my room for a last cigar before bed. We had some private matters to settle in connection with the election.

"You pulled out all right, Van," he said when we were alone. "But there wasn't much margin."

"I trusted Carmichael — I knew John wouldn't go back on me."

We sat and smoked awhile in silence. Now that I had picked the plum, the feeling came over me that Slocum ought to have had it. With the idea I burst out at last: —

"I've been thinking of one thing all along, Slo — and that is: What can I do for you when I am Senator? Name what you want, man, and if it's in my power to get it, it shall be yours. Without you I'd never have been here, and that's sure."

"I never cared much for politics," he replied thoughtfully. "I guess there isn't anything I want, which is more than most of your friends can say!"

"Something in the diplomatic service?" I suggested. He shook his head.

"How about a Federal judgeship — you can afford to go out of practice."

"Yes, I can afford to go on the bench!" he replied dryly. "But it's no use to talk of it."

"What do you mean?"

"You ought to know, Van, that that is one thing that can't be bought in this country, not yet. I could no more get an appointment on the Federal bench than you could!"

"You mean on account of that old story? That's outlawed years ago!"

"You think so? The public forgets, but lawyers remember, and so do politicians. The President may make rotten appointments anywhere else, but if he should nominate me for the Circuit bench there would be such a howl go up all over that he would have to withdraw me. And he knows too much to try any such proposition."

It was no use to argue the question, for the lawyer had evidently been over the whole matter and knew the facts.

"It isn't that bribery matter, Van, alone; I have been hand and glove with you fellows too long to be above suspicion. My record is against me all through. It isn't worth talking about. . . . I have had my pay: I am a rich man, richer than I ever expected to be when I put foot in Chicago. I have no right to complain."

But I felt that, in spite of all he said, that wasn't enough — somehow the money did not make it square for him. As the night passed, he warmed up more than I had ever known him to in all the years we had worked together, and he let me see some way inside him. I remember he said something like this: —

"There were three things I promised myself I would do with my life. That was back in my senior year at Bowdoin College.

I was a poor boy — had borrowed from a relative a few hundred dollars to go through college with, and felt the burden of that debt pretty hard. Well, of those three purposes, one was for myself. First, I promised myself I would pay back my uncle's loan. That was a simple matter of decency. He was not a rich man, and his children felt rather sore at his letting me have those six hundred dollars to spend on a college education. I managed to do that out of what I earned as a law clerk the first years we were together at Ma Pierson's. The next thing I had promised myself was to buy back our old brick house in the aristocratic part of Portland — the house my father had been obliged to part with after the panic of '76. I meant to put my mother and sisters in it. The only sister I have living is there now with her children. My mother died in her old home, and that has always been a comfort to me. . . . You may think it was my desire to do this that made me stick by you when we had that difference about the Chicago and London bonds, but you are mistaken. I went with you, Van, because I wanted to — just that. I saw then what it meant, and I am not kicking now.

"Well, the third aim I set myself when I was speculating, as college boys do about such things, was the hardest of all. The others, with reasonable success, I could hope to accomplish. And I did fulfil them sooner than I had any reason to hope I should. The third was a more difficult matter, and that was my ambition to sit some day on the Supreme Bench. There were two members of our family who had been distinguished judges, one of the Supreme Court of Maine, and another of the Federal Supreme Court, back in the early forties. I had always heard these two men referred to with the greatest respect in our family, especially my great-uncle, Judge Lambert Cushing. Although by the time I came to college our family had reached a pretty low ebb, it was natural that I should secretly cherish the ambition to rise to the high-water mark.

"And," he concluded, "after thirty years of contact with the world, I haven't seen much that is more worthy of a man's ambition in our country than a seat on our Supreme Bench. I have no reason to be ashamed of my three aims in life. Two of them I made — the third I might never have come near to, anyway; but I chucked away my chance a good many years ago. However, I have done pretty well by myself as it is. So you see there is nothing, Van, that you can give me that I should want to take."

He reached for another cigar, and stretched his long legs. It was the first time he had ever spoken to me from the bottom of his heart, and now that he had revealed the truth about himself, there was nothing to be said. He was not just the ordinary corporation lawyer, who sells his learning and his shrewdness for a fat fee. I had run up against that kind often enough. They are an indispensable article to the modern man of affairs; for the strategy of our warfare is largely directed by them. But Jaffrey Slocum was much more than such a trained prostitute: he was a man of learning and a lover of the law for its own sake. I suspect that if he had ever sat on the bench he would have been a tough nut for the corporations. . . .

"There's no better proverb, my friend, than the old one about the way you make your bed," Slocum summed up, rising to go. "It don't trouble you, perhaps, because you are made different. You are made to fit the world as it is to-day."

With that he bade me good night and went away. I sat on by myself for some time afterward, thinking, thinking of it all! Very likely if Slocum could have had his desire, and gone on the Supreme Bench, he would not have found it all he had painted it as a boy. But whether it was foolish or not for him to set such store by that prize, it was beyond his reach, and the man who had done most to put him out of the race was I. I had needed him, and I had taken him — that was all there was to that. He had sold himself to me, not just for money, but for friendship and admiration, — for what men of his kind sell themselves. For in all the world there was not enough money to pay him for selling himself — he had as much as said so to-night. Now, when I wanted to give him the gift that he had earned by years of devotion, there was nothing in my hands that was worth his taking!

Thinking of this, I forgot for the time being that I was Senator from the state of Illinois.

CHAPTER XXXI

FURTHER COST

I go to see May — A cottage on the West Side — May comes to the door — Pleading — Stiff-necked virtue — A discussion of patriotism — We wash dishes and dispute — Old times — One woman's character — Possibilities — Hard words — Rejected gifts — Even to the children — Who shall judge? — Another scale and a greater one

---

THE cab drew up before a one-story frame house that stood back in the lot, squeezed between two high brick buildings. This was the number on Ann Street, over on the West Side, that Will had given me when I had pressed him for his address. The factories had pretty well surrounded this section of the city, leaving here and there some such rickety shanty as this one. There were several children playing in the strip of front yard, and as I opened the gate one of them called out, "Hello, Uncle Van!"

It was Will's second son, little Van. He said his mother was at home, and, taking my hand, he showed me around the cottage to the back door. The boy pounded on the door, and May came to see what was the matter.

"Is that you, Van?" she asked, as if she expected me. "Will said he saw you the other day."

She did not invite me in, but the little boy held open the door and I walked into the kitchen. The breakfast things were piled up in the sink, unwashed. A boiler of clothes was on the fire, and May had her sleeves rolled up, ready to begin the wash. Her arms were as thin as pipe-stems, and behind her glasses I saw deep circles of blue flesh. She had grown older and thinner in the three years since she and Will left my house for good.

"Will's gone to the city," May remarked.

"He don't look strong, May. It made me feel bad to see him so — changed, not a bit like himself."

She seemed to bridle a little at this.

"He hasn't been real well since he had the fever at Montauk. He was reinfected at the hospital, and nearly died. When he got out he tried farming down in Texas, but his strength didn't come back as we expected, and the climate was too hot for him. So went came North to see if he could get some easier work."

"How are the children?" I asked, seeing a strange baby face peep around the corner of the clothes-basket.

"We lost the baby boy while Will was at Montauk. Another little girl has come since then. We call her Sarah."

She waited a moment, and then asked hesitatingly: —

"How's your Sarah? She didn't look well when I saw her last."

"No — she's been delicate some time — since our boy died, last summer. She's gone to Europe with the girls for a change."

Then we were silent; there was not much more we could say without touching the quick. But at last I burst out: —

"May, why wouldn't you take that money I sent you while Will was away at the war?"

"We could manage without it. It was kind of you, though. You have always been kind, Van!"

"You might have known it would make us happy to have you take it. It was only what I owed to the country, too, seeing that I was so placed I couldn't go to Cuba. I wanted then to leave everything and enlist. But it wouldn't have been fair to others. I sent some men in my place, though."

Perhaps it sounded a little like apologizing. May listened with a smile on her lips that heated me.

"You are just like that preacher!" I exclaimed. "You can see no good in folks unless it's *your* kind of good. Don't you believe I have got some real patriotism in me?"

"It's hard to think of Van Harrington, the new Senator, as a patriot," she laughed back. "Those men you sent to the front must have come in handy for the election!"

I turned red at her little fling about the Senatorship: my managers *had* worked that company I equipped for all it was worth.

"I guess there are a good many worse citizens than I am. I wanted to fight for those fellows down in Cuba. And you wouldn't let me do the little I could — help Will to take my place."

"After all that happened, Van, we couldn't take it."

"And I suppose you don't want to touch anything from me now! See here, May, I came over this morning to do something for you and Will. Did he tell you about my wanting him to go down to my place in the country until he got well and strong?"

"He's much interested in this paper, and thinks he can't get away," she said evasively.

"Darn his paper! You don't believe Will was cut out to be a thinker? Anyhow, he ought to get his health back first, and give you an easier time, too."

"I am all right. Will is very much in earnest about his ideas. You can't get him to think about himself."

"Well, I don't mind his trying to reform the earth. If later on he wants a paper to whack the rich with, I'll buy him one. Come, that's fair, isn't it?"

May laughed at my offer, but made no reply.

"If you folks are so obstinate, if I can't get you to go down to my place, I'll have to turn it into a school or something. A fellow I was talking with on the train the other day gave me an idea of making it into a sort of reform school for boys. What would you think of that? Sarah is taken with the idea —

she never liked the place and won't want to go back, now that the baby died there."

"That's a good plan — turning philanthropist, Van? That's the right way to get popular approval, Senator."

She mocked me, but her laugh rang out good-naturedly.

"Popular approval never worried me much. But, May, I want *your* good-will, and I mean to get it, too."

For the more obstinate she was, the more she made me eager to win my point, to bring her and Will back to me. She understood this, and a flash of her old will and malice came into her thin face. She got up to stir the clothes on the fire, and when the water began to run over I stripped off my coat and put my hand to the job. Then I stepped over to the sink.

"Do you remember how I used to wash while you wiped, when we wanted to get out buggy-riding, May?"

"Yes, and you were an awful shiftless worker, Senator," May retorted, fetching a dish-towel from the rack and beginning to wash, while I wiped. "And you had the same smooth way with you, though in those days you hadn't ten cents to your name. And now, how much is it?"

"Oh, say a quarter!"

"Then it must have cost you a sight of money to become Senator."

"It did some, but I kept back a little."

When we had finished the dishes we began on the clothes. A child's dress caught on the wringer and tore. It was marked in a fine embroidery with the initials, J. S. H., for Jaffrey Slocum Harrington — as we had thought to call the little chap. May saw me look at the initials.

"Sarah sent it to me along with a lot of baby things when my Jack came. Perhaps she might like to have them back now."

"She and the girls come home next week. Won't you come and see her? She'd care more for that than for anything."

"You were always awfully persistent in getting your own way, Van!"

"But I didn't always get it, I remember."

"It might have been just as well if you hadn't had it so much of the time since."

"Well, maybe —"

"There are a few other people in the world besides Van Harrington, and they have their rights, too."

"That's true enough, if they can get 'em."

"Maybe their consciences are a little stronger to hold them back from getting things. You never held off long when you wanted a thing, Van. You took the peaches, you remember?"

Her lips curled in the way that used to set me mad for her.

"I didn't eat a peach," I protested. "I gave them to your brothers, and Budd Haines."

"Yes, *you* gave them!"

"I don't believe you think me half as bad as you make me out!" I said, stopping the wringer and looking into her eyes.

"You don't know how bad I make you out," she challenged my look.

It was not hard to see why I had been crazy to marry her in the old days. There was a fire in her which no other woman I ever saw possessed. Jane was large-minded, keen as an eagle, and like steel. But there was a kind of will in this worn woman, a hanging to herself, which gave her a character all her own. Nevertheless, we two couldn't have travelled far hitched together. She would have tried her best to run me, and life would have been hell for us both.

"Well," I protested in my own defence, "there's no man and no woman living has the right to say he's the worse off on my account. I have treated the world fairly where it has treated me fairly."

"So that's your boast, Van Harrington! It's pretty hard when a man has to say a thing like that to defend his life. You don't know how many men you have ruined like that poor Hostetter. But that isn't the worst. The very sight of men like you is the worst evil in our country. You are successful, prosperous, and you have ridden over the laws that hindered you. You have hired your lawyers to find a way for you to do what you please. You think you are above the law — just the common laws for ordinary folks! You buy men as you buy wheat. And because you don't happen to have robbed your next-door neighbor or ruined his daughter, you make a boast of it to me. It's pretty mean, Van, don't you think so?"

We had sat down facing each other across the tub of clothes. As she spoke her hot words, I thought of others who had accused me in one way or another, — Farson, Will, Slocum, — most of all, Slocum. But I dismissed this sentimental reflection.

"Those are pretty serious charges you are making, May," I replied after a time. "And what do you know? What the newspapers say. There are thousands of newspaper men all over this country who get a dollar or two a column for that sort of mud. Then these same fellows come around to us and hold out their hands for tips or bribes. You take their lies for proved facts. I have never taken the trouble to answer their charges, and never shall. I will answer for what I have done."

"To whom?" May asked ironically. "To God? I should like to see Van Harrington's God! He must be different from the One I have prayed to all these years."

"Maybe he has more charity, May!"

"Are you asking for charity — my charity as well as God's?" she blazed.

"Well, let that go! I shall answer to the people now."

"Yes! And God help this country, now that men like you have taken to buying seats there at Washington!"

We said nothing for a while after this, and then I rose to go.

"We don't get anywhere this way, May. I came here wanting to be friends with you and Will — wanting to help my brother. You needn't take my money if you think it's tainted. But can't you feel friendly? You are throwing me off a second time when I come to you asking for your love."

She flushed at the meaning under my words, and replied in a lower voice: —

"It would do no good, Van. You are feeling humble just now, and remorseful, and full of old memories. But you don't want my love now, in real truth, more than you did before." Her face crimsoned slowly. "If you had wanted it then, you would have stayed and earned it."

"And I could have had it?"

Instead of answering she came up to me and took my arms in her two hands and pulled my head to her.

"Good-by, Van!" she said, kissing me.

As I stepped out of the door I turned for the last time: —

"Can't you let me do something for my brother, who is a sick man?"

Tears came to her eyes, but she shook her head.

"I know he's sick, and likely to fail in what he's doing. But it can't be helped!"

Outside little Van was sitting on the ground playing with a broken toy engine. I put my hand on his little tumbled head, and turned to his mother: —

"I suppose you wouldn't let him touch my money, either?"

She smiled back her defiance through her tears.

"You had rather he'd grow up in the alley here than let me give him an education and start him in life!"

I waited several moments for her answer.

"Yes!" she murmured at last, very faintly.

The little fellow looked from his mother to me curiously, trying to make out what we were saying.

So I went back to the city, having failed in my purpose. I couldn't get that woman to yield an inch. She had weighed me in her scales and found me badly wanting. I was Senator of these United States, from the great state of Illinois; but there was Hostetter, and the old banker Farson, and my best friend Slocum, and my brother Will, and May, and their little children, who stood to one side and turned away.

The smoke of the city I had known for so long drifted westward above my head. The tall chimneys of the factories in this district poured forth their stream to swell the canopy that covered the heavens. The whir of machinery from the doors and windows of the grimy buildings filled the air with a busy hum; the trucks ground along in the car tracks. Traffic, business, industry, — the work of the world was going forward. A huge lumber boat blocked the river at the bridge, and while the tugs pushed it slowly through the draw, I stood and gazed at the busy tracks in the railroad yards below me, at the line of high warehouses along the river. I, too, was a part of this. The thought of my brain, the labor of my body, the will within me, had gone to the making of this world. There were my plants, my car line, my railroads, my elevators, my lands — all good tools in the infinite work the world. Conceived for good or for ill, brought into being by fraud or daring — what man could judge *their* worth? There they were, a part of God's great world. They were done; and mine was the hand. Let another, more perfect, turn them to a larger use; nevertheless, on my labor, on me, he must build.

Involuntarily my eyes rose from the ground and looked straight before me, to the vista of time. Surely there was another scale, a grander one, and by this I should not be found wholly wanting!

CHAPTER XXXII

THE END

The senatorial party — Mrs. Jenks's pearls — Gossip — One good deed — The Duchess brand — I take my seat in the Senate — Red roses

---

WHEN it came time to go to Washington to take my seat, my friend Major Frederickson, of the Atlantic and Great Western road, placed his private car at my disposal and made up a special train for my party. Sarah and the girls had come back from Paris in time to accompany me to Washington. The girls were crazy over going; they saw ahead a lot of parties and sights, and I suppose had their ideas about making foreign matches some day. The boy was to meet us there, and he was rather pleased, too, to be the son of a Senator.

Among those who made the trip with us there were Slocum and his wife, of course, John Carmichael, young Jenks and his pretty little wife, and a dozen or more other friends. We had a very pleasant and successful journey. A good deal of merriment was occasioned by a string of pearls that young Mrs. Jenks wore, which had lately been the talk of the city. The stones were of unusual size and quality, and had been purchased through a London dealer from some titled person. Jenks had given them as a present to his wife because of the success of the beef merger, which had more than doubled the fortune old Randolph Jenks left him when he died. The pearls, being so perfect and well known in London, caused a lot of newspaper talk. They were said to be the finest string in the United

States; there were articles even in the magazines about Mrs. Jenks and her string of pearls. Finally, some reporter started the story that there was a stone for every million dollars Jenks had "screwed out of the public by the merger" — twenty-seven in all. (For these days there was beginning to be heard all over the clamor about the price of food, and how the new combination of packers was forcing up prices — mere guess-work on the part of cheap socialistic agitators that was being taken seriously by people who ought to know better.) One paper even had it that pretty little Mrs. Jenks "flaunted around her neck the blood-bought price of a million lives!"

So it had come to be a sort of joke among us, that string of pearls. Whenever I saw it, I would pretend to count the stones and ask Mrs. Jenks how many more million lives she was wearing around her neck to-night. She would laugh back in her pretty little Southern drawl: —

"The papers do say such dreadful things! Pretty soon I shan't dare to wear a single jewel in public. Ralph says it's dangerous to do it now, there are so many cranks around. Don't you think it's horrid of them to talk so?"

Sarah had her string of pearls, too, but it was much smaller than the famous one of Mrs. Jenks. Sarah didn't altogether like Mrs. Jenks, and used to say that she plastered herself with jewels to show who she was.

Well, the pearls went to Washington with us on this trip, and made quite a splendid show, though we used to joke Ralph Jenks about sitting up nights to watch his wife's necklace. The fame of the pearls had got to Washington ahead of us, and the Washington *Eagle* had a piece in about the arrival at the Arlington of the new Senator from Illinois and the "packers' contingent" with their pearls! People used to turn around in the corridors and stare at us — not so much at the new Senator as at Mrs. Jenks's pearls!

I had already taken a house in Washington for the winter, and Sarah soon was busy in having it done over for us. We had shut up the Chicago house, and after discussing the matter with Sarah I concluded to turn over the Vermilion County property to a society, to be used for a reform school. Sarah talked it over with the young fellow I met on the train, who first put the idea into my head, and she seemed to take great pleasure in the plan, wanting me to give an endowment for the institution, which I promised as soon as my packing-company stock was straightened out. Now that I had failed to put Will and his family down there, as I had set my heart on doing, I had no more wish to go back to the place than Sarah had. And as a home to take boys to who hadn't a fair chance in life, it might do some good in the world.

It was a pleasant, warm day when my colleague, Senator Drummond, came to escort me to the Senate. My secretary and Slocum accompanied us up the broad steps toward the Senate chamber. As we turned in from the street with the Capitol rising before us, my eye fell upon a broad advertising board beside the walk, on a vacant piece of property. One of the conspicuous advertisements caught my attention: —

THE DUCHESS BRAND

STRICTLY FARM-MADE SAUSAGE

BEST IN THE WORLD

It was one of Strauss's "ads." Slocum pointed to it with a wave of his hand and glanced at me; and I thought I caught a smile on the lips of my colleague, which might have been scornful. So I paused before we passed beyond sight of the sign of the Duchess brand.

"It was good sausage, Slo! At least it was when *we* made it."

"And it did pretty well by you!" he laughed.

Senator Drummond had moved forward with my secretary.

"Yes! The Duchess was all right." Then we followed the others slowly up the great steps. . . .

In the Senate chamber, in one of the galleries, a group of women were sitting about Sarah, waiting to see me take the oath. One of them waved a handkerchief at me, and as I looked up I caught sight of Mrs. Jenks's pearls when she leaned forward over the rail.

On my desk there was a bunch of American Beauty roses: I did not have to look for the card to know that they had come from Jane.

THE JOHN HARVARD LIBRARY

The intent of
Waldron Phoenix Belknap, Jr.,
as expressed in an early will, was for
Harvard College to use the income from a
permanent trust fund he set up, for "editing and
publishing rare, inaccessible, or hitherto unpublished
source material of interest in connection with the
history, literature, art (including minor and useful
art), commerce, customs, and manners or way of
life of the Colonial and Federal Periods of the United
States . . . In all cases the emphasis shall be on the
presentation of the basic material." A later testament
broadened this statement, but Mr. Belknap's inter-
ests remained constant until his death.

In linking the name of the first benefactor of
Harvard College with the purpose of this later,
generous-minded believer in American culture the
John Harvard Library seeks to emphasize the impor-
tance of Mr. Belknap's purpose. The John Harvard
Library of the Belknap Press of Harvard University
Press exists to make books and documents
about the American past more readily
available to scholars and the
general reader.